CLUTCH

TROJAN #1

S.M. WEST

PLAYLIST

Listen on Spotify

"Cool Girl" – Tove Lo
"Black Sheep" – Gin Wigmore
"Itch" – Nothing But Thieves
"Into the Storm" – BANNERS
"Raging" – Kygo and Kodaline
"Soundcheck" – Catfish and the Bottlemen
"Like I Would" – ZAYN
"September Song" – Agnes Obel
"Butterfly" – Crazytown
"You're the One" – The Black Keys
"Can't Feel My Face" – The Weekend
"To Build a Home" – Cinematic Orchestra
"Touch" – Little Mix
"All We Know" – The Chainsmokers
"You and I" – Ingrid Michaelson

Love is vivid. I never wanted the pale version. Love is full strength. I never wanted the diluted version. I never shied away from love's hugeness but I had no idea that love could be as reliable as the sun. The daily rising of love.

Jeanette Winterson, *Why Be Happy When You Could Be Normal?*

1

STUPID

*P*ansy

"*Why are you so stupid? I could've told you Cody would cheat on you. Pansy, don't be so stupid.*"

Ivy's condescending, nasal voice plays on an endless loop in my head from our conversation last night. Stupid—that's what they all say I am.

Running my hand over the smooth leather steering wheel of my sister's Mercedes-Benz, I snicker. *Who's stupid now, huh?* Okay, it's maybe not the smartest thing I've ever done, but it's well-deserved. She wouldn't help me. She told me I could only stay the night, said I was on my own after that. My *sister.*

She refused to let me crash until I got back on my feet, so she has no one to blame but herself. She keeps telling me to take matters into my own hands and get my life in order. Well, I've taken the first step.

She'll say it's classic Pansy, flying by the seat of my pants—and truthfully, it's the only way I roll. I'm sure I'll pay for my latest plan—I always do—but for now, I don't care. I had no choice, other than sleeping in a shelter, and that would be rock bottom.

Not that I'm better than anyone who needs to use one; I'm not above that. At this point, though, a shelter would break me. I'm already at my lowest with Cody cheating and throwing me out of his place, and now my sister too. It's difficult to accept that I'm alone.

My mother is probably rolling over in her grave. She believed in family and being there for each other, though Ivy apparently missed that lesson.

Instead, the fact that she's successful makes her think she's better than me. I'm shit on her shoe, something disgusting she needs to get rid of. My heart feels like it is being squeezed, as I'm unable to remember a time when we were close.

If Poppy were here, I would have gone to her for help. She'd take me in no matter what. Sure, she'd call me naïve and stupid, but she'd let me lick my wounds and rebuild my pride rather than kicking me when I'm down.

I'm justifying my actions because deep down I'll regret it once Ivy gets a hold of me. She's at a medical conference for the day and won't discover that I "borrowed" her car until tonight, giving me a nice head start.

Shaking off my guilt, I glance around the top-of-the-line sports car. It is one sweet ride. Though it's decked out with satellite radio, I want my jam. Rummaging through my purse with one eye on the road, I find my phone. Syncing it with the Bluetooth while driving will be tricky, but I'm up for it. Pretty soon my tunes will be blaring out of this wicked stereo system.

Juggling driving and unlocking my phone, I enter my password as the car hits what could only be a pothole. For a moment, the bounce causes my butt to lift off the seat, and I release an *oof* as my abdomen connects with the steering wheel. *Ouch.*

The jostling causes my foot to push on the accelerator, and the car charges forth and swerves as I lose my grip on the wheel. In those seconds, everything slows. I'm veering for the side of the road where a hitchhiker is walking, and like a missile, the car's locked on its target. *Where the hell did he come from?*

He glances over his shoulder, and our eyes meet. I'm heading straight for him. Without hesitation, he dives into the thick brush.

Grabbing the wheel, I slam on the brakes, and the piercing

screech of grinding metal reverberates throughout my body as the car comes to a stop. Throwing it into park, I run toward the man now extracting himself from the thick thorns and brambles.

"Why the fuck are you trying to kill me?"

His long, sandy blond hair is in disarray, strands falling from his bun, and leaves and debris cling to his short, dark blond beard. With his hands on his hips and his defined chest heaving, livid blue eyes pin me to the spot.

"I'm so sorry. It was an accident. I was..." I trail off. This is all my fault; if only I'd been paying attention. "I was stupid, and I'm so sorry." Great, now I'm calling myself the one word I detest. I'm *not* stupid.

He starts to brush the dirt from his clothes, and I lunge to help him, but he bats my hand away. "Stupid—that's for sure! Stay the hell away from me."

I should be used to being called stupid by now, but I rear back from the sting of his bitter words. He has a right to be angry, scared, or even in shock—it did seem I was gunning for him. Marching past me, his death glare is another jab to my usually impenetrable armor. He's intent on getting away from me.

"Uh, do you want a ride?" I call after him, wanting to make this right.

"Fuck no."

2

CRAZY

Silas

Fucking crazy woman. I can't get away from her fast enough. Running is an option, but it's hot as hell out here. I wish I'd had my phone on me when those idiots threw me off the bus, and I also have no water. *Shit.* In this desert heat, I'm parched.

Glancing over my shoulder every so often, I check in case the maniac appears. Sure enough, about fifteen minutes later, the silver Mercedes slows to a crawl beside me. The redhead rolls down the window.

"You need a ride?" She smiles as if she didn't almost run me down. She's crazy.

"No. Get away and leave me alone."

She stops the car—in the middle of the road. *Lunatic.* Shaking my head in disbelief, I keep walking, ignoring her, hoping she'll go away. Getting out of the vehicle, she runs to catch up.

"I'm really sorry. Come on, you need a ride, and I'm going your way. I took my eyes off the road for two seconds, and I'm sorry. I promise to drive within the speed limit, keep my eyes on the road, and obey all traffic signs. Please let me make it up to you."

Damn, I do need a lift. I've been trying to hitch a ride for the past two hours with no luck. Who knew world-famous rock stars could strike out while hitchhiking? I thought cars would be lining up -- turns out I was wrong. Now, do I chance it with psycho woman or keep trekking along this hot, dry highway?

I turn on my heel, and the hopeful hazel eyes of the auburn-haired stranger nail me. It's hard to keep my gaze on her cute face when her long legs are showcased in tiny jean shorts. It doesn't help that her button's undone, exposing a tease of her tanned midriff and black panties. Her tight, threadbare t-shirt and well-worn cowboy boots finish off her youthful, fun vibe.

A warm, soft breeze sweeps her long locks into her face. Brushing the strands away, she nibbles on her lower lip. She appears forlorn, like she's the one destitute on the side of the road.

My resolve is crumbling with the innocence radiating off her. She may be wacky, but not in a fear-for-your-life sort of way. My guess is she's just scattered and wasn't trying to hit me.

Besides, I do need a ride, and I have no cell phone. It's one long-ass walk to get to the town where the bus is; best-case scenario, it'll take me the entire night.

"Eyes on the road and no talking," I order.

"Yes, I promise. I'm Pansy." She extends her hand.

With a curt handshake, I contemplate lying about my name, but she doesn't appear to know who I am. She's a stranger, and we likely won't be together long enough for her to figure it out—if she hasn't already.

"Silas," I introduce myself as I head for the car, thinking this ride might be the beginning of my final hours on this earth. I have no clue what I'm in for with this crazy chick.

We drive in silence for maybe ten minutes—though I might be generously exaggerating—before she starts talking, or more like rambling.

"So, Silas, where are you headed?"

"I thought you promised no talking," I remind her.

Her pink, bow-shaped lips puff out a sigh as she confesses, "I suck at no talking, especially when I'm nervous."

Her being nervous leaves me queasy. *Fuck.* Who knows what disaster she could cause with her nerves frazzled? I imagine a major pile-up shutting down the highway for hours. I better ease her anxiety.

"Next town."

"What?" She's puzzled.

"Where I'm headed, the next town." By design, my answer is vague. "I need to get there fast."

"How fast?"

Shit, why'd I say fast? "The sooner, the better, but no speeding or driving like a madwoman."

"Ha. Funny." She chuckles. "There's a shortcut ahead that'll save us about an hour. The road's desolate, a lot less traffic."

I like the sound of that. "Fine."

Anticipating my return to the tour bus is both a relief and a burden. I want to explain to the band. I'm hoping since they have had time to cool down, they'll be willing to hear me out, but the real question is if they will listen to what I have to say.

"Why were you hitching?"

Sighing, I scrub my hand down my face. She isn't going to shut up. "It's a long story, and I'd rather not get into it," I say, hoping my clipped tone will do the trick. No such luck.

"Just curious, because I can't figure out why the lead singer of Trojan would be hitchhiking."

Shit. She's smarter than she acts. I had no clue she knew who I was. "When did you figure it out?"

"I knew you looked familiar when I first saw you, and then it hit me as we were talking."

This broad puzzles me. If she knew who I was, I'm surprised she didn't try to take a picture, ask for an autograph, or maul me—which happens more often than I like to admit. "Why didn't you say something or go all fangirl?"

She grimaces before glancing back at the road. "Well... I'm not a fan."

Raising my eyebrows, I laugh. I love how blunt she is. It's a welcome change from all the ass-kissing.

"Okay, I can appreciate that. So, if Trojan isn't your kind of thing, what is?"

"Um, I'd rather not say. I don't want to insult you or tick you off. You're talented, and millions of people around the world love you guys. It's just not my thing. Besides, why do you care about what I like? You have countless adoring fans."

Again, I laugh at her candidness. "True," I respond unapologetically.

Fame comes with a price, though. In the beginning, I lived for all that shit, the fame and the glory, but now that's what I want to get away from. It's why I dropped the bomb on the guys. It's why I find myself in this car with a pretty, quirky, and possibly crazy woman.

"I do want to know who I've lost one potential fan to," I jest.

Rolling her eyes, she smirks. "My all-time favorite rock star is Eddie Vedder, and before you say anything, I'm twenty-seven, and my older sister introduced me to Pearl Jam. It isn't the band, per se; it's him." Her voice is dreamy, the gifted musician obviously on her mind.

"Good choice. Who else?"

"I'm more a Civil Wars or Lumineers kind of girl."

Nodding, my gaze lingers on Pansy longer than it should. I find her direct nature refreshing, and she's definitely interesting, though I'm still a bit leery. She's unpredictable.

She's also cute, with creamy skin and a light sprinkle of brown freckles on her cheeks and her small, upturned nose. Together with her doe eyes and dewy glow, she appears younger than she is. I'm guessing she isn't wearing any makeup, except for a light pink gloss on her pretty bow lips.

Normally, I wouldn't look twice. She's too fresh, too bright, too innocent for me—but right now, I can't stop myself from staring. I'm enjoying the view. Always being on tour doesn't lend itself to having a girlfriend, so I've gotten used to the groupies.

I tend to gravitate toward the in-your-face type of woman—it's easier to get off and get out. I cringe at that pathetic truth; if I'm honest, it disgusts me.

"You know what? There is one song of yours that I like," she adds. "Actually, like is too tame a word—I love it. I was so surprised to find out it was a Trojan song."

Feigning she's stabbed me in the heart, my hands clutch my chest. "Stop, woman, you're killing me. This is brutal. You're worse than our harshest critics."

"I'm sorry, I didn't mean it like that."

"Well, you can't leave me hanging. I must know which song you love." I grin.

"'Only.' It's so poetic and moving, and every single word speaks to me. I totally understand how it is to feel alone all the time."

Her confession is both unsettling and uplifting.

"I wrote that song."

A strange tingling sensation fills my chest. Her reverent tone moves me. The song never did as well as we'd hoped, a departure from our more upbeat rock tunes. While the critics loved it, fan reception was lukewarm.

It's a personal song, one I wrote around the time I started questioning if I still wanted to be the lead singer of one of the hottest rock bands in the world. It can be a lonely life—it's tough to be thirty, in your prime, and all alone.

"Did you?" Contemplating, she regards me, not the rock star, but *me*, Silas Palmer, the guy. "It's beautiful."

3

UNIQUE

*P*ansy

Wow. I'm blown away to discover one of my favorite songs was written by the man sitting next to me. He's squirming in his seat, likely uncomfortable with the adoration plastered on my face.

"So, Pansy's an unusual name. There's gotta be a story behind it," he inquires, cutting through my thoughts.

"There is." I frown. Of all the things to talk about, they always ask about my name.

"Care to share?" he pushes.

"Not really."

Shaking my head, I stare out at the dark, desolate road. We've been driving for over an hour, and the sun set not too long ago. It dawns on me that taking this shortcut wasn't smart because there aren't many rest stops, and I need to pee.

"C'mon, you promised not to talk, and that's all you've been doing. The least you can do is answer my question."

"Fine," I relent. I guess he's right, considering I almost hit him. "My mom was following tradition. My grandmother had this whole flower/nature thing going on with her daughters' names. My mom was Rose, my aunt was Lily, and my oldest sister is Ivy."

She's the smart one, a neurologist, and the one to ream me out for all my screw-ups. Our mom passed away when I was twenty-two, and she's since appointed herself my mother.

"Then there's Poppy." She's the one with a heart of gold. "She's in Africa building schools. Daisy's next, she's a model in Europe." The beautiful one. "That leaves me, the youngest, and the one stuck with the oddest name." I chuckle weakly.

"Pansy isn't stupid, it's unique."

That's what my mom would say. Pansies were her favorite flower, and she said she had girl after girl, but the name never fit until me. She used to say, "Pansies are beautiful, unique, and resilient like you, my girl."

I miss my mom. I should be satisfied with what she thought of me, but it isn't easy when others think you're the flighty one, the stupid one. I could go on, but this line of thinking only puts me in a foul mood.

I need to be positive for Silas, to make it up to him. He's having a hard time if his deep sighs and clenched jaw are any indication.

"Whatever. So, tell me, why you were hitching?"

Like me in response to his inquiries, it's evident he doesn't want to talk about it. His fists curl, and he turns toward the window. Stealing a few glimpses while his attention's diverted, it's hard to miss how good-looking he is.

He's got the whole hot-rock-star thing down to a T with his long hair, piercing eyes, and neatly trimmed beard. His faded blue jeans mold to his toned thighs and his black t-shirt fits his solid chest perfectly.

He's casual, his clothes like a second skin. Both wrists sport thin brown leather bands, and his long fingers tell their own story with callused tips from playing the guitar.

Clearing his throat, he turns to me. My attention is on the road, but his heated gaze blazes a path along my skin.

"I had news that the guys didn't want to hear. They got angry and kicked me off the bus."

"What did you say?" I ask, without caring that I'm prying.

"Um..." He hesitates, scratching the back of his neck. Our eyes lock, his gaze measured, considering if he can trust me. "I, uh, I told them I want out of Trojan."

For most people, they might need a minute to gather their thoughts, a moment of silence. Not me. Like a bull seeing red, I barrel ahead.

"What? No!" I shriek without considering how judgmental I might sound. "I mean, sorry, you do what you have to, but you guys are wildly successful. Why would you end it all?"

"I'm not telling them to end Trojan; I'm walking away. They can go on without me and find another lead singer."

"Not possible." I can't imagine they'd find someone more talented than the songwriter of "Only."

He chuckles. "You don't even like our songs. You can't say that."

"Yes, I can. You're hugely talented. Why would you walk away from it all?"

"I don't want the fame. It's taken me so far away from why I started the band." He sighs like he's released a huge burden by saying it out loud.

"What would you do then?"

"I haven't figured that out yet. Something to do with music, but what, I'm not sure."

"Wow. And your band didn't take the news well?"

"That's an understatement. I've never seen them so pissed at me, and we've had our moments. All three of them wanted me off the bus. It didn't help that Jared was out of his mind on molly. He threatened bodily harm. Even though I tried to resist, I never stood a chance. It was three against one. The fuckers left me on the side of the road with no phone, no water. They didn't even care how the hell I was going to get home."

"Is that where you're headed?"

"Yep. We just finished our North American tour, our contract's up for renewal, and I figured now was the time to tell them. They were already talking about getting back into the studio to write another album. I couldn't listen to it."

He tugs at his bun and wild golden tresses tumble to his shoulders. Usually, I don't go for guys with long hair—only women should have long hair—yet for the life of me, I can't make sense of that logic as my heart flutters at sexy Silas Palmer with golden locks framing his handsome face.

He's exquisite, and nothing like Cody, my ex-boyfriend of two years. He's shorter than Silas by a few inches, wider, stockier, and his white-blond hair is less than an inch from his scalp. I wouldn't say Cody was my type either, but his boyish charm got me.

A lot of good that did me. He ended up sleeping with his boss, a woman twenty years older and married. I have no clue what's going on in his head, and while I felt humiliated, I didn't love him. That was evident when I discovered them in our bed. Sadly, I'd been using him.

He had a condo, a steady job, and could be fun, whereas I'd dropped out of my second college program. Yes, you heard me—college at my age, and no medical or legal degree to show for it.

Since graduating high school, I've tried to figure out what I want to do with my life. At twenty-seven, I couldn't argue with Ivy when she said I should have that figured out by now. She's right.

Thankfully, I spot a rest stop ahead. It's only a gas station and convenience store, but it'll have to do. We're about two hours from our destination, I need to pee, and I'm starving.

"I'm stopping here." I turn into the parking lot.

"Good idea, I've gotta piss." He jumps out before the car comes to a complete stop and by the time I turn off the ignition, he's already inside.

When I return with my stash of food, Silas is leaning on the car. I wanted something warm, but all they had were nasty hot dogs that were more decayed than the walking dead. As I near him, he pops the final bite of a dog in his mouth. *Yuck.*

"How could you eat that? Gross." I shiver.

"It wasn't that bad." He shrugs.

"Don't complain to me when your stomach aches. I don't want to hear it."

We hop into the car and pull onto the road again as Silas delves into the plastic bag.

"So, what'd you get?" He names each item he pulls out of the bag. "Twizzlers, salt and vinegar chips, Sour Patch Kids, peanut M&Ms, water. You didn't get any protein—how do you expect any of this to fill you up?"

"What are you talking about? The peanuts will." I don't need him criticizing my food choices. "Can you please open the chips for me?"

While he disses my lack of nutrition, he has no problem eating my food. We snack and chat about nothing and everything—movies, what we like, what we don't. He confesses he hasn't seen a movie in over three years, then talks about touring and the lifestyle he leads. While at first it might be glamorous, it would be exhausting after a while.

Then the topic of food comes up, more specifically our favorite foods. No surprise, the pound of sugar I just consumed is an anchor in my belly. Why is it when you're starving, food pops into your mind? It's pure torture.

As he licks the salt from his fingers, the smacking of his lips gets my attention, and the pink tip of his tongue swirls around his finger as ripples of excitement shoot through my stomach like he's licking me.

Eyes on the road, Pansy. Eyes on the road.

4

BRAVE

Silas

"Why are you out here?"

"What?" She sips from the water bottle. "My mouth is wrung out from the sugar and salt."

"I bet," I smirk. She consumed not only the chips but also the whole pack of Twizzlers. "Why are you out here on this road tonight?"

"Um, that's a long story. I'd rather not get into it."

"Come on; I thought we were friends," I cajole, nudging her shoulder. "Tell me."

"Fine, but I'm keeping it simple and quick, and don't interrupt. Actually, don't say a thing even when I'm done."

"Got it." I make the Boy Scout sign with my fingers. She rolls her eyes, correctly guessing I was never a Boy Scout.

"I'm heading out for a new start. My life's a mess. I've been unable to finish a college degree, and not because my grades suck. They're excellent. It's because I can't make up my mind.

"I took a couple of years after high school to figure out what interested me, and I thought I'd found my passion in event planning, so I enrolled in a hospitality program. It took two years to figure out I'd made a bad choice. I'm not an event planner. How I thought I'd enjoy the stress, the personalities, and the last-minute disasters is beyond me. I then took another couple of years to decide I wanted to be a nurse, but again, I wasn't cut out for needles, blood, and people dying. I was miserable, so I dropped out."

"I'm sensing a pattern here," I interject, unable to resist, although I should keep quiet. I'm fascinated by her story.

"Uh-uh, you promised not to say a word. One more thing out of your mouth and I stop talking."

I almost challenge her by saying *I'd like to see that,* because I doubt she can be quiet. It's obvious her story is hard for her to share—she's wearing down the wheel with her roaming hands. I guess she considers herself a failure because of her lack of direction.

To me, she's brave enough to try new things, to want to find her true passion. I lost mine for the band years ago and kept my mouth shut for too long—so long, I ended up carelessly blurting out my departure to my bandmates and closest friends. No wonder they kicked me out.

"Anyway, I'm now less than two weeks out of college and back to square one. About a week ago, I came home early to find my boyfriend in bed with another woman. Even though I wanted to leave, I didn't have anywhere to go. He said I could stay until I figured things out, but that was his guilt talking, and it was such a bad idea. Two days ago, he kicked me out. His new girlfriend didn't like me still living with him, and frankly, neither did I, so I had to go. Then..." She hesitates. "You know what? Forget it. That's enough humiliation for one lifetime."

"Tell me. You can't end it there."

"Fine." Her voice is small. "I went to my older sister Ivy's house, asking to stay with her." She swallows and takes a deep breath before going on. "She refused. She let me stay last night but said I had to be gone today. So, this is me getting gone. Go ahead, say it."

"Say what?"

"Tell me how stupid I am." She turns away from me as her hand wipes at her cheek. *Is she crying?*

"Hey, all I was going to say is your ex-boyfriend and sister sound like dicks, and you should be glad you're getting away from them."

Her burst of laughter comes as a surprise to both of us. With water pooling in her eyes, she smiles, and something strange and intense tugs at my heart. I like making her smile.

"You're right; they're dicks." Her voice is stronger, almost cheerful. "Anyway, now I'm on my next adventure, and I've got no clue where I'm going."

"I don't think that's a bad thing. It sounds exciting, and it's courageous and smart."

"What? Really?" She whips her head in my direction, eyes wide with surprise. I point my finger back at the road, motioning for her to watch where she's driving.

"Yeah. You've got the courage to explore different things, and you're smart for wanting to find your passion. Too many people get stuck in a job because that's what we're all told to do—go to school, find a job, make a living, have a family, blah, blah, blah. You're not following the herd. You've stopped to listen to your heart and figure out what the hell it is you want to do with your life. So, you're not only contributing to society, but it also means something to you. That's smart."

Pansy's smile is blinding even in the darkness of the car, and the faint light from the driver's panel illuminates her glittering eyes. My sense is not many people encourage or support her.

The car begins to shimmy and shake. She whips her head back to the road, white-knuckling the steering wheel.

With a small scream, she cries, "What the hell is going on? I didn't hit anything. It's listing to the right."

"Pull over," I order, helping to steer the car to the side of the road.

The ride is bumpy and jerky as she slowly and carefully brings us to a stop. Simultaneously, we jump out of the car. The front passenger side tire is a sad sight, deflated and misshapen.

"Fuck. Seriously?" I yell, gripping my hair.

"Shit. It's probably from the pothole I hit hours ago."

"You should have been watching the fucking road, and this

wouldn't have happened," I fire at her. Her calm tone infuriates me more. "Who goes straight for a fucking pothole? Now what the fuck are we going to do?"

Pansy gasps, taking several steps away from me. Frowning, she tightens her jaw and purses her lips. "You don't have to be a jerk. I didn't deliberately do it, and I already apologized for it." She folds her arms across her chest. "I'm sure there's a spare. We'll change it and be on our way."

Striding past me, she goes in search of the spare while I stand there stewing in my anger. I just want to get back on the damn bus— why is it so hard? Am I asking for too much? I don't fucking think so.

Her grunting and groaning pull me out of my gloom. This slip of a woman is giving it her all in trying to lift the spare tire out of the car, and she's getting nowhere. If I were in a different frame of mind, I'd find it amusing.

Instead, I'm stunned by her round, luscious ass sticking up in the air. Her jean shorts are so short, her creamy ass cheeks peek out from the denim, as well as a sliver of her black lace panties.

I snarl at my body's reaction to her; angry and turned on are the last things I want to be right now. "Get out of the way." Moving her, I yank the tire, jack, and other necessary items out of the car. "Stand back."

"No wonder you were kicked off the bus," she mutters under her breath.

Stopping, I glare at her. She's straightening her clothes and finger-combing her hair away from her face, oblivious to me. When our eyes do meet, instead of backing down as any sane person would, she stands her ground, chest out, chin up, and glowers back. Her hair's disheveled, cheeks flushed, eyes wild. My cock stirs to life.

Shaking my head at this game I don't have time to play, I grind my teeth and will my dick down. Dismissing her, I get to work.

It's not long before I need help. The flashlight—which was stowed in the car, thank goodness—is tricky to hold between my teeth while unscrewing the busted tire. The light flickers in and out, and I'm unable to steady the beam.

"Pans, some help here would be appreciated." My tone's snarky.

"Do not call me Pans. My name is Pansy. Try asking nicely, and I'll consider helping." She's snooty.

Throwing the tool and flashlight to the ground, I growl, "Fucking forget it. I'll do it myself."

"Good! I'm done with you." She pivots and stomps off into the dark.

Her long red mane sways in time with her ass and curves. *Fuck her.* I seriously don't have the time or the patience for her theatrics. If she wants to act like a drama queen, she can go right ahead, but I won't be her audience.

It takes another twenty minutes to finish the task, and she hasn't come back, which surprises me. I definitely expected her to return. It's pitch black and who the fuck knows what wild animals are lurking out there.

My concern grows the longer I'm alone. She isn't to blame for the flat tire, and the thought of something happening to her because of my rash temper leaves a nasty taste in my mouth and a hollowing in my chest. I'm a bastard.

Throwing the lame tire and other things in the car, I hop into the driver's seat. *Thank fuck she left the keys.* The engine roars to life with a press of the ignition button, and the headlights cast a long shaft of light across the dark expanse.

Not too far off, brown leather cowboy boots dissect the slanted beam, and Pansy's trim frame comes into view. Her long hair is a tousled mess with strands flying in her face, and her shirt molds to her small breasts. The light catches every bouncing curve and appealing sashay of her jean-clad hips as she marches toward the car.

Yanking the driver's side door open, she stands, hands on her hips and eyes narrowed on me. "This is my car. If anyone should be walking, it's you. Get out."

5

SORRY

*P*ansy

"I'm sorry." His voice is low and remorseful—or is that just wishful thinking on my part?

"And that makes it all right?" I understand he was upset, and he had every right to be, but I'm not his verbal punching bag. When he opens his mouth to respond, I cut him off. I'm not done. "Cars get flat tires, and I didn't deserve to be yelled at or mistreated. Now, I'd like you to please get out of my car. This is where we part ways."

He sighs, running his hand through his wild locks as he steps out of the car. I'm forced to step back if I don't want him right on me. Standing less than three inches from me, he tugs on my shoulder, halting my retreat. My body reacts to our proximity, tingles spreading through me.

I tilt my head back to gaze directly into his face. In the faint glow of the interior light, I make out his bottomless blue eyes, and they're searching my face, searching for something.

"I'm sorry. I was a jerk. Totally out of line. Would you please let me ride with you?"

"You've got anger issues," I blurt out, unable to hold back my criticism.

Giving me a faint smile, he nods. "Yeah, I do. I'm working on it, but obviously, I'm doing a piss-poor job."

"That's for sure," I retort. "Get in the passenger seat, let's go. I'm tired, and I'm sure you'll be glad to be rid of me as much as I will be of you."

My words aren't true. While his anger toward me hurt, I also like him. I've enjoyed his company, for the most part. This ride would have been a lot longer and lonelier had Silas not been here.

His eyebrows arch in surprise at my comment, but he remains silent and walks around the car. As the inside light fades, the grease smudge on his cheekbone catches my eye. Without hesitation, I reach for him, my finger wiping at his warm, smooth skin. He stills, a groan escaping his lips as I lick my thumb and try again. It's then that my movements stutter. *Oh, God.* I smeared my spit on his cheek.

His eyes are now heavy-lidded as his hand wraps my wrist, stopping my movements. Our rapt gazes are fixed on each other. The silence is thick, the rapid thumping of my heart and my shallow breathing deafening.

Breaking the tenuous moment, he removes my hand from his face and places it on my lap. "Thanks, Mom," he croaks, clearing his throat as he opens the glove box. "Is there any sanitizer or wipes?"

"Um, yes, here." I hand him the small bottle. My voice is gravelly and strange, even to my ears.

What just happened? Instead of him being grossed out by having my saliva on his face, we had this weird, brief connection—but now it's gone. I'm tired; I must have imagined it.

We slip back into silence and start driving. At first, the comfortable solitude doesn't bother me, but the longer neither of us speaks, the more anxious I become.

Opening the peanut M&Ms, I put a few in my mouth. I'm not hungry, but I need something to do, like driving isn't enough. I scour my mind for something to say, something to fill the silence and put us back into comfortable conversation, but as fate would have it, another disaster unfolds.

The car slows, sputtering and shuddering. Honestly, I can't

believe this. Why is this happening? Having no clue what's wrong, I pull over and the engine dies, plunging us into darkness.

"What happened?"

"I don't know." I flip on my phone flashlight and try to figure out what's wrong.

It only takes seconds, and once I guess at the cause, nausea overwhelms me. My stomach twists as bile climbs up my tight throat. Silas is going to lose his shit.

"We're out of gas," I whisper, staring at the gas tank indicator. Without a doubt, that's the issue.

"Are you fucking kidding me?" He slams both hands flat onto the dashboard.

I shriek and jump at his outburst. "I'm sorry, I wasn't thinking." Guilt coils in the pit of my stomach.

I'm one hundred percent responsible; I should have filled the tank when we stopped at the gas station. Instead, I was so caught up in my road trip partner that my brain left the building.

"That's painfully obvious. Do you ever think?" Snatching my phone, he taps on the screen. "Dammit, no signal. We gotta call a local garage or something." His furious glare causes a sharp jerk in my chest.

Shrinking into my seat, I wish I could disappear. I bite down on my lower lip, trying to stop the trembling as the sting in my eyes and throat intensifies. Tears course down my face. Holding my breath, I struggle to stem my tears and get myself under control.

It's not only Silas and his nasty words that have brought my weeping on; it's the culmination of the past two weeks—shit, the past few *years*—squeezing at my heart, shredding my pride. The growing pressure in my head forces me to gulp for air.

"Fuck, seriously?" His harsh tone and apparent disdain jabs at me as I fall apart.

"Fuck off," I scream. "Get the hell out of here."

He jerks back as I lunge at him with my fists flying, aiming for any part of his body I can reach—his hard pecs, his defined biceps, his strong jaw. With each hit, he grunts, commanding me to stop. His hands cuff my wrists, bringing them together toward my chest. Yanking me to him, one arm around my back and the other tucked between us, he secures my fists.

I slump and burrow into him, sobbing at how pathetic my life is. For once, why can't luck be on my side? Why can't things go my way?

His hold is firm, his inviting masculine scent soothing. My rapid breaths and the pounding of my heart steady with the security of his warm embrace, despite the ache of his rotten words.

"Shh," he soothes, rubbing small circles on my back. "I'm sorry, I really am. We're royally screwed, aren't we?"

He loosens his hold at my push, his soft beard brushing my forehead and a few strands of my hair catch. As we disentangle ourselves, he laughs, releasing my hands.

"I'm sorry." My lips wobble as I flatten my hands on his solid upper body.

"Shh," he murmurs, his finger gently touching my lips.

His rumble vibrates from his chest into my palms and down to my belly. My tongue darts out, grazing his finger on my mouth. Blinking back the dampness in my vision, I sigh at the tangy flavor of his flesh, shuddering as I swallow the taste of him.

His hand moves to cup my cheek, each sweep of his thumb eliciting quivers along my spine. His lips land on mine, sharp and hungry. His beard tickles, intensifying the tingles from within. Sliding his hand to cup the back of my neck, with a squeeze, he pulls me nearer. My eyelids flutter closed.

Lost to the sensation of his tongue licking my lips, I moan into his mouth. His arm tightens around me, his fingers dig into my hip, and I don't want to ever come up for air. I could stay like this forever, lips locked with Silas Palmer—not the famous rock star or the irate man, but sweet, sexy Silas who's sucking on my tongue like candy.

6

DIRT

*S*ilas

Kissing Pansy is different. Better. Not what I'm used to. I make it a rule not to kiss groupies—it complicates things—but on the rare occasion where I've had too much to drink, been lost in the moment and gone in for a kiss, I've regretted it. Usually, the woman wants to eat me alive, consume me, and not in a good way.

This kiss is different. She knows how to kiss. It's soft and teasing. She tastes like milk chocolate and peanuts, sweet and savory. I want to devour her. As I bring her closer, her breasts graze my pecs, and she moans into my mouth, her hands digging into my shoulders. *I've got you.*

I should pull away. I was a major asshole to her, letting my temper get the best of me yet again. It's not her fault I was dumped on the side of the road or that I've got all this anger bottled inside me. Months of keeping your mouth shut when you should speak up will do that to you, not to mention the other shit from my past that only brings me rage.

My dick's hard, straining against my zipper at having her in my arms, but this can't go anywhere. She's vulnerable. She was just crying in my arms, and I was consoling her. Truthfully, I've wanted to kiss her since she stared me down on the road, and now that I have my chance, I don't want to let up. I'm going for broke.

I anchor my hands to her hips and lift, our lips fusing as she willingly climbs onto my lap. Her legs straddle me, knees folded under her at the sides of my thighs, and as she sinks into me, a groan slips out.

Needing to touch her further, my hands roam her collarbone, her skin silky and warm. Threading her fingers through my hair, she yanks me deeper into her mouth. Succumbing to her wet warmth, my eyes close. Our matching sighs mingle and fade.

Flashes skitter across my closed eyelids, distracting and dragging me from my Pansy-induced haze. Confused, I blink a few times. Pansy pulls away, breathless, and her voice sounds confused.

"Silas?"

Flickering red, blue and white beams of a police cruiser illuminate the interior of the car like a nightclub. Her eyes are huge, and her mouth's open in surprise.

"What the hell?"

A cop raps his hand forcefully on our window.

"Oh, my God," Pansy says, her voice shaky.

Opening the door, she climbs out. Keeping my hand on her hip, I step out and pull her close. We peer at the cop standing less than three feet from us, his hand on the holster of his gun. He's a big guy, easily six foot four, and wide.

"Hands where I can see them. Sir, step away from the lady." His voice is a deep baritone, authoritative.

While I'm reluctant to let her go, it's not wise to argue with a police officer. We step apart and make sure our hands are in front of us, easily visible.

"Who's the owner of this vehicle?"

"Um, it's my sister's car," Pansy responds, her voice uneven and small.

"License and registration, ma'am."

She stutters, "U-Um, they're in the car."

Nodding, he instructs us to walk to the front of the car, telling me to place my hands on the hood. Standing back from us, he looks on keenly as she retrieves her identification and hands it to him. Then, speaking to me, he says, "Your identification, sir."

"It's in my front pocket." I cautiously fish it out of my jeans and send a prayer of thanks; finally, something is working in my favor. I'm fortunate to have my driver's license; at least I had that on me when I was tossed.

We silently obey as he instructs us to stand with our feet shoulder-width apart. He pats us down, and while he's rough and quick with me, he takes his sweet-ass time roaming his hands over Pansy's body. I practically swallow my tongue to prevent myself from losing my shit. Finally, he goes to the cruiser, not once taking his eyes off us.

Glancing at Pansy, I try to catch her eye, but she refuses to face me. Her head's glancing down at the hood. I want to say something to reassure her that everything will be fine—after all, we're no longer stranded. The cop will help us get gas, I'm sure of it.

Upon his return, his voice is gruff as he states, "Pansy Dobson, you're under arrest..."

She gasps, and I jerk as he drones on about her rights.

"Wait, this is her sister's car," I stress, taking my hand off the car, completely forgetting my moves aren't mine to make. I'm suspended in some fucked-up moment where I have no free will.

Before I even know what's happening, I'm airborne. The cop has my hands behind my back, and I'm facedown on the ground. Dirt and dust waft into my mouth and nostrils, and his knee drills into my back. I'm stunned—getting flipped onto the terrain knocked the wind out of me. Ringing in my ears drowns all sound, until Pansy's crying eventually cuts through.

"Oh, my God. Silas, I'm sorry." There's something to her voice that suggests she's not as clueless as I am.

The cop reads me my rights and slaps handcuffs on my wrists, hauling me to standing. She's now in my view, hands still planted on the hood, but she's sobbing and shaking.

"Do. Not. Move. Or you'll regret it," he orders her while he drags me to the car and throws me in.

As I struggle to sit, I cough up the crap I inhaled while on the ground. He's fucking manhandling Pansy as if she's a toy, cuffing her and throwing her into the back seat beside me.

"Hey," I murmur softly as she tries to sit up.

"Not a word out of either of you." His voice is ice.

"I can explain," she attempts as he whips around, glaring at us. I'm thankful for the metal grid separating him from us.

"Shut up. Now."

Slinking back into the seat, she squeezes her eyes shut and bites her lower lip to stifle her cries. Anger boils within me at her fear; I want her to feel safe, protected. I am also curious as to what she can explain. It's likely a mix-up with her sister, and this will all be sorted soon. It has to be.

With slow, deep breaths, I try to steady my heart rate as he arranges for the car to be towed. He then calls the police station to tell them he's bringing us in.

We roll into town about thirty minutes later, and the irony isn't lost on me: I desperately wanted to get here, to catch up with the tour bus, and now I'd rather be any place else.

Once we're in the station, the officer deposits us in chairs and walks a few feet away to a desk. Pansy uses the opportunity to whisper hurriedly, "I'm sorry, Silas. It's all my fault. I took my sister's car without her permission. This is her way of punishing me. I'll get you out of this."

I'm dumbfounded by her revelation, and irritation builds at the sheer absurdity of it all. *Seriously?* This is all a case of siblings squabbling, and somehow, I'm stuck in the middle. It doesn't matter that with one phone call I'll walk away from this—I'm *angry*. This is the cherry on top of a fucking shit-tastic day.

"Shut up," the officer barks. He waits until he's satisfied we'll be silent before he turns back to his task.

"How fucking stupid are you?" I say coldly through gritted teeth. "I've had enough of your bullshit. When this is all over, leave me the fuck alone."

7

RIDE

*P*ansy

Silas's cruel, razor-sharp words are a kick to the stomach. I get that he's handcuffed and being threatened with jail time because of Ivy—well, really because of me—but he's no different than the rest of them.

He called Ivy and Cody dicks, but he's the biggest dickwad of them all. I thought he saw me for who I am, that he got me. I believed he was special. He's not. He's no better than them.

When I turn my back to him, he scoffs at what I'm sure he thinks is my immaturity or further stupidity. We wait in silence and are eventually separated when I'm taken to a holding room, where an officer finally uncuffs and questions me.

I should ask for a lawyer, but I'm sure Ivy will show soon. This whole thing reeks of her—never mind the wasted time, money, and energy used to "punish" me in this manner.

During my interrogation, it becomes clear that the officer likes me, or at the very least, he's sympathetic to my situation. He shares tidbits about Silas even though he shouldn't—Silas has been released, his one phone call leading to his ticket to freedom.

I'm glad I'll never see that asshole again. Even if he did write a beautiful song and we had some sweet and memorable moments, I'll never forgive or forget the horrid things he said to me. He called me stupid, again. Enough is enough. I'm done with that.

I finally ask for my phone call, and I'm told to sit tight. Alone in the holding cell, that's what I do: sit and wonder how I got here, if or when Ivy is going to come, and what happens next.

During the night—I have no clue what time it is—a guard comes for me. Fortunately, he doesn't cuff me again, and he leads me to the front of the station.

Ivy's pushes off the discharge desk when she sees me and heads my way. The stabbing staccato of her expensive high heels is the maddening music to my walk of shame. Contrary to my rumpled appearance, she's so prim and proper in her crisp beige suit. Not a strand of her strawberry blonde bob is out of place, and her makeup is flawless. Perfect—that's Ivy.

"Pansy." My name is blasphemy on her lips. "How could you?"

I stare blankly at her, trying in vain to keep my emotions in check. This day has been from hell, and I can't handle much more. All I want is a cardboard box to crawl into and sleep. A homeless shelter sounds wonderful about now.

She natters on about how disappointed she is in me, chastising me for stealing her car. Yes, she says stealing, and she's sure to tell me it doesn't change a thing. She's not supporting me. I'm on my own. The clock in the precinct indicates it's five fifty-three in the morning. No wonder I'm exhausted—I've been up for nearly twenty-four hours.

As we walk outside into the cool morning air, I sigh, stretch, and smile. I wasn't locked up long, but I embrace my freedom. Glancing at my sister, I see her annoyance at me written all over her face.

"Ivy, this is where we say goodbye." My tone is devoid of emotion.

"What? Where are you going?"

"I have no clue, but one thing I know for sure is that I don't want to be around you. I'll always love you, but I don't like you. I'm sorry I *borrowed* your car. Yes, it was wrong and selfish, but I'm sick and tired of you telling me I'm stupid. I'm not. I've got a higher than average IQ and a 4.0 GPA." I only say those things because they matter to her. "Goodbye, Ivy."

"Pansy, stop being stu—" I shoot her an icy glare as I pass her on the steps. "Don't go, let's talk."

"I'll text you when I'm settled."

She calls after me as I head down the road, only concerned with finding a motel. I've got savings, and while I'll have to be smart with my pennies, I need to sleep before I figure out my next move.

I'm not even ten minutes from the station when a black Range Rover pulls up beside me, and the driver's window rolls down. Silas.

"You need a ride?" He grins sheepishly.

Scoffing, I dismiss him with a flick of my hair before walking on. He's crazy. Did he forget what he said to me?

"No. Get away and leave me alone." The fleeting satisfaction of using his words on him warms me.

Behind me, the car door slams, and seconds later, he's at my side, pulling on my hand. My eyes narrow into slits as his twinkle with amusement. He smiles awkwardly, big and bright, trying to soften me.

"I'm really sorry. I'm the fuck-up this time," he confesses. "I met your sister, Ivy, and I get it."

"Ivy has nothing to do with this. *You* called me stupid—I'm not. I'm tired of people treating me like I'm dumb."

"You're not stupid, not by a long shot, and I never should've said that. I'm the one who's stupid."

"No, you're not," I interrupt. I don't like that word being used for anyone. It's wrong and hurtful.

"Fine." He chuckles. "But I do have a stupid temper, and I have no excuse for calling you names. I'm truly sorry. How can I make it up to you?"

I like this side of him; his sincerity restores my belief that he's a decent person. He's got a mean temper, but he can admit his faults. My family never apologizes for their cruel words, even when they know they upset me.

My silence must unnerve him because he laces his fingers with mine, urging me toward him. I resist, needing to keep my head about me. As much as his apology helps, the wound is still there. It's still fresh, and I'm tired, vulnerable. It'd be too easy to let this go. That's what I always do—let people off the hook for treating me like garbage.

"Please forgive me." He clings to me, pulling me closer.

His remorse tugs at my heart. Damn, why can't I be a cold-hearted bitch, make him work harder for his apology? Sadly, it's not my style.

Our chests collide, and my breath hitches. His arms envelop me; his pleading expression weakens my efforts. I'm anchored to him, and his hand caresses my cheek as my body overrides my mind, willingly leaning into him.

"You hurt me." I push hard against him, remembering how his words were blows to my heart, my ego.

I've caught him by surprise, and he stumbles, loosening his hold, but before I can distance myself, his fingers latch onto my hips. Rough, callused tips sink into my exposed flesh, sending an electrifying jolt up my spine. His grip is both firm and gentle.

"I could be halfway home by now, but I couldn't leave. I felt shitty for how I treated you and what I said. If I'd really meant it or if I was a heartless asshole, I wouldn't be here. Okay, I am an asshole for saying what I said, but I'm truly sorry."

I'm now back in his arms, chest-to-chest, and I can't think of one good reason why I shouldn't be here.

"I should stay mad at you," I murmur weakly, letting my stubbornness have its way, one more time.

His smile grows; he's wearing me down, and he knows it. Being in his arms has eliminated any fight in me. Even with his short temper, I like him, I really do, and his remorse is evident in his features and voice.

"Give me another chance?" His tone is hopeful and confident.

"Drive me to a motel and let me sleep, then we'll talk. I'm thinking you can start making it up to me with a ride to my next destination."

My fingers comb through the short, soft hairs of his beard as I pinch his chin with my thumb and forefinger. His lips tempt me. I want to kiss him, but it's not smart. I'm sleep-deprived, and making decisions based solely on my libido isn't wise. Before I can bring his mouth to mine, his lips descend on me.

His tongue swipes across the seam of my lips, and I eagerly open for him, inviting his teeth to nibble on my lower lip. Pulling my lip into his mouth, he sucks and teases a moan out of me. Our kiss is long, languid, and loaded with endless possibilities.

Pulling back, he whispers, "Oh yeah? And where would that be?"

"I'll let you know when I know."

Smiling, his mouth covers mine again. Our lips tangle, tongues twisting as my stomach flip-flops and my heart races with anticipation. His kiss is solace and hope to my weary heart. I don't know if this is it or if there's a future for us, don't know where we'll go or how bumpy the road will be, but I welcome the ride.

8

GOOSEBUMPS

*P*ansy

"This place is shit." Silas is grumpy and throws the car keys on the hotel desk, where they slide along the surface before falling to the floor.

Glancing around the room, it's no different than what you'd find in any of the countless hotel chains across the country, but I guess that's his point. All I care is that it's clean.

It's 9:00 in the morning, and we've been up all night. I feel worlds better with my stomach full but still exhausted. After breakfast, he drove in circles searching for a five-star hotel in this small town in the Mojave Desert. It didn't matter that both his phone and GPS indicated his pursuit was in vain, he kept looking in the same way you seek a pot of gold at the end of the rainbow. Finally, my incessant yawning and eventual dozing prompted him to pick a hotel.

"The room is fine, and it's clean. I just want out of these clothes and into bed."

There's only a queen size bed. There were no rooms available with two beds, and I wasn't going to let Silas pay for two rooms when we're grown-ups. We're just sleeping.

He leisurely roams my body from head to toe, slowing on my thin cotton tee, then sliding to my denim shorts. He lingers on the band of my black panties peeking out from my undone shorts.

I roll my eyes and yawn. While I do like his admiration, I just want to sleep. Perching on the edge of the bed, I pull off one of my cowboy boots and moan in relief as my foot wiggles free from the leather.

He halts on the way to the bathroom, his gaze locking with mine and his eyes darken at my unintentionally naughty noise. He grins, untying his man bun, his tresses tumbling to his shoulders. Changing course, he heads to me.

Without asking permission, his rough, callused fingers wrap behind my knee, sending a shiver through me, while his other hand swiftly removes the offending boot.

"Better?" He roams my bare legs with a lazy, lopsided grin. His rapt attention does all kinds of fluttery things to my insides.

"Much," I say, low and husky, surprising both of us.

He arches a brow; my cheeks heat, and we both laugh. When I'd set out from Ivy's yesterday with a vague destination in mind, only knowing I was headed to the ocean, I had no clue what I was in for.

"I'm glad you're here," he whispers, his lips heading for mine.

Messy locks outline his handsome face, and his neatly-trimmed beard accentuates his full lips. I want his kiss, but I don't. This is happening too fast. I've been nothing but impulsive since meeting him, and hooking up with a rock star isn't part of my plan.

Based on my track record, Silas could easily derail my plan to make something of myself. It would only prove my sisters right, that I *am* a silly scatterbrain who just goes wherever the road takes her.

Stuck in my own thoughts, I'm too late to stop his lips from covering mine. His kiss is strong, but only a tease. Short and sweet.

Before pulling away, his nose skims from my jaw to my ear where his teeth latch onto my lobe. A deep, breathy moan passes my lips at the tingles alighting my spine. My pleasure only encourages him to continue his nips at my tender flesh. Goosebumps erupt along my skin, all the while, his tongue teases with flicks behind my ear, and heat builds between my legs.

My belly twists at how right and how wrong this feels. How did the lost girl of yesterday, looking for a fresh start, wind up weak-kneed and locking lips with a rock star?

He draws me closer, our eyes lock, and our lips meet again as his beard abrades the flesh around my mouth. Each scrape and tickle echoes with a fluttering in my chest and stomach, and every sweep, suck or nip to my mouth further reduces me to blazing need. My hands find his waist at the same time he wedges his thigh between my legs, where I ache the most.

How it happens, I'm not sure, but we wind up on the bed, Silas on top of me, and we're still kissing. Our bodies are fused, his lengthening erection rubbing into my stomach.

On instinct, I slide and wrap my legs around him, wriggling until we're perfectly aligned. My body, with a mind of its own, grinds against him, any reservations forgotten.

He moans into my mouth, and I clutch his hair, urging him on. His touch is hot and greedy, skimming the sides of my breasts, stopping to palm one, feeling its weight, with his thumb flicking at my hardening peak.

I release a pleasurable moan, my insides on fire at his touch as my fingers glide down his hard planes, seeking his belt. I've never done this before, had sex this quickly. I've known him less than twenty-four hours, but my libido is driving this crazy train, and for the life of me, I can't think of one reason to stop.

I don't know what tomorrow holds. We could be at each other's throats in hours. Do we even want to be friends or is there a possibility for more? All I know is that I want to have wild sex with him.

While I'm riding my lust-induced high and buzzing from everything Silas, he draws up abruptly to straddle my hips. His hands fly into his hair as if touching me pains him as he squeezes his eyes shut.

He climbs off me, removing my hands from his belt, and I shiver at the loss of him, my heart plunging to my toes like a stone sinking to the bottom of a pond.

My flight instinct kicks in, and I scramble, awkward and jerky, to get away as heat rises to my face. Silas grips the back of my neck, stilling my getaway, and rests his forehead on mine.

His blue eyes find mine, dark and troubled. On a slow groan, his warm breath tickles my face, and my heart pounds with my desire to flee.

"Fuck, Pansy, we can't..."

"You're right. We can't." I push away, snorting in a weak attempt to make light of this.

My cheeks are on fire, but I refuse to look away from him. I goofed, and I won't make things worse by shying away. This was a silly misunderstanding, no biggie.

"Pansy." His voice is soft.

"It's all good. I'm tired and just want to sleep."

Grabbing my ratty suitcase, I hustle into the bathroom before he can say another word, and slam the door behind me.

With a jagged exhale, I lean against the door and close my eyes. It's not a lie. I am exhausted. While most people are starting their day, I need sleep. I haven't slept for well over twenty-four hours, and this delirium is most probably the cause of my smuttiness. I practically dry humped him. God, could I have been any more desperate?

So much for not going where the moment takes you. Once in the shower, the cool water washes away the dirt and grime of the past day, and I give myself a pep talk. Silas is hot, and while I'm not wild about his anger issues, he is a nice guy. But none of that matters. This is about me. I need to focus on getting settled and devising a plan.

Once in my PJs, I venture into the room to find only the bedside lamp on. Silas is out cold, on his back with his arms to the sides, hair fanned on the pillow, bare-chested, with his full lips slightly parted.

While this thing, our happenstance meeting, has been fun and something I need to dwell less on, I can't deny that he sure is pretty to look at.

&

a shaft of sunlight cuts across my face. Squinting, I roll onto my side. The other side of the bed is empty.

"Good morning, or should I say good evening?" I hear the smile in his tone and I blink, my lips curving to match his smile.

Lazily turning onto my back, I raise my hand to shield the sunlight and gaze in the direction of his voice.

"Evening," I croak, sure that my tangled hair, sleepy eyes, and lines from the pillow on my face are a vision of loveliness. Oh well, I'm not, nor have I ever tried to be a goddess. "What time is it?"

"A little after seven."

Casually sitting in an oversized chair, one toned, jean-clad thigh is flexed, leg bent with his ankle resting on his other knee. With his hair in a bun, he rests his head in his palm, cocked to the side. A playful grin dances on his lips, his twinkling gaze fixed on me.

"Did you sleep well?" he asks.

"Yes. Did you?"

"Yeah, for about six hours." He glances to the empty side of the bed.

We slept. Sure, sleep is the key word, but let's not quibble over semantics. We were in the same bed. I wonder if I drooled or worse? I grimace at the possibility.

As if reading my mind, he teases, "You're cute when you sleep. You make these adorable sighs and *mmm* noises."

"I do?"

"Yeah, they're hot, like you're dreaming something naughty and fun."

His eyebrows rise and fall with his devilish tone, and I plant my face in my palm. "Great, my most embarrassing moments seem to all be with you."

Chuckling, he stands and stretches. His tight black t-shirt inches up to expose a sliver of his taut, smooth belly. "Nah, definitely no reason to be embarrassed. Cute and hot."

He extends his hand, and I nervously place mine in his,

concerned I'll combust on contact. I may be stronger mentally and physically thanks to sleep, but emotionally, I'm still a mess.

Not only am I attracted to him, which I'm epically failing to hide, but I'm also homeless, I have no family support, and no clue what I'm doing. It's enough to make me want to cry or laugh hysterically. When he waited for me outside the police station, something changed between us. Silas became a friend.

Other than my parents and maybe my sister Poppy, I can't think of anyone else who would have waited for me. I know Cody, my ex-boyfriend, wouldn't have. He would have been ticked at the mess I got myself into, and my other sisters, Ivy and Daisy, wouldn't have bothered.

"Time to get up, sleepyhead. I'm starving, and I'm sure you are too." Effortlessly, he pulls me from the bed, and with my hand still in his, he examines my face. "We can order in or go find someplace to eat."

I swallow hard, a ball of nerves lodging in my throat. I do not like this fangirl side of me and vow, then and there, to put a stop to it.

"This place has room service?" Doubtful.

Grinning, he shakes his head. "No room service, but there's a restaurant downstairs, I can get something brought up."

"Don't go to any trouble..."

"It's no trouble. You want to eat in?"

"Yes, please. I need to get dressed and could use another shower."

"Sure, check out the menu." He points to the desk. "Tell me what you want, and I'll take care of it while you shower."

I grab some clean clothes and quickly scan the menu, finally deciding on a burger before slipping into the bathroom.

With a heaving chest, I lock the door and shake my head. What's wrong with me? I'm not usually this flustered by a guy, pretty face or not. They're just people. Although I must admit Silas is different, and it has nothing to do with his rock star status. He's complex, intense, playful, and hard to ignore.

We met under strange circumstances, and for all intents and purposes, we should have parted ways by now. Maybe that's it? The fact that he's stuck around amazes me. He has a life. He has his own problems and commitments, why is he helping me? Why is he here?

Maybe I'm helping him too? Or helping me allows him to delay what's waiting for him back at home?

Once dressed in comfy leggings and a long-sleeve top, I wrap my wet hair in a bun and exit the bathroom. He's put together a makeshift dining table with the desk and chairs.

He spies me standing in the doorway and with a few smooth strides, he's directly in front of me. His hand grasps the nape of my neck, and he leans in to kiss me. His lips against mine are quick and light, so light I wonder if I imagined it. What is he doing to me?

I have to put a stop to this familiarity. This intimacy we have. I can't deny that I like it, but it's also too fast and unsettling. The exact opposite of what I need.

Before I can tell him how I feel, my stomach growls, breaking the moment, and he laughs. Stepping out of his hold, I slap my hand over my belly as if that will stop the animal-like sound.

"You look so good I could eat you," he teases. "Let me feed you."

9

TEASE

*S*ilas

We are famished, and our silence only confirms it. We're focused on eating every morsel on our plates.

"What's next?" I ask, breaking the silence as she pops the final fry in her mouth.

"Next?" She wipes her mouth with the paper napkin, her expression perplexed.

"Where to from here? I said I'd take you wherever you want to go."

I smile at her cute, puzzled features and push the heavy, oversized chair away from the table. She does the same, resting her hand on her stomach while studying me.

"I'm headed to California. To the beach," she confides.

"Why the beach?"

"I love the ocean. I've only been a handful of times, but I've dreamed about living by the beach. I've just never followed through..." Her voice trails off, glancing down to her feet. "Until now."

Her expression is pensive and words measured. I want to hear more about her love of the beach. There seems to be something there.

"Tell me about it."

"What?" She lifts her head to ponder me. "You want to hear about my love of the beach?"

I nod encouragingly. After all, this is why I stuck around, to make sure she got to her final destination safely. If the ocean is where she wants to go, I want to know what's driving her.

"My aunt Rose and her family lived in Galveston, and while we never really had a vacation, for about five years straight, before Aunt Rose passed, we would drive and spend a few weeks with her, my uncle Bob and my cousin, Iris.

"They lived near the beach, and I would spend every waking second in the water. My daddy was an adventurer, and he and I would explore life under the water and along the shore. Did you know Galveston Bay is an estuary?"

She's smiling, and her eyes are shining. I'm not really sure what she's talking about, but her enthusiasm is vivid and contagious.

"What's an estuary?"

"It's a coastal body of water where the sea meets the mouth of a river, and the fresh and salt water mix. It's connected to the Gulf of Mexico with a variety of marine life and marshes." Her hands rapidly move as she brings them together and moves them around in circles.

"I didn't know that."

"It's beautiful and fascinating."

"Sounds like it. Well, as you know, California has a long and magnificent coast. How does Santa Monica sound? My place is steps from the beach."

"I'm not staying with you, Silas. I can't." Her gaze meets mine.

"Why not?" As the words cross my lips, I cringe at how creepy that sounds. "That came out all wrong. What I mean is, since you don't have a place to stay, you could crash at my place until you get settled. It's big enough."

I've already fucked this up by moving way too fast with her earlier today. I've got to slow the fuck down. With my lifestyle and having to be cautious because most people want things from you, I only know how to do hook-ups. Before we went to sleep, I started to make the moves on her, on autopilot, even when I knew it was wrong. I'm going to have to learn how to take direction from her. We may have met under weird circumstances, and I'm surprised that we're still together, but I want to get to know her.

"Santa Monica sounds good, but you can drop me at a motel," Pansy says.

Shaking my head, I bite my lower lip to keep from arguing with her. I like the idea of her going my way, and I'm grateful as fuck that she didn't want me to take her back the way we came. I would have gone back to Vegas if that's what she'd wanted, but I'd have hated it.

Once released from jail, my manager, Bianca, was waiting for me. My bandmates were already in LA, and she was there to take me home. I insisted on staying, telling her that I'd find my own way home. It took some convincing, but Bianca eventually arranged for a car rental and left.

"Okay. When do you want to go?"

"I call the shots?" She raises an eyebrow and cocks her head, baffled.

"Yup. I already said it but it deserves saying again, I'm truly sorry for being a jerk and calling you stupid yesterday."

I do regret my rash and cruel words. I didn't mean it, not for a second, but as usual, my anger got the better of me. It happens more often than I like to admit. While no excuse, the crap with my band and my shit luck with Pansy on the road were weighing me down. I haven't handled stress well recently, especially when feeling out of control or trapped. Unfortunately, I took it out on Pansy.

"Silas, you don't have to keep apologizing. We're good."

We share a smile, and I drink her in as she stands, hesitant. I love the cute-as-fuck shorts she was wearing yesterday, showcasing her long, bronzed legs, but what she's wearing now, fuck me. Her pants are painted on her and from the looks of things, she's not wearing underwear. Or if she is, it's one of those string-like contraptions that resemble dental floss. Her toned legs, displaying every flex and tightening of her muscles, and her heart-shaped ass are mesmerizing.

With a deep breath, I force myself to get a grip and keep this clean.

"We can leave tonight or tomorrow. We're only a little over two hours away. The choice is yours."

"I don't know about you, but I'm not tired, we could leave tonight."

In less than thirty minutes, we're packed, checked out and in the rented Range Rover. Before getting on the highway, we stop to get gas, and I can't help myself. I head to the convenience store and grab some things for Pansy.

Slipping into the driver's seat, I hand her the plastic bag with a silly grin on my face, before putting the car into gear. She peers inside and releases a belly laugh that causes me to laugh too. She pulls out the Twizzlers, salt & vinegar chips, Sour Patch Kids, and peanut M&MS, and lines them up on the console between us.

"Oh my goodness, seeing all of this kinda makes me sick. I can't believe I ate all that. My teeth still ache."

"I can't believe it either. I'm surprised you still *have* teeth." She rolls her eyes, and I wink. "Do you want me to get rid of the junk?"

"No way." She scoops up the items and dumps them in the bag, giving me an evil eye. "I didn't say I won't eat it. Just not now."

"Whatever. They're your teeth." I glance her way. "I've been thinking. We're going to be getting in late. Stay at my house for the night."

"No way. Thanks for the offer, but I couldn't."

"Yes, you can. My place is huge, and you don't have a place to stay."

"Silas, this is my last chance to get it right." She turns her head to look out the window.

"Help me out here, I don't get it. How does staying with me get in the way of you figuring things out?"

"I don't even know you." Her tone is defensive and irritated.

"Sorry. It's just that I need to do this on my own. Outside of my parents, I've always been accused of flying by the seat of my pants and not following through on things. I need to prove I'm responsible and can make something of myself."

Her tone is emphatic, and her distress is clear. I don't want to add to it, but I want to understand. "Can I ask a question?"

My tone is cautious, and she turns, her gaze on me. "What?"

"Who are you proving this to? Your sisters or yourself?"

She shrugs and twists back to the window, her voice low. "Both, I guess."

"I know you didn't ask, but I think the only one that matters is you. What do *you* want?"

"I want to make something of myself. Look at you. You're thirty, and successful. I'm twenty-seven and don't have a home, a career, or even an inkling of a future. I want more."

"Don't use me as your role model." I squeeze her knee, and she pivots in my direction, our gazes meeting. "I'm switching gears, too. I think life is meant to be like that. It's not a pre-determined route or straight path with no detours or U-turns. Sure, for some people, that's how it goes, but I think a little of the unknown is exciting and some of the unexpected or mishaps along the way are moments to learn and grow. Do you regret what you've done to date?"

She crinkles her nose and twists her lips in contemplation. "Well, when you put it like that, no. But Ivy, in fact, all my sisters have their shit together. They all have careers and are doing something with their lives."

"And you will too. You're still young, and it's not like you're letting life happen to you. You're making choices."

"I guess you're right." Her smile is faint. "They just make me feel like a failure. I'm tired of feeling that way."

"Don't listen to them. Listen to you. That's all that matters."

I'm surprised at how honest and open I am with her. I understand her struggle. Family plays such a big part in how we see ourselves. It's hard not to care what they think. Trust me, I know. I'm working on my crap with my parents, and it isn't easy. If I can help her in any way, I want to.

My parents are at the root of my anger and my distaste for this life. My dream of a band and being famous has become a nightmare because of my family. It sounds like we could help each other if I don't let my anger get the better of me.

10

CARTWHEELS

*P*ansy

"Thanks, Silas."

His candid pep talk surprises me and makes me feel better. He's right. I don't want to follow a path or live a life set out by others. I will make my own way.

"Anytime." His dimples pop as he smiles. "So back to my invitation. Staying the night doesn't mean you're not doing this on your own. What's wrong with a friend helping another friend? Come on, stay with me."

"I can't. I'll stay in a motel for now, and once I get a job, I'll find a place to live. I've got some savings, so I'm okay for two or three weeks, a month tops. That's plenty of time." I don't want to be too harsh, but I also don't know him at all. "Besides, do you really want to take in some strange woman? You're a rock star for crying out loud, what if I'm some stalker?"

He laughs. "I think we've already established that you're not a fan, so I don't think I need to worry. Stay with me." His voice is smooth and inviting. "At least until you've got a place, or longer if you want, so you wouldn't have to touch that money."

It's tempting to take him up on his offer. While I'm not scared of living on my own -- I've done it before -- it's the uncertainty. I've never lived farther than a twenty-mile radius from where I was born, and now, I'm moving to another state with only a suitcase and a rock star as my acquaintance.

"I guess." I waver. "Although, there's always plan B if I run out of money." With my uncertainty of staying with him, I attempt to joke.

"Plan B?"

"Forget finding a career; I'll marry a rich guy and spend my days barefoot and pregnant."

It was an ongoing joke between my parents. Mom raised four girls while Dad had a daily escape to the office. She would say that she should've married a rich man, at least then she could get a nanny and would have no problem being barefoot and pregnant.

The hint of nostalgia tugs at my heart. I miss my parents. My dad died of a heart attack when I was in my early teens and my mom of cancer about a decade later. They were in love until the very end, and while we weren't rich, we didn't lack for anything.

Silas's mischievous glint has me straightening in my seat, anxious for what he may say next.

"I could help you with the marry a wealthy guy part, but we'd have to ditch the rest."

"You don't want kids?"

"Nah. I've got firsthand experience with how people can fuck up their kids. I don't want to be responsible for messing up an innocent child."

I'm surprised by his revelation, and the weirdest part is, he strikes me as needing a family. He'd told me about wanting to leave the band and the rocker lifestyle, and I suspect that while he has plenty of people who call themselves friends, he doesn't have people he can trust and confide in. People who'll always have his back. A family.

I inwardly cringe; I could use one, too. I may not be alone as I have three older sisters, but our relationships are varied and for the most part, distant. I've spent years trying to ingratiate myself into their lives and change their perception of me as the flighty, stupid one. The spoiled baby.

I have no clue why I was their shared target other than being the youngest. My parents doted on me, much to the detriment of my sisters. I understood their animosity, I just didn't deserve it. I didn't ask for my parents to treat me differently.

"You're not your parents, Silas," I reason.

I may be overstepping, but it needs to be said. It's too easy to be trapped in the confines of the past, whether it's the pigeonhole your family or friends put you in or some notion you bestow on yourself. We all have the ability to break free, and sometimes, all it takes is someone telling you that you can.

"Yeah, well, I still don't want kids." His jaw tightens, ticking as his lips thin and his thumb and index finger pinch at his short beard.

With his eyes off the road, our gazes collide, and the connection is rife with emotion, laden with much more than our two days' worth of knowing each other. There's something between us -- even with our different lived experiences, we share something common and unspoken.

"Stay the night." There's a vulnerability in his voice that I'm certain he doesn't let many see. I ache for him as my barricade of independence crumbles a bit more.

We drive along the winding highway, the violet sky shifting, deepening until darkness covers everything except the stars, with the sound and scent of the surf in the background.

Inside, I'm a bundle of nerves, the battle of staying or going grows tenfold as we turn onto a street of homes facing the ocean. A thirty or forty-foot expanse of carpet-like sand lies between the houses and the sea. This is *my dream*; the sand and surf at my door. I'll never want to leave.

He parks along the curb in front of a beautiful modern beach house made of glass, and white stucco with terraces on every level. One side of the building is a monotone candy cane of clear and frosted glass, four stories high, and just behind is a hillside, lush with palm trees and bigger homes.

Following Silas up the walkway, I pause every few steps, confused.

I don't get it. It's not a mansion, although it's obvious this place cost millions, but even at that, it's like he's an average Joe.

He inserts the key and stops to examine me, his eyes narrowing at my fidgeting and sweeping glances.

"What's wrong?"

"Um, where are the paparazzi or guards or gates? I know we're not in LA, but you're a rock star, why is there no one around?"

He chuckles, opening the door. "I pay a lot to keep this place a secret. I've got a home in LA that's registered as my place of residence. There have been some close calls, but the good thing is that I'm on tour so much this place is a secret. I have to be around a while before the paps realize I'm home."

"Hmm." I find that fascinating considering how popular he is. You'd think the media would be all over him.

We're standing in an open foyer with high ceilings, at least fifteen feet. A middle-aged woman and man of Mexican descent, if I had to guess, stand to the side with smiles for Silas.

"Jorge and Lucia, *hola*."

Silas shakes the man's hand and then kisses and hugs the woman before introducing them to me as his housekeeper, cook, and all-around everything. He speaks of them like family. They live with him and keep the house running while he's on the road.

Out of my periphery, a swath of black fur bounds into the room, barking. It's a black Labrador Retriever.

"Come here, Boy." Silas slaps the tops of his thighs.

As the dog charges for him, he braces with his arms open, eager and willing to get some love from his pet. At the last minute, the animal changes course and runs to me.

With no chance to steady my legs, the dog jumps, paws landing on my stomach, and in slow motion, I rock back and forth on my heels, trying to stay upright. The dull yet hard claws of the dog scrape my flesh under my shirt, and I laugh and hiss at all the attention bestowed on me by this friendly, four-legged creature.

"Silas, she's gorgeous. She's yours?"

"Yeah." He's got an amused smirk on his face and hands on his hips. "Gee, man's best friend, huh? Until a hot chick enters the scene."

"What's her name?"

"It's a he and his name is Boy." His expression is filled with yearning as Boy showers me with affection.

"Boy? What? You can't be serious! That's not a name for this beauty." I feign indignation.

"Sorry to disappoint, but that's his name." He shrugs, unfazed by my outrage.

Crouching down, I pet Boy and peek at the anatomy while the dog pants and licks at my face. Giggles erupt within me at how happy she is to see me. My laughter intensifies upon my discovery. As I stand, Boy saunters to her master, and they share a loving, playful reunion.

"I hate to break it to you, but Boy is a she, not a he." I deliver the news to Silas, who stops mid-stroke on Boy's back.

"Not funny."

"I'm not joking. She doesn't have a penis."

Jorge coughs at my use of the word and Lucia stifles a giggle. In catching her eye, we share a small smile, and she confesses, "I didn't have the heart to tell him. We always took the dog to the vet for him, so he never knew."

Now it's my turn to stifle my laugh, but I lose the battle and fall onto my butt in a fit of giggles. Silas looks from Lucia to me, at first in disbelief which morphs into hilarity at discovering how inept he is at deciphering his dog's gender.

"Damn, I'm an idiot." Shaking his head, he wipes the few tears of laughter from his eyes. "Has he had his walk yet?"

"No, *she* hasn't. I was just going to," Jorge responds.

"I'll do it." Silas gives the dog another pat. "Lucia, would you please show Pansy to one of the guest rooms?"

"*Sí*," she answers at the same time I ask, "Can I come?"

He nods and saunters off with Boy and me trailing him through the house. I try to take in the beautiful yet austere décor, but it's all a flurry. Grabbing a Frisbee, he slips on flip-flops, and since I'm still in my beat-up cowboy boots, I take them off.

My bare feet wriggle in the cool, damp sand and I sigh content-edly. I can hardly believe I'm on the beach. Thrilled to be here, I launch into back-to-back cartwheels, with Boy barking and running around me in excitement.

Above the wind and the surf, Silas laughs and calls my name. He must think I'm crazy. Once upright, he catches up to me, still chuck-ling, and throws the Frisbee for Boy.

"That looked like fun, although I have no clue how to do what you did."

"A cartwheel? You don't know how to do a cartwheel?"

"Nope." He shakes his head.

"I could teach you if you want."

"I'd like that, but not right now. I just want to walk along the beach with you." His voice softens as he takes my hand. "How does it feel to be on the beach?"

"Amazing. There's nothing quite like the smell of the salt air and the sound of the waves."

"True. Now that I'm back, I realize I missed it."

"Your house is stunning," I gush, unable to contain my awe.

"It's okay." I move closer to hear him over the waves.

"Okay?"

"It's just a house." He shrugs, and the gesture matches his nonchalant tone. "I'm not here that often, and while Lucia and Jorge are, the place is too big." He adds with a mumble, "And lonely."

My heart aches for him. I get it. No matter how beautiful the house is, there would be no joy if you had no one to share it with.

Tugging him closer to my side, we bump arms as I lean my head on his bicep. "Thank you for inviting me to stay with you."

It's not smart, and it's temporary, but being here with Silas feels good.

"I should be thanking you. Something tells me I'm getting more out of this than you are."

"How do you figure?"

"I guess because I see all this through your eyes. It's like I'm seeing it for the first time and I like it. Who knows what else you'll make me see differently?"

11

CENTERED

*S*ilas

I wake with unease sitting heavy in my stomach. After Boy's walk last night, Pansy crashed, and I called my manager to arrange a meeting with the band. It's time to face the music.

These past couple days with Pansy, while not always smooth, have been an escape from all of that. Everything with her is simple and refreshing. My fame and fortune don't matter to her.

Once we'd wrapped our North American tour — that last night in Vegas was supposed to end things on a high. The crew and our manager had already headed back to California, and we were staying one more night to celebrate the success of our tour. If only I'd waited until we got home to tell them I wanted out.

Now that I'm home, I can't hide anymore. I need to settle things with the band before I can move on.

Seeking out Pansy, I find her on the deck doing yoga. Seeing her sexy body stretched, flexed, and fluid makes me hard. Her long auburn hair is a wild mass on the top of her head, her skin glowing from the exercise.

She doesn't realize it, but even in her current state of change, while she tries to figure out her life, she's centered and peaceful. Way more together than I feel. It calms me, fills me with a warmth I haven't felt in a long time, to just be near her. I silently admire her form as she finishes her final pose.

"Good morning," she says, her voice breathy.

Her bright smile and the biggest eyes I've ever seen nail me, slowing my heart rate and speeding it up all at the same time. Her smile shouldn't be so disarming. Something so simple, yet rewarding.

Save for Lucia and Jorge, it's unusual for anyone to genuinely be happy to see me. Sure, many praise and fawn over me, but it's not real. This is real. This beautiful woman with happiness shimmering in the depths of her eyes has no clue of the gift she's just given me.

"Hi, I see you've accomplished a lot already." I gesture to the mat she's rolling.

As she walks past me, she dabs the towel to her damp chest, her mat tucked under her arm.

"Yes, I couldn't stay in bed with the ocean just outside my door. I walked Boy this morning before yoga. It was amazing. Now I'm smelly and sticky. I need a shower and breakfast." I follow her inside and close the glass door behind us. "I need to start looking for a job, and there are a few places for rent that I've found on Craigslist."

Her tablet sits on the table, and I swallow my words of protest. "Okay, I can help." Awkwardly rubbing the nape of my neck, I try to find the courage to make my request, knowing it's weird, and if I'm honest, selfish. "Ah, I've got a favor to ask."

"Shoot."

She pulls clothes from the drawers, and there's a strange fluttering in my gut. Her things are in my drawers, and I fucking like it. At first, I wasn't sure if bringing her to my home was a good idea. Only a handful of people, those closest to me, have ever stepped foot in my house. This is my sanctuary.

But when showing her around last night, I wanted her here. I wanted her to like my home. It's been years since I've given a fuck what anyone thinks. And now, with her unpacked as if she may be staying a while, I feel like I've won the lottery.

"Um, I gotta go meet with the band to talk through my exit strategy, and I'd like you to come with me."

"What? Why?" she asks, and my lips mash into a firm line, realizing I may need to persuade her. "Sorry; I mean, I'll come with you, but why do you want me there? I don't know them, and I'm not sure what I can do."

"I could use the moral support. We haven't talked since the road, and my manager says they're still angry. I could just walk, but that could make things ugly, and they could drag me through the courts, which I'd rather avoid. We need to hash this out, and I'd feel better if you were there."

Understanding dawns in her eyes. "Of course. Let me get ready, and then we can go."

"Thank you, I really appreciate it." With a nod, I leave her to dress.

Once breakfast is done, we're on the road to LA. We are meeting on supposedly "neutral territory," although I'm not sure how my manager's office is neutral when she has a vested interest in me staying with the band.

As the elevator doors open, Bianca, my manager, is there, waiting.

"Silas." Bianca leans in for a kiss on the cheek, but not before giving Pansy the once-over. "And who is this?"

"B, this is Pansy. Pansy, my manager, Bianca Ramirez."

"Hi, nice to meet you." They shake hands with tight smiles.

"Silas, this is business, why would you bring a friend? No offense." She briefly glances at Pansy. "She's not going in with you."

We follow her down a hall. "Bianca." My voice is cold, and I'm aware that I need to keep calm. "I asked her to come, and she's staying. She'll wait outside the room."

"Fine." She flips her long dark hair over her shoulder and crosses her arms.

Bianca can be a ballbreaker, that's one of the reasons she's such a great manager, but I don't appreciate it right now, especially as it's directed at Pansy.

"Bianca," I grind out, ready to lose my shit, but Pansy places her hand on my arm and gives me a gentle rub.

"Silas, I'm good. Go on in, and good luck." She gives me another one of her blinding smiles and my anger begins to fade.

With my hand on her hip, I bring her close, planting a quick kiss on her cheek, and she squeezes my bicep. Her cheeks are coated with a tinge of pink. Bright and fresh.

Bianca clears her throat, spinning on her heel before prancing into the conference room. She expects me to follow, and as much as I'd like to put her in her place by not obeying, I want to get this over with.

Glancing over my shoulder, my gaze lands on Pansy sitting on the couch. She pulls the tablet out of her bag and places it on her lap. She's continuing her search for a job and apartment while I'm in the meeting.

I enter the room, all heads swivel in my direction. Jared, Eli, and Gray sit around the large mahogany table.

"About fucking time," Jared angrily spits out.

Obviously, our time apart hasn't helped to calm him. Next to me, he's a hothead and unpredictable. We used to be tight -- in fact, we started the band together -- and I've known him the longest. But he's changed, and I suppose so have I. Sex, drugs, and rock 'n' roll, possibly in that order, are all he cares about.

"Jared." Bianca's voice is tight. "We talked about keeping this civil. Don't start or else you leave."

As much as I didn't like the way she treated Pansy, Bianca's exactly what the band needs. Some days, it's like herding cats, with each of us wanting different things, and other days, it's like refereeing a WWE match. She has the determination and attitude to keep us in line.

"Hey, Si," Eli greets me, lifting a few fingers in a wave.

As usual, he acts like Jared isn't even there, not having time for Jared's outbursts. Eli's the most mature of us all; he has to be since he's a single parent to an adorable four-year-old daughter, Crystal.

He got a groupie, Melanie, pregnant, and even though he soon discovered she was a junkie, he did the stand-up thing. He stuck by her through the pregnancy, got her clean, and made a conscious effort to be a father.

Melanie stayed clean for her pregnancy, but not even six months after giving birth, she started using again. She died two years ago of a drug overdose. Now Eli's priority is his little girl, and he doesn't have time for band drama.

Gray dips his chin but remains silent. He's the youngest and newest, and also the silent type. But when he does speak, it's usually spot on.

Our original drummer, Rich, left nearly five years ago now. At the time, he had a difficult choice to make: his love of music or his life. He had to get clean if he was going to live to see another day.

Now more than ever, I can relate to Rich. While my choice isn't life or death, it's for my well-being. I love music; it'll always be part of my life. I love nothing more than getting lost in words, creating a piece of music, but the band and fame are no longer what I want.

"Hey, guys, I just want to hash this out and come to an agreement that'll work for all of us." I pull a chair out and sit. Jared leans in, his dark, angry eyes intent on me.

"Fuck that shit. You don't give a fuck what we want." He runs a hand through his long black hair. "This is all I've ever wanted, and you fucking know that. You used to want it too, now what the fuck, man? You don't give a shit about us?"

"Jared, let him speak." Eli is calm; he's had time to think about what I said. I may be jumping the gun, but he might even see my point of view.

"Yeah, man, let him talk." Gray's cheeks redden to almost the same color as his hair. He usually goes with the flow, but when he speaks, we listen.

"Like I said the other night, music is in my blood." I start with our common bond, our love of the words, the tunes. "I'll never stop writing and playing, but this life – the tours, groupies, media..." I release a long exhale. "It's no longer what I want. I can't do one more tour, one more interview. I'm tapped out. What do I need to do to get out in the best way possible? In a way that we can part as friends, and my departure doesn't hurt your future success?"

Jared starts spewing his hateful garbage about how selfish I am, and there's nothing I can do, while Bianca and Eli interject and try to shut him up. It's going to be a long afternoon.

Three hours later, after several shouting matches, a tossed water bottle aimed at me and endless cups of coffee, we reach an agreement. I'm not wild about it, but it's the best option to get out of this quietly, quickly, and hopefully, amicably. Although I've no doubt, it won't be easy.

12

NASTY

*P*ansy

The conference door flies open, and a six-foot-three tattooed beast with wild dark hair and leather pants charges out. Startled, I almost drop my tablet, but manage to catch it on a gasp.

Stopping, he pivots in my direction; his dark, intense eyes narrow, his jaw ticks and he balls his fists. Ice chills my spine.

"Who are you?" The question would be innocent if not for his menacing tone.

"Pansy," I whisper, forgetting my voice.

"Who are you waiting for?"

"Silas." One-word answers are all I can muster with my heart jackhammering against my ribcage and echoing in my eardrums.

Then recognition hits me. It's Jared Grange, Trojan's bassist and the other rock god women throw their panties at. Like Silas, I've certainly appreciated his beauty, but I've never given him a second thought until now.

Now I'm scared shitless, and I don't know why. Well, that's not true, I do. He's intimidating, the anger rolling off him hot enough to start a fire.

"Why?"

Finding my voice and my nerve, I sit up straight and square my shoulders. "What's with the twenty questions?"

The sides of his lips twitch in amusement as two other guys and Silas exit the conference room. I recognize them as the other members of Trojan. The guys stop to gauge the situation, glancing from Jared to me and back again. Jared turns his gaze from me to Silas and laughs.

"Fuck, now I get it. This is all about pussy, isn't it? Where'd you find her?" He jerks his thumb in my direction and Silas growls.

"Her name is Pansy." Silas inches closer, his voice clipped.

Bianca quickly assesses the situation, and before I can blink, she's in between them with her long, black-manicured fingers splayed on each of their chests.

"Down, boys." She nudges Jared back a foot or two while giving him a sharp glare.

"It's Pantie or Pussy or whatever the fuck her name is." His tone is nasty as he gestures to me again. "She's the reason he wants out. Where the fuck did you meet her and why this one?"

Every single word out of his mouth is toxic and makes me ill. He's talking about me as if I'm not even there and he thinks that I'm not worthy. *Fuck him.*

"Shut the fuck up," Silas shouts, pushing past Bianca. She stumbles back, allowing him to close the distance from Jared.

I jump from my seat, but I'm not quick enough, and neither is anyone else. Silas grips the neck of Jared's shirt and slams him against the wall. Jared's laughing, taunting Silas. His dark eyes are glassy, and it's then I realize that he must be high and he's enjoying the fact that he's pushed his friend to the edge.

Bianca rushes between the men and Silas gives a bit, allowing her to push between them.

"Stay the fuck away from her," Silas says, his teeth bared and his top lip tight, almost white.

Now at Silas's side, I clasp the sides of his face and turn him to face me. Having been on the receiving end of Silas's wrath, I can see he's barely hanging on, one of his anger meltdowns approaching.

While I'm not a fan of his eruptions, I'm not scared of him. He's had many opportunities to physically hurt me and even in his rage he hasn't.

"Silas," I soothe, rubbing my fingers along his cheeks. "It's okay. He's not worth it." Whether it's my voice or my presence, something gets through to him. His gaze shifts to me and softens, despite his clenched jaw and fists.

Releasing and pushing off Jared, Silas pulls us away. "Are you okay?" He caresses the side of my neck, and I shiver.

Nodding, I steer him to the couch, even farther away from Jared, who's watching with avid interest. I don't know why he hates me and why he's concluded that I'm the reason for the band's breakup. Silas came to that decision before he'd even met me. But either way, unease coils in my gut at feeling like an animal in a predator's snare.

"Silas, call me when you're done with her, I want to give her a go. I bet her poontang sure is sweet. I can almost taste it." Jared winks at me, his tongue snaking out like he's licking me. "I'll see you soon, darlin'."

"You motherfucker, I'm gonna kill you!" Silas lunges for him, and I wrap myself around his arm.

"Jared, enough!" Bianca shouts, her beautiful features twisting into outrage and something else. Hurt?

It takes Bianca, both guys, and me to hold Silas back as Jared saunters away, his wicked chuckle echoing down the corridor.

"I'm sorry for that asshole," the brown-haired guy says as he releases his hold on Silas and turns to me.

"I'll go talk to him," Bianca mutters, giving me a tight smile before heading after the jerk.

I'm speechless. I want to both cry and kick Jared's ass, and it doesn't help that Silas is wound tight and furious.

"He's an asshole," I confirm, and the clean-cut, brown-haired man grins in response.

"Hi, I'm Eli Lansing." He extends his hand, and the red-haired guy follows suit and offers his hand.

"Hi, I'm Grayson Bennett, but call me Gray." His blue eyes

shimmer while he shakes my hand, but it's brief. He drops my hand and quickly averts his gaze as if he's shy or anxious.

"Hi, Pansy Dobson. Pleased to meet you," I lie, not about meeting them, but there's been nothing nice about this whole encounter.

"Fuck, Pansy, I'm sorry. Had I known he was going to be a colossal dick, I'd never have asked you to come." Silas scrubs his hand down his face before pulling me to his side.

While I'm comforted by the gesture, I'm also uncomfortable because it's intimate and I've no clue what we are to each other. We're acquaintances, maybe even friends, but that's it at this point. He's acting like I'm more and I'm unsure as to how to feel about that, especially since Jared just accused me of breaking them up.

"It's fine." My voice is dismissive. I just want to forget about it.

"Silas, get Otto to do up the papers and send them to me as soon as possible," Bianca cuts in, all business.

None of us saw her return, but all the guys are now gawking at her as if she has three heads. She really is stunning with her olive skin, dark brown eyes, full lips, and high cheekbones, and when you think hourglass figure, I'm pretty sure Bianca is the poster child. But even with all her beauty, she looks indifferent, almost cold.

"Easy, B," Eli cautions. "He'll get it done. You can back off for the day."

Silas's eyes widen; his jaw slackens and shoulders relax at Eli's defense of him.

"Did you find him?" Gray asks Bianca.

"No, I gave up. Let him cool off," she says, exasperated, although there's almost a pained tinge to her words.

Eli claps Silas on the shoulder and says goodbye to both of us, taking Gray and Bianca with him.

"Can we get out of here?" I ask once they're gone.

Silas nods, and the walk to the car is silent. I can almost hear the wheels turning in his head as he mulls over what's on his mind. I wait until we're in the car and on our way to his house to ask.

"So, how'd it go?"

"Not as I'd hoped, but better than expected." He fiddles with the satellite radio before continuing. "They want one more album and an LA concert for our final farewell. With that, they'll let me walk away with what's rightfully mine."

"That sounds fair."

"Yeah, it is. Although when we do an album, it's intense. Long hours, little to no sleep for days. But I can do it." He's trying to convince himself.

"Well, let's look at the bright side, there's an end in sight. Will they find another lead singer?"

He laughs, but it's not light, more sardonic. "That's the thing. Eli and Gray are considering other things too. It might be the end of Trojan."

"What? Why did they leave you on the side of the road if they were thinking the same thing?"

"I think I scared them. It forced them to consider other things. Eli has a daughter, and he wants to spend more time with her, and Gray, I'm not sure where his head's at, but he's got something in mind. But when Jared lost it, they just followed suit. He can be domineering and intimidating."

"You think?"

Silas chuckles at my sarcasm. "Yeah. I get why it went down the way it did. I could've handled it better."

"And Jared, he's the only one who wants to keep going?" I don't know why I'm asking about that asshole. I don't care what he wants.

"Jared doesn't know what he wants. He likes the pussy, drugs, and parties. I used to be him, so I understand that he's not there yet." My stomach sours and my heart twinges at Silas comparing himself to that jackass. "The problem is that he's high more times than not and I'm not sure if he's even in it for the music anymore."

His tone is solemn, darkness blanketing a starry sky. He cares about them, even Jared -- perhaps especially Jared. While he wants out, it must be sad to have something you created come to an end.

Minutes from Silas's house, we stop at a restaurant, two streets over from the beach. The *Help Wanted* sign catches my eye, and while Silas is in the bathroom, I talk with Betty, the owner.

She's a short, round woman in her early sixties with cropped white hair and she smells like freshly baked cookies. She encourages me to apply, and I use my tablet to email her my résumé on the spot. By the time he returns, I'm convinced I have the job.

"Black coffee for you, my boy?" Betty points her pencil at him.

He nods. "Yes, thanks."

"And Pansy, what'll it be?"

"I'll have a latte and a slice of lemon meringue pie." I feel like celebrating, splurging on the pie even though I don't have the job yet.

The minute Betty leaves, I'm unable to contain my excitement. "You'll never guess what just happened!"

Silas matches my enthusiasm with a twinkle in his eye and flash of a dimple. "What?"

"I think I have a job!"

"You do?" He scrunches his brow, cocks his head to the side, confused.

"Betty, she's got a position open, and we just got to talking."

"I told you that you're more than welcome to stay at my place and take your time figuring out what you want to do."

Heaving a heavy sigh, I purse my lips. He means well, but his disappointment is written all over his face, and it's a total buzzkill. It also ticks me off because this is something I want to do, and I'm tired of everyone telling me that every choice I make is stupid or wrong.

"Silas, we've already been through this, please don't do this again. I'm moving out, the sooner, the better, and I need a job. This is a good thing."

"Fine," he says, although I can tell by his short tone and hard expression that it's anything but fine. "I just want to say, one last time, you don't have to move out. Save every penny." His voice is now softer, almost pleading.

"Silas, I know this is coming from a good place, but I can't take this handout from you."

"It's not a handout; you'd be doing something for me too. I enjoy your company and I want to get to know you better."

"I want that too."

It's not until I actually say the words that I realize it's true. I do. I've been on the fence even though he wants more. Or at least that's what I'm getting from his intimate gestures. I've been fighting it with everything I've got because I don't want to fall into my old habits.

I'm not boy crazy, but whenever I've had a man in my life, I usually move in with him, and I get comfortable. So comfortable that I stop trying. I don't want to do that anymore. Besides, who knows if Silas and I are even meant to be together?

"I need to do this on my own. It doesn't mean we can't hang out."

He looks away, playing with a few sugar packets, and his jaw ticks, his annoyance evident. I have the urge to appease him and cave, but I won't this time. I'm sticking to my guns and doing what's right for me.

"Okay." His thumb gently rubs the tops of my knuckles.

"Thank you." I smile, bolstered by his sweet gesture.

He doesn't return the smile, but his eyes fix on me. How did we get here? I can't help but wonder, what do we have in common? If we hadn't run into each other in the desert, there's not a chance in a million years that our paths would have crossed. Or maybe they would have?

We have an undeniable attraction, that's the easy part, but aside from that, is there something here to build on? He's everything I'm not – rich and famous. He's already made a name for himself and conquered the world, where I'm still struggling to figure out my shit.

I think he gets my drive. While it may not seem like a big deal to most, it is everything to me. Growing up with disparaging comments from my siblings cut deep, and I want to heal, to prove to them and myself that I count. I'm worthy of being here, just like everyone is.

13

PROMISE

*P*ansy

"You have a good night, darlin'," Betty hollers.

"Thanks, Betty. You too." I stroll from the office, having just finished my shift.

It's been almost a week since I started working and while it's long days, I like it. Betty is a sweet woman, and the staff is friendly. It's been non-stop today, and I'm ready to crash. Since Silas hasn't started the album, he's been picking me up, but he can't tonight. He had a meeting in LA, so Jorge will be here in about twenty minutes.

Rather than wait outside in the heat, I pop into the kitchen and find Bunny, our chef, plating a dish.

"Hey, Bunny, got any crazy plans for tonight?"

He looks away from the plate with ribs and cornbread, his smile big and bright. "Flower girl," he says with a wink. "My ass is stuck in this kitchen until closing."

Callie, my new friend and co-worker, enters the kitchen and lightly hip-checks me. "Janis is *still* not here."

I shake my head and sigh. "Do you need help until she shows up? I've got time until my ride gets here."

"No, I'm good, hon," Callie says.

Janis is another waitress, and even though I'm new, it's obvious that she's a problem. She's always late and never penalized for it. While she's a single parent and has difficulty finding a sitter, she seems to get paid for her full shift no matter how late she is. I'm convinced she's bumping uglies with Ralph, the assistant manager.

Callie takes the two plates from Bunny and leaves. I have no clue why he's called Bunny, and he refuses to tell me. In fact, he out and out ignores me every time I ask, and trying to get the 411 from Betty is like trying to get into the Pentagon. Not going to happen.

I imagine it's something sweet and romantic because how else do you rationalize a six-foot-tall, two-hundred-and-fifty-pound, fifty-year-old African-American man being called Bunny?

"I thought JJ was working tonight?"

"That boy called in sick, again." We share a skeptical look. "He's not long for this joint, let me tell you."

"That sucks, Bunny. You have a good night."

I plant a kiss on his cheek, and he gives my shoulder a light squeeze.

"You too, flower girl. Say hi to Jagger for me," he jokes, referring to Silas.

Everyone who works at Betty's knows who Silas is and knew him well before I worked here. Both Betty and Bunny are fans and take any chance they get to rib him.

I laugh and leave, finding a spot at the counter to chat with Callie while I wait. She's making lattes when a tall, lean, dark-haired man stands beside me.

"This seat taken?" he asks, peering down at me and the empty stool beside me.

"No, it's all yours." I gesture to the spot, and he smiles before awkwardly cramming his lanky limbs into the confines of the diner stool.

"I'm Vincenzo Lupo, but call me Vinny." He extends his mitt-sized hand, his elbow knocking my arm as we shake.

"Pansy."

"This is my first time here. What's good to eat?"

"Pretty much anything. Well, that's not true. Don't have the nachos or tacos. Bunny's a great cook, but he's definitely not from the hacienda, and no matter what we say, he refuses to believe it."

He chuckles, his dark eyes twinkle, and his mouth spreads wide to reveal a gleaming row of straight, white teeth.

"All right, a burger it is." He slaps down the menu, and I have to fight the urge to spring into action and put his order in.

Janis arrived while I was in the back, and now she's flitting around, flirting more than working.

"Janis, a burger for this gentleman," I call to her because Callie's no longer in front.

Janis absentmindedly nods as she's busy trifling with Ralph, the manager who should have left hours ago.

"He may be thirsty, too; you might want to take his drink order." I can't resist reminding her that she should be working.

Vinny chuckles beside me, and Janis narrows her heavily made-up eyes at me; then she spies him, and as predicted, her expression shifts from annoyance to opportunist. Vinny is good looking, with deep-set eyes the same color as his black coffee colored hair, golden skin, a cleft chin, and an athletic build.

"I'm fine, thanks." He waves her away. "Just some water, please."

She spins on her heel and puts an extra something-something into her hips.

"So, you come here often?" he asks.

Water sprays from my mouth, my laughter following fast behind. With the back of my hand, I wipe at the drops running down my chin, shaking my head in disbelief and embarrassment. He hands me a napkin.

"You didn't just say that to me."

"What?"

"That's the oldest and lamest pickup line *ever*."

"What?" His eyes widen, dawning with understanding. "I wasn't trying to pick you up. No, it's just that you know the waitress and what's on the menu and..."

Saving him from his verbal diarrhea, I interject, "Vinny, now you're just insulting me. You weren't picking me up?"

His mouth opens and closes, his eyes darting all over the place as he squirms in his seat. Even though we've only just met, this guy is so easy to read. He's trying to decide if he should shut this down, find another seat, or run.

"I'm kidding. Relax. For a split second, I did think you were trying to flirt. Rather badly, I might add. I work here. My shift just ended and I'm waiting on my ride."

He nods, and a small smile breaks through his uneasy features. He leans his forearm on the counter, and it's then I notice a white cloth wrapped around his arm, from his elbow to wrist.

"What happened?"

We both glance at his bandage, and he grimaces on a slow exhale.

"Diving mishap. I cut it along some coral, and it tore me up pretty good."

"You dive?" I ask, fascinated.

"Yeah. I'm a marine biologist. I teach at UCLA, and if I'm lucky, get to spend the summer researching with other scientists."

"Wow. A marine biologist. What's that all about?"

"The simple answer is that it's the study of marine organisms and sea life."

"Does that mean you're in the water a lot? And how do you study them?"

"Not always in the water. It depends on the area of focus. Some marine biologists teach, some are dolphin trainers, others work for corporations..."

"Wow, really?"

Vinny chuckles. "Yeah, it's fascinating and diverse. You could manage a marine wildlife sanctuary, or work in a museum, or do research. It sounds glamorous, but it's a lot of hard work, and in some cases, long grueling hours in the lab."

His burger arrives, and we continue to talk. He graciously answers all my questions between mouthfuls.

"You mentioned diving? What's involved with diving?" I ask.

"Well, you need to get certified to dive. It's important you have all the proper gear and know what you're doing."

"Tell me more."

Vinny continues with more on how to get your diving certification, and the thought of deep diving, learning about the ecosystem under the sea, excites me. My phone buzzes, signaling that Jorge is here.

"Vinny, I've got to go, but I want to know more, and I definitely want to get my diving certification. What should I do?"

"If you're serious, I'll arrange the diving; I just need your contact info. And if you change your mind, that's okay too. We've only just met and sometimes, once the thrill wears off and things sink in, you might change your mind. If so, no prob."

He hands over his phone, and I put my number into it, also sending a text to me so that I have his number. "Thanks again. Talk soon."

I wave goodbye to Callie and hop into the car with Jorge behind the wheel.

The house is in dark when we get home, and Boy greets me with a brush against my bare legs and a wag of her tail as I slip off my Chucks.

"Jorge, thank you. Good night."

"Night," he says, heading down to their apartment. "See you in the morning."

I've been trying to find a place, but so far, I've had no luck. Santa Monica is expensive, and anything in my price range is a dump. The longer I stay here, the harder it will be to leave.

I traipse up the stairs, ready for a bath and bed when the music hits me. I tiptoe toward the music studio where I find the door ajar. Silas sits at the piano, his profile's silhouetted by the moonlight filtering in through the wall of glass.

This is where he goes to make his music. To escape and create. It's simple and sparsely decorated with his musical instruments and the magnificent view of the ocean and sky as a breathtaking backdrop.

In addition to the piano, a worn-out guitar case rests against the wall, a music stand in the corner, and a small desk with a pencil and papers strewn about.

Silas is oblivious to my presence as the melodic notes float through the air. I sway to the beat, mesmerized by his grace when the tune registers. "September Song" by Agnes Obel. My breath catches because this song reminds me of my mother. Even though she wasn't alive to hear it, she loved piano pieces.

Tears prick at the corners of my eyes, and I sniff to keep them from falling. Stopping mid-note, Silas turns to me, and his serious expression softens. I'm drunk on him.

Relationships with the opposite sex have always been fun, nothing more. I don't do casual, and I wasn't driven to have a boyfriend, it didn't matter to me. Yet with Silas, whatever is between us has the potential to be huge and life-changing. Even uncertain of this volatile, creative, and sweet man, I'm drawn to him.

"Hey, you." The rasp of his voice sparks heat within me.

"Hey, I thought you were in LA." Taking one step into the room, I plant my back against the wall, not daring to go any farther.

His brow arches before he turns to pull the cover over the keys.

"I was. Got back about an hour ago. I had dinner with Bianca and my lawyer, Otto, to go over the agreement."

"How'd it go?"

"Fine, but slow. We still have to go back to the label for their consent, and it's not likely they'll agree to everything. So, it's a work in progress, but we'll get there."

"What you were playing was beautiful."

"Thanks. It wasn't mine."

He now stands in front of me with his hands in his pant pockets. He's more dressed up than I've ever seen him before in black dress pants, a blue button-down shirt, and his hair back in a low, tidy ponytail.

"I know. Besides the guitar and piano, do you play anything else?"

"The bass and ukulele."

"Wow."

We are only ten feet apart, but it feels both close and far. He strides slowly and deliberately toward me.

"How was work?" He places one hand on the wall beside my head, and his other tucks stray strands behind my ear. His blue eyes flash with fire, and I hold his stare.

"Fine," I whisper as he leans in, licking his lips as to his intent. With a firm hand on his chest, I halt his progress.

"I missed you." His low, smooth voice intensifies the mass of butterflies stirring inside me.

"Silas, what are we doing?" I'm overwhelmed by our attraction and perplexed. Should I even be rooting for *us*? We're such an unlikely pair.

"This is me getting to know you better." He smirks, running his thumb along my collarbone.

Pushing him back, I step from between him and the wall and head to the view of the gentle, rolling waves beyond the glass.

"No, that was you trying to kiss me. That's different." I twirl to face him, back against the cool glass.

Still by the door, he studies me with his thumb lightly grazing his lower lip. "I've kissed you before. I liked it." His voice deepens. "Really liked it. I want us to give this a try."

He advances on me until he's only a foot away and gazes down at me. I tilt my head up to meet his eyes. Why is my heart racing when he hasn't even touched me?

"What do you mean by 'this?'" I dare to ask.

I need him to be crystal clear. Even as I try to keep our attraction at bay, terrified of screwing up this chance at getting my life right, I want him. Even if he's not part of the plan. No guy is at this point.

What scares me the most is that he's not just some guy. I could easily date, and it would be light and fun, but not with Silas. I could get lost in him and abandon my goal. Together, we're more addictive than anything I've ever had.

"I haven't had a serious relationship since high school. Once I started the band, music was my only focus. And once my career took off..." He pauses, pulling me in for a hug before bringing us to sit on the piano bench, side-by-side. He swallows hard and wipes his palms on the tops of his thighs.

"I was a dog. I've slept with lots of women, groupies, and I didn't ask their names and didn't want their numbers. It was about getting off and nothing else."

I slide a few inches from him, and he takes my hand. What he did before me shouldn't matter. We didn't know each other, but it's hard to hear.

If I'd known him then, I would have wanted nothing to do with him. He sounds like the type of guy I'd steer clear of. Silas wouldn't have been my type. I'm not sure he is now, but I'm willing to find out even if it hurts.

"Go on," I encourage him.

"Like everything else, it soon became old, and I was lonely. Sex was no longer enough. I wanted something more. I want a relationship, and you're the first woman in what feels like forever who I want to explore that possibility with."

"Silas, I'm not going to deny that I feel the same way about you." A slow, sexy grin breaks across his face, and I rush to get it all out. "But I'm also uncertain. I want, no, scratch that, I *need* to focus on me, to figure out what I want to do with my life. I'm worried you'll be a distraction. A wildly sexy and sweet distraction, but one nonetheless."

Silas chuckles and lightly kisses my lips before pulling me up with him from the bench. He tucks me into his side and opens the glass door to the balcony.

"I'm relieved that you feel the same way, but I don't want to be just a distraction."

"I don't mean it like that." My palm burns on his hard chest, and like an electric shock, my body buzzes. "You're more than that, and I guess that's what's holding me back. That's why I need to move out and do this on my own. I can't be so wrapped up in you that I forget about my dreams."

"Okay, let me make you a deal. Let's figure out together what we have here, and I promise not to let you give up your dreams. I'll put your dreams before anything else."

14

TENSION

*S*ilas

"Otto, no fucking way."

It's my third call of the day with my lawyer about the album agreement. All this time, I thought Jared would be the holdout, the one stalling or causing problems, but he's not.

Surprisingly, he's agreed to everything. It's the record company. They want not only our last album but a full tour. Like we haven't already given them a pound of flesh and then some over the past decade.

Trojan made them a fucking shit ton of money, and always delivered on our commitments. Even with that, it doesn't seem to be enough. If we were tanking on the charts and not selling songs, we would be history. *Fuckers.*

"Otto, I don't care what you have to do, I'm not doing a world tour," I yell, clenching the phone so tightly I feel it give. "Fucking fix it," I shout, tossing the phone across the room, where it hits the wall and shatters into pieces. There's a gasp from the doorway. Turning, Pansy stands wide-eyed, gaping at me.

"Silas, you okay?"

"Fuck, no, and I don't want to talk about it."

While my irate tone has nothing to do with her, she steps back out of the room as Lucia rounds the corner, bumping into her.

"Oh, sorry," Pansy says, clasping her chest with one hand and the other steadying Lucia.

"It's all right, *mija*." Lucia waves it away, looking from Pansy to the smashed phone on the floor, then to me. "I'll call Bianca to get you a new cellphone. Your mother is on the phone."

"You've got to be shitting me," I grind out and Lucia tsks disapprovingly.

"No, Silas, I no joke. Here." She hands the portable house phone to him while using her feet to sweep the electronic bits into a pile. Pansy readies to follow Lucia out the room, but I say, "Please stay."

With one hand on the doorframe, she hesitates, but it's only for a second before she nods and steps back into the room.

A heavy, dark tension slides down my spine, and I close my eyes to find some peace before hearing my mother's voice. I already feel my blood boiling from my call with Otto, and I have selfishly asked Pansy to stay in hope of her being a calming influence on me.

I feel the heat of Pansy's stare, and I can't blame her for being wary of me. A part of me wishes that she hadn't witnessed my outburst or what's about to come. This is going to be unpleasant. A call from my parents always is, and Pansy's about to get a front row seat to this crap.

"Hi, Mom."

"Silas, why haven't you called?" Her tone is accusing and whiny. "Bianca told us you had some trouble with the band. Is everything okay?"

Gritting my teeth, I mentally remind myself to speak to Bianca, *again*, about not sharing shit with my parents. No matter how many times I tell her to not divulge information, she does. She has a soft spot for them, but I haven't shared the full truth about them.

"I've been busy. We're going in a new direction with the band, and it's taken up a lot of my time."

As I've learned over the years, it's best to be vague when it comes to my career. My relationship with my parents is tenuous, at best. I don't know how I went from having a great childhood and loving parents to this. If I think too much about it, my anger consumes me.

While I was a struggling artist, they didn't support my career choice and cut me off. But once I became rich and famous, my parents wanted to patch things up. At first, I was ecstatic, but it soon became clear that I was a meal ticket, no longer a son.

Over the years, I kept my loss and disappointment bottled up inside where it morphed and grew into rage, only adding to my desire to leave this life. When I told Pansy I was working on my anger, it wasn't a joke. I've done group therapy and hated every fucking second of it.

Sharing my feelings and my triggers was bad enough, but listening to others' problems didn't work for me. Then there was individual therapy, but the doctor was too good, got too close to the wound, so I quit.

Looking back, that wasn't smart. If I'd continued, I most probably wouldn't still be struggling with how to tell my parents what I feel.

"What direction?" she asks.

I could fluff this off, but I'm tired of avoiding confrontation with them. It inevitably comes to a head. I'm thirty, and it's my life. They'll support me, or they won't. I slump back onto my desk.

"We're doing one more album, and then I'm out of Trojan." I'm matter-of-fact.

"What?" she shrieks. "You can't do that!"

I laugh, but it's not jovial. It's dark and pointy, every chuckle cutting like glass at my insides. This is what I expected. I'm just an ATM.

"I can, and I am." I bang my fist on the piano keys, the sharp sounds causing Pansy to jump.

"Silas, this makes no sense. I'm getting your father so he can talk some sense into you."

"Mom..." She's no longer on the phone, but I hear her shrill tone as she fills in my father.

"Silas, why are you throwing away your dream?"

My father's voice is authoritative. He thinks he calls the shots. No *hello*? Or *please explain to me why you want to do this*?

Pansy furtively glances my way as she wanders around the room. She's distressed from my outburst and the acrimony in my tone. When we make eye contact, she motions as if she should leave. I shake my head. No way.

While I'm not enjoying the talk, and don't want to subject her to this, I also don't want her to leave. Having her here is keeping my anger in check. I shudder to think what state I'd be in if she wasn't here.

"Dad, this is my decision. It's happening. I don't need to give you an explanation."

"Silas." His tone is terse and frustrated. "You can't do this."

"This conversation is done." Ending the call, I hang my head, my jaw so tight that a headache's coming on.

"Are you okay?" Pansy asks.

"No. I need to get out of here."

I want to beat the shit out of something. Having Pansy close helped but given my track record with her, I don't want to take this out on her.

"I'm going for a swim."

"Do you want me to come?"

Any other circumstance and I'd jump at the chance to have her in the water. But I'm not in the right headspace.

"Nah, gotta go."

"Okay. Come find me if you need me." Pansy has no clue how much that means to me.

I don't even bother to change my jeans and shirt. The need to run is overwhelming. Slipping on my running shoes, I hit the beach, and every step along the wet, hard sand is one less punch I want to deliver. I don't know how long I run, and once done, it's better, but there's still rage within me.

Without a care for who is around, I whip off my clothes, leaving only my boxers on, and dive into the ocean. After minutes of swimming, I feel better. More tired and less angry, although not completely over it.

With a damp matted mess for hair and a towel slung over my shoulder, I search until I find Pansy in the kitchen.

She's with Lucia, and their backs are to me, and it looks like Lucia's teaching her how to make something.

"I used to do this with Silas," Lucia says as she pulls the sugar out of the cupboard.

"Really? When was this?"

"I've known him since he was eighteen. He moved in with us not too long after he started the band."

"He lived with you?"

"*Sí*. He was on his own, him and Jared, but things were hard. The boys were just starting out. Jorge and I were friends of Bianca's parents, that is how we met him."

"Bianca?"

"*Sí*, I've known Bianca since she was in diapers." Lucia twists the long strips of dough and Pansy follows her every move. "While the boys were on their own, we wanted to help them. They stayed with us for a while."

"I thought it was the other way around," Pansy says. "I thought Silas met you and hired you to take care of his house."

"No, *mija*, we took care of him first. He's always been a good boy, a sweet one. He's a son to me. His parents..."

Lucia shakes her head and pauses. Pansy stands still, as if she dares not move for fear of breaking the moment. I too am transfixed -- even though I know how the story ends.

"Things are hard with his parents. When we met him, he was not on good terms with them, but then he was. Now it has turned again. I don't know what it's all about, and I don't push, but it's eating at him."

"How so?"

My stomach twists, the acid bubbling and churning with the truth. I should interrupt, but Lucia is doing me a favor. She's explaining things to Pansy that I intended to, but can't seem to bring myself to do.

"He's having a hard time with them. He is quick to temper and very angry," Lucia says, rushing to add, "And he has every right to be. I don't understand it all, but... *Mija*, I should not be saying this all to you. It is not my place. I try not to push Silas, but let him know we are here for him if ever he needs us."

"I'm glad he has you."

"*Mija*, I'm glad he has you, too." Lucia smiles and pats Pansy's hand.

"I don't know how I can help. I don't even know what's wrong."

"Ah, but you do help. Silas has a lot of loss, and he struggles to find those he can trust. He trusts you."

"He does?" I hear the smile in her voice.

"*Sí, mija*, you are good people and Silas sees that."

Pansy laughs, and that's my cue to join them.

"Hey, what's cooking?"

My eyes lock on Pansy's warm ones while slipping my hand around Lucia's waist to plant a sloppy kiss on her cheek.

"Silas, you are wet!" Lucia pushes out of my arms, rubbing her cheek as if my affection bothers her, but her eyes shine with a tender gaze for me. "Go and get some clothes on."

I'm still only in my boxers, and wet. Pansy notices too, blushing with her gaze anywhere but on me.

"Sorry, I couldn't help myself." Lucia and Jorge are very important to me. They are family.

"Everything okay?" Pansy asks, cautiously.

"Yeah, better now. First, it was crap about the album, the label wants more, and then... the call from my parents."

"It's a lot for one person to deal with."

"It'll work out," I say, wanting to believe. Turning to Lucia, I ask, "What can I do to help?"

"Go wash your hands and put some clothes on first. Then you can help Pansy with these."

"Yes, ma'am," I say in a playful tone.

Pansy giggles, and this time she roams my body, and my cock

twitches at the desire in her eyes. It's definitely time for me to take a cold shower.

15

RIGHT

*P*ansy

  Squeezing the excess water from my hair, I grab my bag and exit the change room. Vinny is waiting outside with my books and gear. Since we've met, we've spoken many times, with some conversations lasting as long as an hour. I'm not sure if marine biology is for me, but from everything I've read and the information he's shared, I think this may be it.

"So, what do you think?" he asks as we walk to his car.

It's a beautiful sunny day with a light breeze. I could easily spend it on the beach, in the water, but I can't. I have to work, and even more so now that I've started my diving certification course. It's not an easy process, nor is it cheap, but I want to do it.

I can't believe I never thought of professions to do with the ocean, especially with my affinity for the water. Now that I'm aware of the possibilities, it seems so obvious.

Today's class was the first time in the water. In a pool, not the open water. It will be this way for a while. The day's lesson was the basics of snorkeling.

"Good, but it seems so easy."

"Don't let that fool you." Vinny chuckles. "Some of it is common sense, but there's much more to diving than just that. It can be risky, even leading to death if you don't know what you're doing."

"I know. I'm taking it seriously."

He opens the passenger door for me and walks around to the driver's side. "What does Silas think of all this?"

Vinny and I have talked about more than just diving and marine biology. He's easy to talk to since I have no fear of failure or of disappointing him. Not that Silas has put any expectations on me, in fact, it's the opposite. He supports me in every way. It's my own expectations that scare me.

Ignoring the twist in my chest, my guilt, I say sheepishly, "I haven't told him yet." Vinny glances at me, his interest piqued. "I will, soon, I just didn't want to say something and then discover it's not for me."

"Have you done that before?"

"Unfortunately, yes. My adult life has been trial and error. I like to think there was a reason for it, besides the wasted money and time."

"Everything happens for a reason," Vinny says philosophically.

"I like to think so."

Vinny drops me at Betty's with ten minutes to spare. We make plans for the next diving class and the rest of the day is a blur. Busy and exhausting. I welcome the end of my shift, and for a split second, I fantasize about the bubble bath I have plans for when I remember my date with Silas.

After declaring that he wanted us to be an *us*, he insisted on doing things right. His idea of right is to go on a real date. We're also celebrating that they have finalized the contract. He even asked me to schedule my shift around the signing tomorrow.

Jorge picks me up, and I manage to shower and get dressed before Silas. I haven't seen him yet. Lucia *ohs* and *ahs* over my floral maxi dress, which isn't anything fancy. It's the only thing I possess that's even remotely appropriate for a date.

I think Lucia is just as excited as I am and is making me nervous as she flits around the room making work for herself.

Silas clears his throat, announcing his presence, and I tear myself away from the captivating ocean view to another equally-appealing one. He's in all black. Casual, yet classic, in dress pants and a dress shirt with the top two buttons undone and sleeves rolled up his forearms. The dark contrasts perfectly with his glowing skin, golden hair and light eyes.

The throbbing pulse of my heart echoes deep within my core, and my sex clenches as I drink him in. He's striking.

"Pansy, you're beautiful," he says, desire coloring his voice as he steals my thoughts.

"I could say the same about you."

Now in front of me, he takes my hand and lightly kisses me on the cheek. "And you smell like I could eat you, too," he whispers for only me to hear as my heart leaps and goosebumps prickle my skin.

This is going to be a long and agonizing night. All I can think about is having Silas. I'm hungry for him. Dizzy with want. This is so unlike me. I've never felt so consumed with such strong desire, and the night's only just begun.

"Wait, before you go," Lucia says, aiming her phone in our direction. "I want a picture of you together. You make such a beautiful couple."

I blush, and Silas agrees, pulling me into his side. With his arms around my waist, my hand on his strong forearm, we smile for the camera.

"Perfect." Lucia claps her hands, beaming from ear to ear like a proud mama capturing her child going to prom.

Our goodbyes are sweet and happy, and the mood lingers on our drive to the restaurant while Silas fills me in on the final details of the contract. Once he signs, he'll be locked away writing the last Trojan album.

I don't know what it all entails, but he's told me many times that it's all-consuming, and while he's committed to doing it, I get the sense he's torn. I'm not sure why, but I can tell his heart's not fully into it.

His phone rings and Silas glances at the car screen to the name:

Mom and Dad. A fleeting look of irritation washes over his features before he hits talk.

"Hello." His voice is even, almost charming, belying what I just witnessed.

"Silas, honey, we've got a problem," a woman, who I am guessing is his mother, says.

"What's wrong?" His concern is subtle but evident in not only his tone but also in the way he sits up straighter in his seat.

"The monthly transfer isn't in our account. Did you forget to do it?" Her pitch is high and whiny.

"Mom, I've told you this before. They're pre-authorized transfers for the first of every month, I can't forget, it's automatic. It'll be there the first business day of the month. You've got a couple days, that's all. Don't worry." His fingers tap aggressively on the steering wheel. "Are you okay until then?" With a quick look at me, he smiles, but it doesn't reach his eyes.

"Oh, okay. No, no, as long as it's there on Monday, we're fine. Sorry to bother you, honey."

"Okay, no problem. All right, Mom, I have to go."

"Bye, honey."

"Bye." He exhales a shaky breath, and his jaw tightens.

"Do you want to talk about it?"

We've only talked a bit about his parents, but I've put enough together to figure out his wealth is a big factor. Not for Silas, but for his parents.

"Nah, I'd rather not. Tonight is about us."

"Okay."

"But, thank you. It means a lot to know I can talk to you." He reaches across the console to squeeze my knee.

The car slows, and he turns, driving up to the front of the restaurant. Media with their cameras and lights are camped out by the entrance.

"Shit. Stay here even when the valet opens the door. Don't get out until I come around."

I heed his caution and anxiously await the unknown. This is the first taste of his fame. It unnerves me. Somehow, the media caught wind of the band's impending breakup, and the first of many articles ran days ago.

Silas has been on high alert around his home and may have to stay at his LA home for a while to throw them off his trail. Now that the media know he's back in LA, they'll be watching more closely.

Opening the door, he ushers me forward, partially covering my face. Intrusive questions bombard us.

"Silas, who is she?" Hands shove phones and other devices in front of us, and flashbulbs blind us.

"Silas, can we get a shot of you and the lovely lady?"

"Silas, why's Trojan breaking up?"

"Is Jared causing more trouble?"

"Who is she?"

"Silas, Silas, can we get a picture?"

Once inside, I'm trembling and sick to my stomach. It was a mob. There is a muffled buzzing inside my head, and I feel faint.

Tucking me into his side, he guides us through the restaurant, where I vaguely make out singers, actors, and other famous people, none of them fazed by our entry or the media scrum just outside.

"Water, please," Silas orders, ushering me into the banquette and sliding in beside me. "Are you okay?"

The waiter quickly fills the glass in front of me, and I guzzle the cool liquid, washing away some of the unease. "Yeah, I will be. I don't know how you do it."

"Yeah, it can be insane. I'll get Bianca to figure something out for when we leave."

My stomach sinks at the thought. Do we have to leave? Unless... I scan the beautiful restaurant, rationalizing that I could easily live here. There's food, comfy seating, and bathrooms, what else do I really need?

"Don't worry," Silas reassures me, softly rubbing my hand while tucking away his phone. "It's taken care of."

After a few minutes of his soothing voice, the chaos of the paparazzi is forgotten. Dinner is lovely, and Silas is attentive, holding my hand throughout our meal and leaning in every so often to kiss the side of my neck or the back of my earlobe. At one point, he even nuzzles into my hair, inhaling deeply.

My heart's in a constant state of flutter, at times threatening to explode from my chest, especially when he slides his hand under my dress to caress my knee and thigh.

My breath catches, anticipating his travel north, but he never does. He's content to deliciously rub small circles on the inside of my knee with an occasional squeeze.

He's driving me crazy, and he knows it. I can't help but think that he likes what he's doing to me. His sexy grin and the mischievous glint in his baby blues say it all. I'm wet and horny, and if we weren't in a room filled with strangers, I'd rip my dress off and beg him to fuck me.

"You were gone before I got up this morning. I thought your shift didn't start until lunch?" he asks.

"Do you remember Vinny, the guy I met at Betty's?"

"The professor?" His fingers tap along my bare thigh like he's playing the piano.

"Yes." Wiping my mouth with the napkin, I twist to face him. "He's helping me with my diving certification."

With a blank face, his ministrations on my leg cease. "What does that mean?"

"I'm taking diving courses, and he helped me figure out where to look and things like that."

"Why didn't you tell me before now?"

"I didn't say anything because I wasn't sure about it."

"And now you are?" His question makes me feel wishy-washy, although I'm sure that's not what he intends.

I look away, and he squeezes my knee, letting up once I face him. "I think so. I'm enjoying it. I didn't mean to keep you in the dark, it's just that I wanted to be certain before I said anything. And Vinny's safe..."

Before I can continue, he screws up his face and throws his

napkin on the table. "What? And I'm not?" His tone rises as he edges to leave.

"Wait, Silas, listen." My fingers dig into his arm, and he stills, giving me his full attention. "Vinny's just an acquaintance. If I pursue this and find out it's not for me, I don't care if I disappoint him. But that's the last thing I want to do with you. Disappoint you."

"What?" His eyes fly wide, stunned, and he inches closer to me. His hands on me, again.

My breathing evens and the pounding of my heart settles. I'm nervous with my confession, but also relieved because he's no longer upset, only concerned. I can still fix this.

"I didn't want you to think I was rushing into anything or being flighty if I decided marine biology wasn't for me." My voice cracks.

If I bail on this, it won't be the end of the world, but it'll be another hit to my already downtrodden hopes for an exciting and fulfilling career. Another point for my sisters' believing I'm stupid and flighty on the imaginary scoreboard against Pansy succeeding in life.

"You're not flighty. Never." Everything about him is tense, yet his eyes flicker with warmth.

"Remember some of the things you said to me when we first met?" I challenge.

His cheeks reddened, and he smirks. "I'm an idiot. I think we've already established that." Pulling me into the crook of his arm, he hooks his forearm over my shoulder.

"That's true." I giggle, settling into him.

"I'll never judge you and I sure as shit won't be disappointed. I admire you."

"You do?" I tilt my head to gaze up at him.

"Yes. You're following your heart. Just because you don't get it right on the first try doesn't make you a failure. You have courage and that alone tells me that you're going to succeed, and when you do, you'll be a rock star in your field. I just know it."

My heart swells, and words fail me. I've never had someone believe in me unequivocally and unconditionally.

"We'll both be rock stars," I whisper, leaning to kiss the underside of his jaw, then his mouth.

"You're my rock star," he mumbles against my lips before deepening our kiss.

Breaking apart, he smiles, holding my chin in his grasp. "I want to hear everything you've been holding back on. Please, tell me."

We sit for hours, well past finishing our meals, and talk. I share every little detail, boring and otherwise, about marine biology, my diving classes, and how I've got no clue about where this will all lead.

We stop to share a dark chocolate mousse garnished with blackberries. The chocolate is decadent and the perfect ending to a wonderful date. But the sweetest and most memorable part of the night is Silas. He has a way of making me feel like the only person in the room, and no matter how small or insignificant what I'm saying is, he makes me feel like it's the most important thing in the world.

16

LONGING

*S*ilas

Dinner was amazing, even with the call from my mother and the media. We had a breakthrough, or at least I hope we did when she opened up about her hopes and fears for marine biology.

At first, she gutted me when she said Vinny was safe. But once she explained, it made sense, and I feel worlds better today. Even with that, I need to know more about this Vinny guy. I'm getting Otto to do a background check.

In my brief ten years in the limelight, we've had to learn some harsh lessons about human nature, and we can never be too careful. Chances are Vinny has no clue that she's with me or that I'm famous, but that doesn't mean he's not some scumbag looking for something more from her.

Pushing away the negative thoughts and the possibility of this being bad, I focus on the way Pansy's face shone when she talked about her classes. She was happy, even when talking about how frustrating it is to not be in the water.

We're now on the deck outside her room, having a nightcap after

our fantastic evening. Pansy walks out in sleep shorts and matching
tank, ready for bed. Fuck me.

A tease of a smile plays on her bow-shaped lips, and matching
her playfulness with my own, I wink and twitch my lips up. I curl my
finger for her to come to me. I want to do this right and take my time,
but even so, I can't help myself.

When I decided to quit the band, I hadn't considered what would
be next, just that I needed out. I wanted an end to the lifestyle; something vital was missing. Now, having met Pansy, *fuck*, as crazy as it
sounds, I think she could help me find the answer. She could *be* the
answer.

Still, I've got no clue what that means, and if I told her, it would
scare the shit out of her. It does me. I drink her in as she stands there.
I love the cute-as-fuck shorts, showcasing her long, bronzed legs. I
open my thighs, inviting her closer, and once she's there, I rest my
hand on her slender hips, tugging her to me. I situate her between
my legs and heat radiates off her, as does a fresh, clean scent.

Taking both her hands, I hold them between us and she nibbles
on her lower lip, her cheeks flushed, and her warm hazel eyes are
questioning. Unable to take much more, I haul her onto my lap. With
a shallow, breathy gasp, her hold tightens as she struggles to right
herself.

Releasing one of her hands, I swing my arm around her waist and
drag her against my chest. She straddles me and our gazes darken. If I
were a betting man, I'd wager we're both thinking about that night in
the car on the road. She was on my lap, chest-to-chest, making out.

That invisible and mighty pull that bloomed not long after we
met has been simmering under the surface for weeks, drawing us
together.

Our lips find each other; oddly, she's reticent, tentative, the opposite of the look she just gave me. Her kiss is soft and gentle, chaste,
but it isn't enough. I want more. My tongue breaks through her
closed lips with ease, her willingness evident.

Our tongues explore each other's mouths, and I'm finally able to
put a name to this weird, insistent hunger I've had since we first met.

Longing. I've been craving her taste, wanting another chance to kiss her, to have her in my arms.

Pansy's hands clutch my shoulders, fingers burrowing into my flesh as her mouth and tongue take on an urgency, probing and tasting me.

She feels it too. Her craving is present, taking hold in the way she rocks back and forth on my lap, her fingers clawing at my body like she wants to climb inside.

And her mouth, *shit*, that sweet as fuck mouth. Kissing's not enough for her, she again intends to consume me from the outside in, and she's driving me fucking crazy. But most of all, her sex rubbing my hardening cock is both amazing and agonizing.

Gripping her hips to stop her momentum, she gradually settles on me; the brightness in her doe eyes diminishes, and a frown clouds her pretty features.

Mistaking my clenched jaw for distaste instead of my attempt to keep my arousal in check, she tries to escape my lap. *Not a chance.* Clamping her waist, I pull her to me, our lips not even an inch apart.

"Don't go anywhere."

"Silas, I... ah, I got carried away."

"We both did. As much as I want nothing more than to have you, we're doing this right."

I won't treat her like the nameless and forgettable groupies that I've fucked. I have no clue what the future holds but dammit, there is something here. Our chemistry is fucking amazing. Our meeting was an immediate spark, and since then, it's only grown and intensified.

It doesn't matter if we're laughing, kissing or fighting, we're on fire, and I want a chance at this, whatever this is. She's easy to talk to, doesn't take my bullshit or care that I'm famous. She likes me for me.

"I want you. So much. We could fuck right now. But..."

"Whoa, who said anything about sex?" The shrill pitch of her voice is a knife in my ear.

Clumsily, she attempts another escape and my heart races at the prospect of this going downhill. I tighten my hold.

"Exactly, no fucking. We're going to do this right." My sharp tone causes a tiny pause in her struggle, but she soon resumes her efforts to flee.

It's half-hearted, though. If she really wanted out of my arms, she would be, and we both know it.

"Pansy, wait. I want to wait. We're going to take this slow. I promise you, we will only do what you're comfortable with and when you're ready."

She must like what I've said because she smiles, nods and then snuggles into my arms. "Thank you," she says into my neck.

"You don't have to thank me. We've got all the time in the world. We'll take our time."

Lifting her head, she peers up at me. "I don't want to wait too long." Now she's teasing. "I'm just scared."

"Scared?" I straighten, pulling her with me.

"Not of you," she says in a rush to reassure me. "Of us. Do you feel the intensity? The sheer power when we're together?"

I swallow hard and nod. I thought it was just me. Closing my arms around her, I bring her to me, and she rests her head on my chest. I'm too overwhelmed to speak. I just want to hold her, and she sinks into me, wanting the same.

17

CONNECTION

*P*ansy

Silas waits on the edge of the deck while I finish my yoga. I fell asleep in his arms last night, and at some point, he must have carried me to my bed. I awoke this morning under the covers, alone.

My mind was a mess when I took Boy for her walk, feeling both elated about our dinner and conversation, and also somewhat confused and disappointed. I wanted him last night. Like *really* wanted him, yet I put the brakes on things. I can't make sense of that.

Other things in life have left me uncertain and questioning, but never sex. Not because I don't take it seriously because, in fact, it's the opposite. Sex has never been casual to me, and it isn't with Silas, yet I stopped us from going too far last night. It would've been my unraveling. He does things to me with just a look that no man has ever done before. It's intimate, astonishing and has the power to derail me.

In the light of day, I'm ticked at myself and almost regretting how it ended. How messed up is that?

"Morning," he says as I roll my mat.

He's dressed in his usual jeans and a t-shirt, and his hair is up in a man bun. He strolls to where I stand and pulls me into a hug.

"Morning." I sink further into his embrace.

"You sleep okay?"

"Sure did, and you?" The strong, welcoming smell of cedar is in the air.

"Yeah. You still up for coming with me to sign the contract?"

"Absolutely, my shift doesn't start until this afternoon. Let me just shower."

He watches me while I gather my things for the bathroom. "Breakfast is ready when you are, and then we'll go." With a smile, he's gone.

❦

*CW*e arrive at the record label's office an hour later and are greeted by a throng of reporters. Fortunately, security is tight, and they can't get too close.

There were articles and pictures from the restaurant last night in today's paper and online. I have been dubbed the mystery woman and Silas warned me that it's only a matter of time before they figure out who I am.

While I am better prepared this morning, I'm still somewhat shaky as we enter the elevator. Bianca's eyes bore into me, her expression flat and uncaring. She probably thinks I'm a wuss. Like I care.

We are nothing alike, and except for Silas, we have nothing in common. Besides the obvious, physically she's everything I'm not with her big breasts, perfectly polished façade and curves upon curves; she's also quiet and cold. I don't have an opinion of her either way, and something tells me that she doesn't think I'll be around for long, so why bother getting to know me.

Like before, they go into the conference room, except this time they're all on their best behavior, laughing and joking, even Jared. The signing goes off without a hitch, and to celebrate, there's champagne. Silas pulls me in to join them.

Except for Bianca and Jared being cold and standoffish, the others welcome me with open arms. Jared's harsh gaze tracks me from the minute I step into the room. I refuse to let him unnerve me. I may not know anything about him, but I can tell he's scared and lashing out.

The funny thing is, I can see how close Jared and Silas are. Jared's insecurities and tantrums seem to feed Silas's loss and anger.

I don't think they're necessarily bad for each other, but this isn't a good time with so much change, and the two of them together could be a bad thing. I only hope making the album is quick and painless.

I can't help but think of all the time they'll be spending together and what that could mean for Silas getting out from this world. Silas's arm is wrapped around my middle, my back to his chest, and he nuzzles into my neck.

"I'm so glad you're here," he whispers, his warm breath coating the column of my neck.

"Me too. I want to know everything there is to know about you." I squeeze his arm around me.

"I feel the same way. I want every little detail about you," he says.

"Pansy, how are you?" Eli asks as he joins us. His smile is bright and warm, swimming in the depth of his green eyes. "Are you settling in okay?"

"I'm good, thanks. Yes, I've got a job, and I'm looking for a place to live." Silas grunts beside me, and Eli arches his eyebrows as I roll my eyes.

"Silas has a problem with me moving out, but he'll get over it."

"I see," Eli says. "I have a guest house out back that I don't use, you could live there if you want."

"No fucking way," Silas says before I can respond.

"I think what he means to say is thank you, but Pansy wants to find her own place," I say, my tone reproachful.

"Yeah, what she said," he grumbles, and we laugh.

Riding the high of the champagne and the jovial spirit in the room, I plant a light kiss on his lips, tasting the toasty, citrus flavors of the bubbly. His fingers dig into my hips, keeping me there as he deepens the kiss. I could get lost in him.

The connection is broken when Jared yells "Get a room!" and we break apart to find all eyes on us. My cheeks flame and Silas grins with a *can you blame me* shrug. Eli chuckles and with me still anchored to him, Silas carries on as if nothing happened.

Shortly after, I ask for the bathroom, and Bianca offers to take me. The walk down the hall is awkward with stilted chit-chat, but on the way back, she gets to her point.

"Pansy, what are your intentions?"

She pulls on my shoulder to stop me. We're only feet away from the room, but far enough that no one knows we're out here.

"My intentions? What are you talking about?" My arms fold over my chest, not liking what she may be insinuating.

"I'm just going to say it like it is. He's rich and famous. You're a nobody. I'd be foolish not to ask if you're hoping to hitch yourself to him. I'm telling you that will never happen."

"I don't expect you to believe this, but I don't want Silas's money, and his fame means nothing to me."

She cackles with a wry grin. "Right. And how do you explain that when you're living with him and mooching off him?"

Her question hits where it counts, and I flinch. "I'm looking for a place of my own, and I've got a job. I can understand how it may look, but it's not like that."

"Sure. That's what Silas said. You've got dreams of your own." She's condescending like I'm some child wishing for a unicorn. "You might want to consider getting on with your life, sooner rather than later."

"Besides being hugely insulted, a small part of me actually likes you for looking out for him. He needs that, but I can assure you, his fame doesn't matter to me and I guess you'll have to take my word for it. Time will tell."

She arches a penciled brow and purses her lips in skepticism.

"Bianca, let Silas and I figure out our shit, and you worry about controlling the media storm and whatever else it is you do. Perhaps you should focus on your job?"

Without waiting for a response, I march past her back to the bathroom. I'm not running away. I just need to calm down. It won't help anyone for Silas to see me like this.

He's protective and will know something is wrong. He will go to battle for me, and it may cause problems. He's on his path to freedom and a new beginning; I don't want this meaningless clash to ruin things.

"That was hot." Jared's deep voice comes from behind me as I exit the bathroom.

My steps falter. I don't want another confrontation. Ignoring him, I keep walking. One was enough for the day; I'd rather not go two for two.

"I heard you and B going at it. You're something else. Fucking loved the claws."

His innuendo pisses me off, and I fall for the bait, swiveling on my heel to face him.

"Jared, what do you want?" I ask with a bite.

He chuckles, his obsidian eyes penetrating, even darker with the thick black eyeliner surrounding them.

"Nothing, I want absolutely nothing," he murmurs, stepping into my space until I'm backed into the wall.

He's got me caged. His body is twice, if not three times, the size of mine and he's everywhere, surrounding me. My pulse speeds up, and my mouth dries. It's not really fear, as there's a room full of people no more than twenty feet away -- I could scream if I needed to -- but rather, his proximity has me on edge.

"Get off me." My voice pierces like shrapnel, hoping to cut him.

He winces and shakes his head, then chuckles as I push on his immovable chest, leaning further into me.

"We could have a blast. You're feisty, but with the wrong guy. Silas is fun, but compared to me, he's boring."

His fingertips trace the scooped neckline of my blouse and bile bubbles in my throat. "I'm not going to repeat it, get off me."

I'm giving him another chance, only because I want this to end without incident, although Jared has other plans. When he leers at my chest as if he has x-ray vision and his fingertips move south, I snap.

With a pounding heart and clenched stomach, I calm my mind

and focus. He's at least a foot taller than me, so I push onto my toes, bend my leg, and put everything into slamming my knee into his junk.

Upon contact, he releases a string of expletives, doubling over and backing away. But not before he slams his fist into the wall, mere inches from my face. I shudder, sucking in a sharp breath at the near miss.

His loud bellow is obviously heard as a few people exit the conference room. Silas is among them. Examining the situation, he has no problem figuring out what happened and makes a beeline for Jared.

Yanking him by the collar, Silas pulls Jared to standing. With his forearm holding Jared against the wall, he draws his other arm back, clenches his fist, and delivers a blow to Jared's jaw.

Jared releases a pained grunt, his head bouncing off the wall, and Silas positions his arm like a slingshot, ready for release. I latch onto Silas's flexed bicep. "No!"

Silas stills, the humming of his wired and explosive body seeping from him to me. I'm as loaded as he is, our connection alive and his burning energy courses through my veins. It would be so easy to give into the violence, to let Silas go at Jared, but I can't let that happen.

"Silas, please. I took care of it. He's not worth it." My plea may be futile with the adrenaline coursing through him, but I have to try for his sake.

If he continues to hit Jared, it could have serious repercussions. He could damage his hand, the agreement with the band, and maybe even his freedom.

Excluding his heaving chest, Silas is frozen with his arm still raised, poised with intent and Jared pinned to the wall. Jared's too focused on the pain radiating from his cheek and between his legs to fight or even reason with Silas, which is a good thing. Something tells me he'd make matters worse.

"Silas, stop this now." Bianca cuts through the tension-filled moment, her tone grating like nails on a chalkboard. Her timing sucks. Her bullish attitude could work against what I'm hoping to accomplish.

Resting my head on his back, I wrap my other arm around his middle and breathe him in. His woodsy masculine scent is soothing.

"Please, don't do this." I murmur into his back for only him to hear.

His shoulders deflate, and he drops his arm, slowly backing away from Jared, and then pulling me to face him.

"Did he hurt you?" His hands cup the back of my neck, his eyes are soft and concerned.

"No, I'm fine. I took care of it."

"You sure did." He grins and draws me closer to him, his lips skimming my forehead. "Let's get out of here."

"I'm so with you."

As we push through the small crowd that's gathered, Silas twists to glare at Jared. "This isn't over." Each word bleeds fury. "We're having words."

Surprisingly, Jared nods agreement before turning his head to the side and closing his eyes. A small exhale of relief leaves my body. Words I can handle, fists are another story.

Eli and Gray catch our gazes, their expressions a mixture of outrage and concern. Silas shares unspoken words with them, and they too nod. Bianca nabs my arms before we enter the elevator, and her features are etched with worry and remorse.

"Are you okay?" she asks, her question directed at me.

"Yes. Just a little shaken, but I don't think he meant any harm."

Silas growls, pulling me into his arms. "Fuck that, Pansy. He was way out of line, and he's not getting off easy."

"I agree," Bianca is quick to add.

"So do I. He doesn't get a free pass, and I took care of things on my end, but I don't really think he was going to take it any further. I can't explain it, but I think he was testing me."

Both Silas and Bianca stare at me with puzzled looks. It's not something I can easily convey; it's just a feeling, a sixth sense deep in my gut. It felt as if Jared was pushing for a reaction from me, and as I kneed him, there was this glimmer of surprise, pain, and also relief in his eyes.

"All right," Bianca says. "Please let me know if you need anything, and I'm going to talk to him too."

"Thanks, B." Silas tightens his hold, and the elevator closes, cocooning us in a brief, quiet moment.

As of now, I'm not sure about this. About Jared. Silas hasn't said it outright, but I know Jared is important to him, even if he is an arrogant bully. I'm not sure if I can play nice with the asshat, even for Silas.

18

SMITTEN

*S*ilas

The day I've been dreading has come. It has been only four days since the signing of the contract, but since then, Pansy's found an apartment only two streets from Betty's.

Turns out Callie, the hippie chick she works with knew of an available apartment in her building. Pansy got first dibs, and of course she loved it. And the worst or best part, depending on who you ask, is that she can move in right away.

We're on our way up the narrow stairs -- the elevator is broken -- so she can show me the place. I will hate it no matter what.

She's on the fifth floor of the six-story building in a studio apartment with just a partition separating her tiny bedroom, if you can call it that, from the living room. Pansy loves it, bouncing around and gushing with Callie over this or that. The place is nothing to write home about.

There's a barely-there galley kitchen, no room for a table, and old colorful appliances. Her place is basically one room that serves as the living, dining, *and* bedroom, with a bathroom no bigger than a shoebox by the front door.

"Well, since I don't have any furniture, I'm already moved in." Pansy giggles, dumping her beat-up suitcase on the floor.

Leaning on the wall with my arms crossed, I sulk. Callie flits around the room, her bangles jiggling with every move. It's annoying as fuck, and I growl in irritation.

She glances from Pansy to me a few times, but neither of us says a thing. Pansy ignores me. I'm a dick by not trying to hide my displeasure.

"You let me know if you need anything," Callie says. She lives on the fourth floor and has offered to help Pansy get settled. *Isn't she so sweet?*

"Cal, thanks so much, I'm good for now," Pansy replies.

"Okay, hon. Talk soon." Callie hugs Pansy. "Bye, Silas." She waves from the door, her cheeks flushed and eyes glassy. It doesn't matter that we've already met a few times, she's still star-struck.

I dip my chin and remain silent. If I open my mouth, I'm liable to lose it and insist Pansy come home with me.

In about a week, I'll be holed up with the guys and who knows when I'll get to see her. At least if she was at my house, I could see her when I came home to crash. Now, who fucking knows when that will happen?

"Do you want to grab a bite or just go straight to IKEA?" Pansy cuts through my miserable thoughts. All I want is her.

She needs a bed or futon or whatever the fuck we can squeeze in here. It's the one concession she gave me; I'm allowed to get her a few things for this place. She insists she'll pay me back, but doesn't have it right now. She's not paying me shit, but I let her think I'm on board with that.

Nabbing her around the neck, I bring her to my side, where I love to have her, resting my nose and mouth on the top of her head. My senses fill with vanilla almond, and I inhale deeply, wanting her scent to invade all of me.

"Let's eat."

I want nothing but to eat her, hold her tight and devour her. Keep her with me. It's foolish and irrational, and something I would never say to her, but history has shown me that distance can make for drastic changes in relationships.

On the way to lunch, I try to push my concerns aside and concentrate on having a meal with my girl. Sitting side by side on the picnic table, she bumps my shoulder with a sexy smile on her face and puts a fry in my mouth.

"I know it's going to be tricky to find time for each other with all that's going on, but it can work if we both want this." Her salty finger traces my bottom lip, brushing at my beard. "Now's our chance to prove it. Silas, it's not impossible."

She plants a light peck on my lips, the salt of the fries mingling with the undeniable sweetness of her cherry lip gloss.

"I want this. I'll always make time for you," I growl into her mouth before stealing another kiss.

She squeals as I grip her waist and bring her into my lap. She sits sideways, and my dick jerks, hardening at her bottom pressing against it. My feverish arousal tunnels my vision, and I forget we're in public as one hand roughly palms her succulent ass and the other bands her throat. Brushing my thumb against her fluttering pulse-point, I guide her lips to mine.

The idea of stopping stirs in the back of my mind. I may be disguised with a beanie and sunglasses, but our affection will draw attention, and I could get recognized.

Those thoughts vanish when she latches onto my head, and our lips lock; her nails sink into the wool beanie, leading our hot kiss. She wiggles her bottom, trying to get closer, and I groan with the friction and pressure against my groin. Tasting her is both bliss and torture because now I want her even more. I've wanted her from the day we met.

I've never felt this way about anyone before. Being with her is easy, exciting and at times wild and uncontrolled. She's unpredictable and fun, sweet, loving, and caring. All the things I've never had.

Someone clears their throat, and she jerks back on a gasp. Her eyes are glazed, pupils dilated, cheeks flushed, and lips parted.

Without any words, I help her off my lap and stand beside her, discreetly adjusting myself.

We grab the remains of our food, and dispose of it in the trash before heading to the car. Pansy laces her fingers with mine and giggles.

"What's so funny?" I ask, peering down at the glow on her face.

"Sometimes, we're like two horny teenagers." Her eyes flash with desire. "I've never been so smitten with someone before."

"Smitten?" I joke.

She lightly hits my stomach, leaning into me as we near my Jeep.

"You know what I mean, don't be an asshole." There's a glimmer of a smile in her tone.

Laughing, I wrap her in my arms, inhaling her again. "I'm smitten with you, too."

I match her beaming smile with one of my own as my gaze drops to her mouth. I press her closer to me, tightening my hold.

After furniture shopping, which was successful in that she got what she wanted and she let me pay, I drop her at Betty's for her shift. I am now going to see Jared. Pansy was worried when I told her my plans, but she understands why I have to talk to him before we start writing the album.

She begs me to stay calm and not to hit him, and I promise. Even though I'm pissed and would like to rearrange his face for what he did to Pansy, I don't want to fight with him. When she told me everything, I was enraged, sickened, and fucking sad.

For all his douchebag moves over the years, and he's had a few -- heck, so have I -- what Pansy described didn't sound like him at all. He was never one to disrespect, scare, or fuck, nearly assault a woman.

Media's camped outside of his place when I arrive. I didn't tell him I was coming, so I have to stop at the gate and call in. He has a 40,000-square foot compound with twenty-eight bedrooms on one and a half acres, perched on a hilltop in Bel Air.

It is fucking obnoxious, impressive, and has been featured in

Architectural Digest. If I didn't know better, I'd think he was compensating for something, but the sad truth is he's filling his life with things, with what he didn't have growing up in foster care, and for what he's lost.

It hits me as I walk up the marble steps to the front door that the end of Trojan is another loss for him. Something I'm taking away. It was my decision, and to some extent, Eli and Gray were already along that path, too, but for Jared, he wasn't even considering it.

"Well, well, well," Jared greets me at the top of the stairs, bare-chested in jeans and black combat boots. The large wooden double doors are wide open, with him in the middle, arms stretched out. "Took you long enough. What is it? Four days? I thought you'd have been here the same day to finish the ass-kicking your girlfriend started."

His provocative tone fails to entice a comeback from me. Beneath his flippant attitude, he cares. Turning his back to me, he leads the way into his place and down the hall to the great room. And great it truly is, with twenty-foot ceilings, marble, glass, and wood everywhere.

"Pansy told me everything."

"I'm sure she did. Drink?" He pours three fingers of scotch for himself.

Shaking my head, I widen my stance and study him. He looks like shit; his dark hair is tangled and greasy, dark circles rim his eyes, and he's sporting a good start to a beard.

"What the fuck, Jared?"

"Look, I'm going to make this easy for you." He downs his drink in one gulp with a slight grimace as he swallows. "I was out of line. I was a fucking asshole, and Pansy had every right to skewer my balls." Instinctively, his hand adjusts his crotch, and I squirm a bit at the memory.

"Damn straight she did." Pouring himself another drink, I grit my teeth from saying something.

"Look at it from my side of things. She comes out of nowhere, and you're quitting the band, shacking up with her... I'd be an idiot not to consider that she had something to do with it."

"I already told you, I'd been thinking about walking long before Pansy. And as for her coming out of nowhere, if you dumbasses hadn't dumped me on the side of the road, I'd never have met her."

As I say the words, a shudder runs through me at the unthinkable. Never one to believe in fate or a higher power, I can't help but believe that no matter what, our paths would have crossed.

"Yeah, yeah, you've said this all before. But I needed to find out for myself."

He starts to pour his third drink, and I can't stay silent. "Jared, lay off. That's enough of that shit."

Raising an eyebrow while his dark eyes bore into me, he lowers the tumbler of amber liquid. "What are you, my dad now? Silas, you and I are tight, but you aren't my father or even my brother. You may be able to dismantle Trojan and rock my fucking world to the core, but you don't get to tell me how to live my life or what the fuck I put in my body. Got it?"

His words sting. Jared is family. "Fuck, Jared, that's not what I meant. You're fucking killing yourself. When are you going to forgive yourself? Just take it easy."

"Whatever." He tosses back his third drink and throws the glass against the wall, shattering it.

I wince at the anger rolling off him, recognizing it, but also not. We both have shit we're dealing with, or in Jared's case, choosing not to deal with, and I want to help him, but there isn't anything I can do. I know his story, and nothing can be fixed or undone. In fact, it's out of his hands too.

"About Pansy, I fucked up, but I had to know what the hell her deal was. B tested her in her way, and I was doing the same. I had to know if you were a meal ticket for her, or if her interest in you was real. I figured if she were after a payday or fame, one rock star would be as good as another, and so I made a play."

"And what did you figure?" I know the answer, but I want his take.

"She's into you, man. For sure. She never took the bait." Standing up, he places his hand on my shoulder and squeezes. "I'm a jackass, and I'll make it right with her."

"Yeah, you will."

19

BALLS

*P*ansy

The warm sea breeze and the bright sun wash over me the moment I exit Betty's. Silas's leaning against his car, a smile sprawling across his lips at the sight of me.

In a few quick strides, he meets me halfway and pulls me into his arms. "God, I missed you," he mumbles against my lips, hot and soft.

It's meant to be a quick hello kiss, but it's too good to stop. My fingers curl into his shirt, pulling him in as my tongue delves into his warm mouth. Minty fresh and all man.

"Me too, I've missed you so much."

"Hello, beautiful." Silas checks our surroundings, always on the lookout for cameras or fans, especially with the recent media attention on Trojan.

The last thing we need is our picture splashed all over social media. So far, we've managed to keep our relationship on the down low, and we want to stay that way.

"Pansy! You're still here. Wait." Vinny's long strides eat the asphalt and Silas tightens his grip on me.

"Hey, Vinny. Silas, this is Vinny."

"Nice to meet you," Silas says, taking Vinny's hand.

"I've heard a lot about you," Vinny says.

"I wish I could say the same." His subtle dig, delivered in a dry, flat tone, is not lost on me. I've shared more openly with him about marine biology, but limiting what I say about Vinny. I don't want him to feel Vinny is any more than a friend because that's all he is.

"Vinny came by to find out how my meeting with his friend went," I rush to say guiltily. "His friend's a marine biologist for a company in San Diego."

"I see," Silas says, a slight frown on his lips

"Anyway, Pansy says you've got plans for tonight, so I won't keep you." Vinny looks to me. "Just reminding you that I can't take you to class tomorrow."

"Oh yeah, Callie's taking me. Thanks."

"Great. Have a good night and nice to meet you, Silas."

"Yeah, you too, Vinny. We'll have you over or something; I'd like to get to know you better."

Silas is unusually silent until we near his house. "I can take you tomorrow, you know." He rubs the center of his chest as if it aches. "After the weekend, it will get harder to see each other."

"Okay. I didn't ask... I don't want it to look like I depend on you for anything. You're my..." I pause, and he glances, quizzically at me. "You're my boyfriend, and I don't want it to seem like I'm using you for anything else."

He parks the car, jogs to my side, and hauls me to my feet and into his arms. One arm firmly bands me and his other cups the side of my face.

"I'm your boyfriend?" There's a hint of amusement in his tone, and I nod. "I like that. A lot. And as your boyfriend, I want you to use me any way you want."

"Really?" I laugh with a slight reddening to my cheeks. "I like that."

"Good. So, it's settled? I'll take you tomorrow?"

"Yes, please. I'd like that."

With a light kiss on my lips and then the tip of my nose, he releases me. Once in his house, my nerves kick in when we hear voices. The band is here for a barbecue.

When he first mentioned it, I welcomed it, wanting to get to know the band better, especially Jared. I hate what he did, but I am willing to give him another chance.

Jared and Gray are on the deck off the living room drinking beers. With a brief hello, I promise to return once showered. By the time I'm back, Bianca, Eli, and his little angel, Crystal, have arrived. Jorge and Lucia have also joined us, and everyone is in great spirits.

"Hey, Pansy." Eli leans in for a hug, and Crystal stops her brief mauling of Boy to smile at me.

"Hi. Hey, Crystal, beautiful girl." I kneel beside her and Boy eagerly rolls onto her back, paws in the air, so we can both pat her belly. Crystal giggles while her chubby fingers thread and tug at Boy's thick fur.

"Hi, Pansy." Bianca approaches, wine glass in hand and a tentative smile.

"Hi. How are you?" We got off on the wrong foot. She made snap judgments about me, and I've been tempted to do the same about her. But I want to get to know her.

"Good. How are you doing?"

"I'm good, thanks. How are things coming along for the album?"

"The boys will be in the studio soon, and that's a good thing because I think the anticipation is getting to all of us."

"Yes. Silas is both anxious and dreading it, but I think it'll be fine." I'm trying to be upbeat and show her that Silas matters to me. I don't know why I feel like I need to prove that to her, but it's there.

"Silas has mentioned you've started diving class?"

"Yes. I'm really enjoying it, but it's stressful with the expenses." I realize my goof when she purses her lips.

"Why are you worrying when you're living with Silas? He's got you covered." Her insinuation of my freeloading ways is clear in her tone, and it takes everything in me to not get my back up.

"I'm not living with Silas, and even if I were, I'd pay my way."

"Oh. Sorry. Silas didn't tell me that you had your own place."

There's something in her tone that suggests something more, but I can't put my finger on it. Does he tell her everything? I want to ask but choose not to. It would only push us into the defensive bitch zone, and that wouldn't be good for any of us.

"I'm my own person, Bianca. I don't know what assumptions you may have made about me, but I'm not with Silas for any other reason than I like him."

"What the hell?" Silas's gruff tone startles me; I turn to see Silas and Jared approaching and twist back to Bianca, who is unfazed.

"Silas." My warning tone tells him not to fight my battles. "Everything's fine."

He opens his mouth to say something, and before he can, my mouth crushes his words, consuming them. Without protest, his fingers dig into my backside, pushing me against the hard planes of his body. God, I've missed him. I instinctively wrap my legs around him, his impressive arousal rocking against my core.

What's he doing to me? I'm never one to shy away from displays of affection, but I've always kept it respectable. Silas is a whole different beast. With him, everything leaves my mind, and all I want is to climb inside of him.

"Fuck me." I vaguely make out Jared's expletive followed by a chuckle. My sole focus is on the fire burning within. Silas's mouth is destroying all my senses.

"Really, Silas?" Bianca chimes in, pulling me out of my stupor.

"Bianca, why don't you just lay off for once," Jared says harshly.

Her eyes narrow on him, her lush lips now a thin line as she steps back. Intense glares are traded as neither dare to back down. I drop my legs from Silas's waist; these two are mood killers.

"Guys, chill. We're here to have a good time," Gray says, cutting the tension, hooking his arm around Bianca and pulling her away.

"Jared, why don't you go easy on her?" Eli asks with Crystal now on his hip.

"Why does she always have to be in bitch mode? You used to be fun."

Jared's disdain's evident in his surly demeanor. He runs a rough hand through his dark hair, his lips tight and jaw clenched. His eyes land on mine and instantly, his features soften, a smile spreading across his face.

With Silas beside me, his chest to my back, he stiffens, tightening his grasp on my waist. "Jared," he warns.

I gently rub Silas's arm to ease his concern, and his gaze flicks to me.

"Relax, let me talk to him." I motion to Jared, needing to clear the air.

"You behave yourself, or this whole thing is off," Silas threatens Jared before kissing me on the forehead.

Jared chuckles, but he doesn't fool me. His shoulders are tense, lips tight, and his laugh doesn't meet his eyes. He tracks Silas's retreat.

"How are your balls?" Might as well cut to the chase.

Jared's eyes widen; tilting his head back he laughs, holding his stomach as he bends forward. I join in because mission accomplished, the tension has broken, and most of all, he didn't react negatively, which was a definite a possibility.

Everyone turns to Jared, stunned by his laughter. Obviously, it's a rare occurrence. Silas steps in our direction, but I deter him with a subtle shake of my head.

Jared straightens and lightly taps me on the shoulder as he calls to Silas, "Damn, I can see why you like her so much."

Silas is not amused, and he doesn't even try to hide it with his territorial stare, the sharp tilt of his chin and subtle broadening of his shoulders. With an open and easy smile, I try to put him at ease, and he dips his chin with a flicker of a smile for Jared before turning back to Jorge and Lucia.

"My balls are just fine, no thanks to you," Jared quips. "But I deserved it. I was an asshole and way out of line. I could say I was high and blame it on that, and while that's true, I won't. It's because I was pissed, blamed you for some of the shit that was going on, and didn't trust you."

His candor surprises me and puts me further at ease. "Why? I had nothing to do with Silas's decision to leave Trojan."

"I know." He hangs his head. "You were easy to blame. Silas wanted out, and truthfully, I'm not surprised. He's been different for some time now and seeing that he knows what he wants, and you're obviously part of that, it's just..." He shrugs, tugging his hair and at a loss for words.

"I get it." I let him off the hook. He's more open with me than I dared hope for, and his love for Silas is clear in his voice. "And do you trust me now?"

He lifts his head. "Not quite yet, but I'm getting there. I can see how much you mean to Silas and I think you care about him. Not who he is to the world, but *him*."

"I do care about him, a lot. What about you? What's next for you?"

He jerks his head my way, looking me in the eye, shocked that I care to ask about him. My guess is these guys don't have a lot of people that truly care about them. Most see them as a meal ticket, or a moment of glory to brag about, not as a person.

"That's the thing. Between you and me, I have no fucking clue and it scares me shitless."

Jared and I talk for a bit, about nothing serious or heavy, but we joke and get to know each other better. During dinner, my phone rings and I excuse myself to answer it.

"Hello."

"Pansy?" Ivy asks, and unease slithers down my spine.

"Ivy?" I don't know why I play coy when I know it's her.

"Pansy, where are you?"

Always one to forgo pleasantries, she gets to the heart of the matter. I suppose with her being a doctor, it serves her well to get straight to business, but it would do wonders for her social life if she tried being nicer. A hello and how are you goes a long way.

"What do you mean, where am I?" She snorts, and before she can fire a nasty comment, I continue, "I already told you I'm in LA."

I deliberately didn't give her specifics of my whereabouts. While there is a slim chance of her showing up or coming to get me, there is still a chance.

"Send me your address." Her voice fades as she moves the phone away. She's talking to a nurse or someone at the hospital, her tone more domineering if that's even possible. Picking up where we left off, she says, "I need your address."

"Why?"

"Pansy, stop this. You've made your point. You want your independence and have something to prove, fine. But what if there's an emergency and I need to get to you?"

Rolling my eyes, I answer, "You have my number. You could call or text."

"Why are you being difficult? I'm not coming to visit if that's what you're worried about. I just want to know how to find you, if I have to."

"Fine." I rattle off my address, all the while knowing this is a mistake.

Turning off my phone -- one call from Ivy is enough for one night -- I tuck it into my purse and return to dinner. Silas seeks me out, and I smile, letting him know all is fine. A call from my sister shouldn't shake me, but it does. I have a good thing going here, and the last thing I need is my sister crashing into my life and wrecking everything.

20

FLUSH

*S*ilas

Pansy sits curled on the outdoor couch with Crystal snuggled into her, sleeping. Eli watches with adoration on his face, and I sure as fuck hope it's for his daughter and not my girl. I nudge his shoulder, and he chuckles.

"She's awesome, but you saw her first. I'd never make a move." Eli holds his hands up in the air. "She's all yours and the feeling's mutual by the looks of things."

"You bet your sorry ass it is." I bump him again, beaming that he thinks Pansy's just as crazy about me as I am about her.

Eli laughs, shaking his head as he walks over to Pansy and his daughter. The two share some whispered words before he carefully lifts his little girl into his arms and says goodbye.

"And then there were two." I snuggle beside Pansy, my arms around her.

"Did you have a good time?" She cuddles into my side.

"Yeah, it feels like I'm fixing some of what I fucked up by springing my shit on them."

"Good. I had fun, and I think everyone did, too. Well, except for Bianca and Jared, what's up with them?"

I roll my eyes and sigh; I don't want to talk about Jared and Bianca. "That's a long story. They've never really gotten along, although I think it's because they're a lot alike."

"They seem to rub each other the wrong way."

"Yeah, you could say that," she shrieks as I stand with her in my arms. "Enough about them, it's time for us to go to bed."

She tightens her hands around my neck and melts into me. And as much as I want to have her right now, take her and mark her as mine, I'll settle for just having her spend the night with me, sleeping. I want her. I always do.

*

*W*hen I wake, Pansy's already up, likely walking Boy, doing yoga, or swimming, in any order. I love having her in my space. My only wish is for it to be permanent.

During the shower, a song hits and the urge to write is strong. I head to my music studio where the words and the melody pour out of me, and time has no meaning.

Minutes, or maybe hours later, my fingers dance along the keyboard, finishing up the last few notes. The song's not complete, but close. I'll play it for the guys, and together, we will finish it.

While this is our last record, I love making music, and since Pansy's come into my life, I'm brimming with song ideas, scraps of paper everywhere. So much so, half of me is eager to get in that studio and write, but the other half is reluctant to lose the limited time I have with Pansy, getting to know her.

"I love that. Is it new?" Pansy surveys me from the doorway in a faded black one-piece swimsuit that's seen better days. All I see is her toned bronze skin, calling to me.

Crooking my finger, I beckon her, and she obeys. With each step to me, streams of sunlight flit across the crown of her head, deepening the warm, red tones of her long locks.

I pull her onto my lap, and her delicious bow-shaped lips curl up as her eyes widen, darkening to moss green. Her warm, almost bare back leans against my chest, and I swear our heartbeats are synchronized.

"Silas." My name is almost a tremble on her lips.

"Hey," I whisper, and she smiles.

I place her hands on the keyboard, my larger ones shadowing hers, and we play a few bars of the song I just wrote. The one she just overheard. It's about her.

"Hypnotizing." She sways with the beat.

"Very hypnotizing." *She sure is.*

Lightly kissing her shoulder, my tongue licks at her salty skin, and she shudders and sighs, sinking into me. With her surrender, my hands have a mind of their own, gripping her waist and lifting her to sit on the piano with her legs bent, her bare feet grazing the keys.

"Silas," she exhales, her hands latching onto my shoulders.

Seated at eye level with her sex, I glance at her, seeking permission. The tiny nod and nibble on her bottom lip is all the go-ahead I need. My fingers gently knead her thighs before pulling her legs wide apart.

She gasps as my hands glide up the inside of her legs. Eager to taste and touch, my tongue kisses, nips, and licks at the soft, silky skin of her thighs, the sea salt mingling with a flavor that is undeniably Pansy. She tastes like fucking freedom.

I continue to rub my palms along her thighs, to the juncture of her legs and pelvis. I'm overwhelmed with desire, burning inside as my thumb slowly swipes her mound through the already-damp bathing suit. I'm not sure if it's wet from the ocean or her excitement.

She releases a breathy moan, dropping her head forward, her hair falling around us like curtains. Licking my lips, I plant a wet, open-mouthed kiss at the apex of her thighs and groan at her musky, intoxicating scent. She sucks in a jagged breath and curls her fingers and toes.

"Silas," Lucia calls from down the hall, nearing the room.

My head snaps up, and I quickly adjust my semi. Pansy scrambles to get off the piano; dissonant notes fill the room, and she lets out an expletive as her toes hit a few keys. With a chuckle, I help her to her feet as Lucia rounds the corner.

Lucia glances between us as Pansy averts her gaze, her fingers absently running through her hair. "Sorry to interrupt," Lucia says.

"You weren't interrupting," Pansy is quick to say, and Lucia's smile is knowing.

"I have made brunch. Come." Lucia beckons for us to follow.

"Thanks, Lucia." With my hands on her petite shoulders, I bend to kiss her cheek before turning to Pansy. "Let me just make one quick phone call, I was supposed to meet up with Gray, but I'm going to push it until I take you home."

Pansy looks to be getting ready to protest, not wanting me to change plans for her, but Lucia cuts through, "All right, but hurry or everything will be cold." She takes Pansy with her.

My call is quick, and Gray is cool with the change in plans. That guy is so easy-going. I don't know how he puts up with us. With the exception of him, each of us has had our share of drama and through it all, he has been solid. I hope when all is said and done, I still have these guys in my life.

I come into the kitchen and find Jorge sitting at the table sipping coffee; he nods to me but remains silent. Pansy and Lucia are seated with their backs to me, talking.

"*Mija*, you should move back in," Lucia says, and I decide to remain quiet and see how this plays out.

I'm not above letting Lucia try to persuade her to come back, even though we haven't talked about Pansy's living arrangements, or how much I want her here. But Lucia knows me, and it wouldn't take much for her to figure out it's what I want.

"Like I told Jorge, I can't right now. I need to do this on my own. I don't want to be a burden to Silas or to take from him. I want our relationship to be equal."

I want to interject, tell her how wrong she is, and that we *are* equal, but Lucia beats me to it. "Child, you're no burden. You're a blessing."

"Lucia," Jorge warns. "Leave it be. Let them figure it out." He peers over their heads imploring me to make my presence known.

"Jorge, I'm only trying to make her see they are good together and it could be better if she came back. For all of us."

"You're only saying that because you want her here."

"And you don't?" Lucia challenges and I bite my lip to stifle my laugh.

Shaking his head, his eyes narrow, but in a loving way. "*Sí*, I would like her here too. She helps me with Boy."

Pansy laughs, and I hope she knows that Jorge is only deflecting to hide how he feels. He's not one to show his emotions.

"You two, stop. I'm not ruling out coming back, someday, but not for now. Besides, Silas and I are only just starting out. Who knows where this could go."

"*Mija*, I can tell you where this will go. I have two eyes and can see clearly. I see the way he looks at you. You have his heart."

"What?" She nervously laughs, squirming in her seat. "I don't know about that. I think you're reading way too much into this."

Lucia laughs, "All right, *mija*, you tell yourself that."

Deciding to end my eavesdropping, I cough and enter the room. Pansy's cheeks are pink, and Lucia's eyes gleam like a victor from battle. We both know her message is received and now it's up to Pansy and me.

21

SOMERSAULT

*P*ansy

We pull into the driveway of his beachfront property in Laguna Beach, and it's stunning with the rocky bluffs, canyons, and secluded coastline.

This weekend is our getaway before the band starts working on the album. While it's hard to give up the lost income, I want this. Some time with Silas before things change, again.

He's divided about his obligation. At times, he seems happy, almost energized by it, but then it's like he's going for major dental surgery without the anesthesia.

His 5,000-square-foot home is out of this world, nestled along the coastline with a spectacular view of the Pacific. The inside is wood beam ceilings, hardwood, granite, and floor to ceiling windows every-where. But the outside steals the show with the stunning view of nature's wonder. A deck spans the entire house with oversized couches, a fire pit, and an infinity pool bleeding into the horizon.

"Are you hungry?" His arms fold around me from behind.

The setting sun paints the sky in warm tones while the waves lap lazily at the shore. Boy sits on my feet, whimpering and shifting with Silas's light jostle.

"I'm starving, but I don't want to tear myself away from the view."

"I'm glad you like it. I don't come here nearly as often as I should."

"When was the last time?"

"Ah, I think two years ago."

"What?" Incredulous, I twirl to face him, forgetting about Boy, who now snorts, shakes his body, and saunters off. "That's a crime. If I lived here, I'd never leave this place."

"Well, if you lived here, I'd never leave either."

"Cheesy," I say with a laugh.

"I don't care how corny it sounds, it's true."

My heart flips. The Silas I'm getting to know is sweet, caring, and easy going, nothing like the angry man I met on the road. I want to know what causes those outbursts, but I won't push. Hopefully, he'll tell me when he's ready.

"Let's eat. I've warmed up what Lucia made us."

Dinner is delicious, and I'm stuffed. Silas suggests s'mores on the deck, but I protest just wanting the sea air. Outside is chilly, and he lights the fire pit before we curl on the sofa with Boy wedged between our legs. Scents of cedar and sunshine, all Silas, surround me. Perfect.

"Have you decided to major in marine biology?"

"Yes. I've decided on UCLA. I'll have to take out a loan, but it's an investment in my future."

"Let me help you."

"No. I can do this."

"Fine." His body hardens, to match his tone. "I've no doubt you can do this on your own. Truly, you can achieve anything you set your mind to. I only want to make it easier for you."

I wish I could bottle his unwavering belief in me and take it out if or when self-doubt settles in.

"I know it seems like I'm being difficult, but I don't mean to be. It's just that my family, well, most of my sisters don't have any faith in me. In my abilities to achieve anything, and I suppose this is my way of proving them wrong."

"Okay, I can sort of understand that. But know this, you don't need to prove anything. This is your life."

He holds my face, really looking at me like I matter. There's a tightness in my chest, but not a bad kind, more the anticipation of something great.

"Silas," is all I manage to say, a reverent whisper.

"Remember this." His hold is firm and gentle. "You can do whatever you put your mind to."

His confidence in me is heady. His eyes are lit with lust, the contrasting light of the flames magnifying the hard and soft, firm and fluid of his facial features.

He licks his plump lips, and inching forward I graze the underside of his jaw with mine. The soft hairs of his beard tickle my lips, and we both shudder. His hands drop from my face to my hips as his fingers press into my flesh.

I kiss him once at the tip of his chin while my fingers trail his jawline, and I turn to face him fully. There's a flutter between my legs as he grips my ass with one hand and the other slides along my ribcage to rest just below my breast.

Silas Palmer is an amazing kisser. The best I've had. I've never been one to lose myself in a kiss. Sad, but true. My mind can wander like a wayward child, flitting from one inane thought to another at the most inopportune times, but not with Silas. With him, I forget my name.

"Let's head in," he mouths against my lips.

"Yes," I murmur before going back to kissing him.

Hoisting me against his solid frame, he expertly navigates his way from the deck to the bedroom. Once there, he places me on the bed and doesn't waste any time peeling down my jeans and underwear to mid-thigh, where they rest as his hand delves between my legs.

His deft fingers part my lips and effortlessly glide over my clit. With a few tantalizing strokes, a tease, he stops to pull my jeans and underwear all the way down and off me.

"Take off your top," he commands as he pulls his t-shirt over his head.

His masculine beauty hits me square in the chest, my heart tripping over itself at the magnificent landscape of his lean, cut torso and his light blond happy trail dipping below the band of his jeans.

"Pansy." His voice lowers to a sexy whisper as he leans in over me. "Do I need to help you?"

Arching a brow, he presses his mouth to mine while his hands cup my breasts through my blouse, his fingers pinching my nipples, and I cry out in pleasure.

A cocky grin breaches his lips. "Pansy?"

"Help me," I beg, giving him what he wants, his sexy grin widening.

In no time at all, I'm bared to him, and his hot mouth's on mine as demanding hands skate from my rib cage to stomach to between my legs. On a throaty sigh, my eyes flutter closed while his rough fingertips stroke me.

Rocking two fingers in and out, his thumb swirls and presses on my bundle of nerves, and everything spins. His mouth captures my release as his magical fingers stoke the fire burning within, and my body continues to burst with spasms around his digits.

"Pansy." He pulls out of me.

With heavy eyes, I'm transfixed on him sucking my arousal off his fingers. Needing to reciprocate, I sit up and palm his heavy erection through his jeans, before pushing to standing, and together, we make quick work of discarding his clothes.

I greedily go for his hard cock, wrapping my fingers around him and smoothing my thumb over his engorged crown. Settling on my knees, I wrap my lips around him, and my name breaks the barrier of his lips on a growl.

"Fuck, Pansy."

He wraps his fingers in my hair, his body tightening, thighs taut, stomach flexed, as he guides my speed, fucking my mouth. I take him as deep as I can, his head sliding down my throat as I breathe through my nose, trying not to gag. Never one for giving head, this is an experience all unto its own. The power I have, knowing he's at my mercy, is exhilarating, and only serves to fuel my arousal.

One hand fondles his balls, and when I flick my tongue over his head, dipping the tip into his slit, his body jolts. "Pansy, you... gotta... stop. If you don't...I'm gonna..." That's what I want. I pick up speed, pumping faster, sucking stronger, twirling my tongue around his sensitive head as I tug on his balls. "No, I want inside you."

He reluctantly pulls away with a pop from my mouth as his cock releases. Before I can react, or say a thing, he plants me on the bed, spreading my legs wide, hovering above me. He holds his cock in one hand, sliding it over my core, and I'm ridiculously awed by his wet, swollen head running through my folds, sending hot shivers through my body.

"Let me grab a condom," he painfully grinds out, halting his pleasurable moves and pulling back.

I wrap my hand around his wrist, making him pause and glance at me. "I'm on the pill. It's okay."

He blinks before his eyes narrow a fraction, and he leans in, now fully understanding what I mean.

"Are you sure?" His eyes latch onto mine, searching for my truth. "I'm clean, I've never gone without wrapping up before," he adds like it needs to be said.

Neither have I and I can't explain why, but the thought of anything between us feels wrong, despite the small voice in the back of my head telling me not to do this. He's a rock star cliché, likely unable to say how many women he's slept with. I don't even know when the last time he had sex was and if he always uses condoms. But I want to believe him, and I can't bring myself to listen to any logic right now.

"Yes."

I pull at his arm as he readily takes his position over me, his fingers swiping through my slick arousal while the tip of his cock dips inside me. He pushes further in, his heavy-lidded gaze swimming with a naked desire.

"Silas, oh my God."

He fills and stretches me with his intense thrusts, sinking into me, and my eyes snap shut, my mouth falling open on a jagged breath.

My hands fasten onto his hard, flexing arms, nails digging into his flesh.

The wet heat of his mouth finds mine, and he consumes me while keeping a smooth, addictive rhythm with his body. One hand holds himself above me while the other cups the back of my neck, our mouths fused.

Our frenetic union steals my air and leaves me on a knife's edge, craving something that is just beyond my reach, that can only come with my release. I'm so close and don't know how much more of this I can take. Silas removes his hand from my neck, his fingers now circling my clit.

"Fuck, oh my, don't stop," I cry.

"I've got you, baby."

He rolls my bundle of nerves between his fingers, round and round, and I swear I'm going to lose my mind. I'm full of him, he's everywhere, and I'm begging for release.

"I'm so close, so close," I moan.

His lips suck on mine while his fingers pinch my clit, pushing me over the edge. My core clenches around his cock, and my whimpers of pleasure break our kiss.

He hammers into me as I orgasm, and his body stiffens with his own release, my name a primal call on his lips. We cling to each other, his thrusts slowing, and eventually stopping as my spasming lessens around him. He rolls onto the mattress, taking me with him as his cock slips out of me.

"Pansy." He kisses the top of my head. "Fuck, baby, that was phenomenal. You're phenomenal."

A smile crosses my lips. I can't really argue with him. Hands down, the best sex I've ever had.

"You weren't bad, either."

He swats my ass and rolls on top of me again. "Not bad? Do I have to prove myself to you?"

"Ah, no. You've wiped me out and ruined me for all others."

22

MISS

*P*ansy

The next two days in Laguna Beach are idyllic and over way too fast. We spend our days taking long walks, swimming, or reading together in the hammock on the beach.

At night, we cook, sit on the deck with the sounds of the crackling fire and crashing waves, and have plenty of sex. Silas even plays a few songs, and we finally have those s'mores.

Any doubts I had about having both a career and Silas are erased. I'll work extra hard to stay focused, but I can't give up Silas. He's not perfect, and neither am I, but together we're magnificent.

The end comes too quickly, and Silas drops me back at my apartment with promises to talk daily, at the very least. He does drop hint that if we lived together, it would be easier, but I ignore his comment.

To make up for the missed shifts, Betty gave me an entire day, and while it's welcomed, it's long and grueling. It's just before my dinner break when a UPS guy comes in with a package.

"Pansy Dobson?" he asks.

"'That's me." I put the dishes on the counter and meet him on the other side.

"Package for you, sign here please."

I do as he asks, and he hands me a nondescript package the size of a shoebox.

"What is it?" Janis asks, inches from my face.

"Who's it from?" Callie asks excitedly.

I shrug, having no clue. Callie offers scissors, and I cut away the tape. Inside is a small white card, and I immediately recognize the slopes and scrawls of Silas's writing.

You're the most beautiful person I know.

S xo

Butterflies stir low in my belly, and there's a strange tingling in my chest to match the huge smile pulling at my lips. Callie *aww*s and swoons over my shoulder, having read the card. Twizzlers, peanut M&Ms, and Sour Patch Kids fill the box, and I laugh, ripping open the Twizzlers and shoving a sweet strawberry twirl into my mouth.

"What?" Callie is puzzled as she peers into the box looking for more. "You better be careful with those. Ralph has a sweet tooth."

"I'd like to see him try."

Not a chance anyone is getting their clutches on my sugar stash, especially considering it came from Silas. Today is his big day, and it's not only sweet but also special that he took the time to show me he's thinking of me.

"That's from Silas?" Janis asks, puzzled. "The guy's a freaking millionaire for crying out loud, you should tell him to try for diamonds or something more worthwhile."

I scoff, shaking my head, and turn my back to her.

"You guys serious?" Callie asks, following me back to where we keep our stuff.

It's a good question. I suppose we are, although it's scary to think of us like that. "Yeah, we are."

"You're one lucky girl."

"Yeah, I am."

Over the next week, Silas and I text and talk, but aren't successful at finding time to see each other. I try not to let it get to me -- we knew this would happen and it doesn't change how we feel about each other.

He continues to surprise me with thoughtful gifts every few days at Betty's. From flowers, to a mug, or a book on marine biology, all his packages include cute one-liners:

I miss your lips.

Did you save me some M&Ms?

I'm thinking of you.

My bed's lonely without you.

Think of me today.

Each note brings a smile to my face and a pang to my heart. I miss him even though we're not that far apart. I count the hours until we will talk and the days until we will see each other again.

Jorge usually drives me to and from work if Callie can't. Today, I surprise Jorge and Lucia by splurging on an Uber to Silas's place. My shift doesn't start until lunch, and I hope to have an hour with Silas.

Both Lucia and Jorge are thrilled to see me but sad to say that Silas isn't home. He hasn't been home in days, but they assure me that it gets like that when he's writing.

Since I'm here, I walk Boy on the beach, and we go for a swim. It's while I'm in the water that I spot him sauntering my way. I ogle him with his golden hair, bare chest, and board shorts, and my body thrums the closer he gets, the heavy ache building low within me.

"Good morning." He wades into the water.

Before I can respond, his lips are on mine, kissing me like it's been years. He pushes me backward, deeper into the water until I'm chest-deep and he's holding me by the waist.

"Hi." I'm dazed and breathless.

He smiles, kisses my cheek and slips his hand under my swimsuit to squeeze my ass cheek. I copy him, wriggling my hand into his shorts and digging my fingers into the firm flesh of his ass. We laugh, and it's then I notice the dark circles under his eyes.

"When was the last time you slept?"

"I've had naps here and there over the past few days. I'm exhausted. Eli called a break because he needed to see Crystal. I have the rest of the day. Can you play hooky with me?"

"I can't."

Sinking his fingers into my dry hair, piled high on the top of my head, he cocks his head to the side and purses his lips.

"I didn't think so but thought I'd ask. I miss you so much, my beautiful girl.'"

He pulls me into his chest and kisses the top of my head. I sink into his warm embrace and try to keep the tears back.

This man never ceases to surprise me. I never knew how much I needed someone like him, until now. His lips peck at the corner of my mouth before he breaks away to study me. My eyes glitter with the threat of tears. Shit.

"What's wrong? Fuck, did I do something?"

"No, not at all. These are silly tears of joy. I'm glad to see you. I miss you, too."

He pulls me in for one more hug. "Come sleep with me for a bit." He burrows his face into my neck, his moist lips sucking on my skin.

My heart sinks. "I can't. I've got work."

He groans, the rumble vibrating from his mouth to my neck and down into my chest. I shiver, holding him tighter.

"Since when do you work Thursdays?"

I usually don't, but I need the extra shifts. "Sometimes I do. I tell you what -- I'll lie down with you for a bit. Let's go to your room."

"Those are words I'll never tire of." He nips at the sensitive spot where my neck meets my collarbone, sending a jolt to my groin.

Once in the house, he takes a shower while I grab a bottle of water in the kitchen. When I get to the room, he's already in bed. I slip under the cool, crisp sheets and he folds his arms around me. His head nestles between my breasts, and before long, his soft, sleepy breaths skate across the thin fabric of my shirt.

I wish I could stay with him. Forget about work and my obligations, but as tempting as it is, I have to leave.

23

DISAPPOINTMENT

*S*ilas

"Silas." My mother's voice slices through my dream of Pansy.

Blinking, I open my eyes, only to see my mother hovering above. A groan escapes my lips at my nightmare. Why the hell do I have my mother in a fantasy about Pansy? Turning over, I bury my head into the mass of Pansy's hair and sigh on the exhale. She's real and in my bed. It wasn't all a dream.

"Silas, get up, now," my mother says. Shit, she's real and actually standing in my bedroom.

Pansy stirs, rolling over to face me with a gasp, eyes wide and confused at the strange woman hovering over us. Clutching the sheet to her, she buries her head into my chest. "Who is that?"

"Silas, tell your friend to leave."

Does she think I'm fifteen and this is her house? Irritation prickles at my skin.

"Mom."

"Oh my God, that's your mom?" Pansy squeaks into my flesh.

"Pansy, you stay." With a reassuring rub on her back, I carefully extricate myself from the bed.

Pansy pulls the sheet over her head, curling into a fetal position. My mother scowls with her hands on her hips and lips pursed.

"Oh my God." Pansy jolts from the bed forgetting her embarrassment. "I'm late! I fell asleep."

Grabbing her phone, she groans at the time and rests her head in the palm of her hand.

"Who on earth is this girl?" my mother asks.

"Let's go." I pull my mother to the door and turn to Pansy. "Jorge will drive you. Call Betty and come down when you're ready."

"Who is that?" Mom asks. "You're just leaving her in your room? Silas, we've talked to you about strangers in your home."

I growl -- Pansy's in earshot -- and pick up the pace, tugging my mother along and closing the bedroom door behind me. Like they know anything about me. If they did, she'd know that I never have strangers in my home.

"Why are you here?" My teeth clench so tight my jaw aches.

"Silas, don't speak to your mother like that." My father stands at the landing.

"This may be hard for you to understand, but this is my house, and you can't come barging into my room like that."

I usher them downstairs and into the kitchen, refusing to say a word until we're far enough away that Pansy won't be further insulted by what I'm sure is to come. We pass Jorge on the stairs, and tell him to be ready for Pansy.

"What are you doing here?" I head for the freshly-brewed coffee. Lucia is an angel.

"You're making a mistake about quitting the band, and since you won't talk to us, we decided to come to you." My father pulls a chair from the kitchen table, positioning it so he's facing me.

"And why is it a mistake?" I don't know why I'm bothering to ask; I already know what they'll say. But I'm obviously a masochist, giving them another opportunity to hurt or disappoint me.

"Have you thought about this long-term? Trojan is on a high. Why would you walk away from the goldmine in front of you?"

My father is animated, his hands moving as fast as he's talking.

All the while, my mother is nodding furiously, her ponytail swishing back and forth like a fly swatter. They are worse than the record label, if that's even possible, wanting every penny they can get from me.

"None of this is about the money. I've got more than enough even if I never work another day in my life." I don't plan on it, but I'm trying to make a point. "I could live comfortably for the rest of my life."

"Silas, you're short-sighted. This is yours for the taking. You don't leave money on the table."

"I don't want the money."

He abruptly stands, taking two strides toward me, fists clenched. "Why are you so damn selfish?"

It shouldn't hurt. His words should bounce off me like a ball hitting the rim of the basketball net. Quick, painless, and rebounding, but they don't. Each word pelts my bruised chest, heavy with all this shit I've carried with me for too long.

It never used to be like this. I don't know why things changed, but it happened one day five years ago, when out of the blue, my parents asked to be power of attorney on my accounts. They claimed it would be easier on me if they had access. Loud, jarring alarms bells went off that day and haven't stopped ringing since. I'm still waiting for an explanation, a reason to stop the incessant warning and anxiety within, but I fear it'll never come.

My father's lecturing pulls me back to the nightmare unfolding in my kitchen.

"We've supported you, and all we're asking is for you to do the same for us. You're such a disappointment," my father says.

Ready to volley my response, both their eyes narrow on something behind me and I turn to see Pansy, dressed in shorts and a black Pearl Jam tee, with her hair piled high on her head in a messy knot, standing in the doorway. She's flushed and her usually open expression is pinched. She must have heard.

I hold my hand out to her, and she tentatively comes my way, her gaze on my parents. Wanting to move past this and hoping her bright and happy disposition will shift the mood, I welcome her presence.

"Mom, Dad, this is Pansy." I want to say lover because girlfriend sounds so immature, yet lover doesn't begin to capture what we are.

"Hello." Her delivery is flat, but not rude.

She definitely heard and part of me is embarrassed. We haven't talked that much about my parents although my guess is she's aware of the tension. It's hard to miss.

My parents stare at her, discriminating, but neither says a word. Like a fist to the gut, I suck in a breath and want to punch back. How dare they be so fucking rude to her?

"If you're not going to acknowledge her, get the hell out of my house."

Pansy squeezes my hand and sucks in a breath. Looking to her, she's shaking her head. "It's okay. I called Betty, I need to go. Talk to your parents." Before I can protest, despite their snub, she turns to them and says graciously, "It was nice to meet both of you."

Not waiting for a response, she twirls on her heel and leaves. I don't want her to go, and quickly follow her out of the room.

"Pansy, wait." I tug at the back of her shirt and pull her into me. "Don't go."

She twists to face me, hands flat on my chest and leans in. "Silas, I have to, and they obviously want to talk to you."

"When does Betty need you?"

From the way she averts my gaze, it's obvious she has time. "Since I missed the lunch hour, I've got about two hours before she needs me. But Silas, my being here is not helping."

"Stay for me." My gut churns at the plea in my tone.

I hate that they're here and are likely going to hound me for more money. And most of all, I hate that she's leaving.

"Silas, call me, but I have to go."

"Fine, just leave."

She flinches, eyes widening at my cold, firm tone. "Silas, go talk to them. They're your parents, don't let this misunderstanding ruin your visit."

"You don't understand..." I start to explain, roughly running my hands through my hair when my anger gets the better of me. "Fuck it, just go."

"Silas, don't be like that. It'll be okay."

My eyes darken, narrowing at her. I'm fed up with my parents always fucking shit up and now, Pansy's inadvertently defending them, on top of the fact that she's leaving. I point at her; she's become my target.

"Don't even start with your unicorns and rainbow bullshit. You've got no fucking clue if everything's going to be okay."

Turning around, I walk away. She stuns me by grabbing my arm and moving in front of me, a mixture of concern and sadness clouding her features. She stands on the balls of her feet, her delicate fingers trace my lips, her eyes never leaving my mouth. A small smile ghosts her lips, and there's a stirring low in my belly as she presses into me; her lips barely brush mine like an already forgotten goodbye.

24

HISTORY

*P*ansy

It is another busy day at work, even with the reduced hours. I work extra hard, feeling terrible for having fallen asleep with Silas and missing my shift. I can no longer harangue Janis, I'm no better than her.

Once work is done, I go home and jump in the shower. The banging on my front door easily breaks through the water raining down on me. Whoever it is will just have to come back. I'm not getting out. I've got about four minutes left to leave in my conditioner.

But they don't get the memo to go away, continuing to bang on my door to the point that I fear my neighbors will call the cops or complain to the landlord. What the hell?

Not wanting trouble, I turn off the water and wrap a towel around me while scurrying to the door. My hair is slathered with product, and I'm ticked. It could be Jason Momoa for all I care, they are going to get an earful.

I yank the door open, and my fury meets a sudden death when I lay eyes on Silas with a bouquet of Twizzlers, Sour Patch Kids, and peanut M&Ms in hand. Despite his sheepish grin, he doesn't look good. Not even a hint of his smile meets his eyes and his wild mess of hair, while sexy, only adds to his lost and lonely expression.

"I'm sorry. I'm a colossal asshole, and I'm here to grovel." He draws his lower lip into his mouth, and his gaze is earnest and warm. With a faint smile, he hands me the candy.

Earlier, at his house, his rebuff hurt. I was tempted to match his anger with my own, but I also knew his parents had a lot to do with his short fuse and desire to lash out. While he's been vague with me about his parents, it's clear they're a sore spot for him. And now, after having met them, I see why.

"What if I don't care for your apologies or groveling?" My sassy response garners a half-smile from him.

I can't stay upset with him when pain and remorse etch his usually playful, twinkling eyes. It isn't his fault that his parents are dicks. But he's going to have to work on his knee-jerk, anger-filled reactions.

"I deserve that."

He cautiously steps toward me. I open the door wider, motioning for him to enter while holding the towel to my chest.

"Come in. Let me just rinse off and get some clothes on."

"I could help," he says, the glimmer returning to his eyes.

"Ah, as much as that could be fun, we're not there yet. We need to talk first." I waggle my finger at him, and he groans, but nods.

Once I've rinsed the conditioner, I dress quickly and join him on my small love seat. My hand rests on his hard thigh, and I give him a squeeze.

"Have you slept at all today?"

"Nah, my parents are still at my place."

"Silas, you need some sleep. Talk to me first and then let's get you to bed. So, your parents are here." I trail off, waiting for him to fill the void and tell me more.

"Yeah." He rubs the back of his neck and releases a small puff of air.

There's silence as he seems to deliberate over his words, or perhaps where to begin?

"You haven't said much, but from what you've said, I figured your relationship with your parents was strained. And while I don't know why, now that I've met them, it makes more sense. Can you tell me more? I want to understand. Be there for you."

He studies me, his eyes roving my face, searching for something. Taking my hand in his, he interlaces our fingers.

"I don't deserve you."

"Stop right there. We all deserve people to care about us even when we're difficult or not nice."

We share a smirk before his expression shifts and his brows knit as his jaw clenches. Resting his head on the top of the couch, he closes his eyes.

"I had a ridiculously easy and happy childhood. My parents were firm but great. Even in high school when I got into a band and was pushing their boundaries, they were fair. So I never saw it coming, and I guess that's where I'm stuck."

"Saw what coming?"

He lifts his head and pivots slightly to face me. "After high school, I wanted to start a band. I didn't want to go to college, and they were shocked and disappointed. They thought my music was a hobby, not my calling. Because I wouldn't do what my father wanted, go to college and pick a reliable nine-to-five profession, things got bumpy. I think they figured that I'd change my mind and when they realized that I was serious, they gave me an ultimatum. College or I was out of the house. I left."

"What? They kicked you out?"

"Yeah. It was rough, at first. Until then, I was pampered, and I had no clue about life and hardship until I found myself on my own. I had to bust my ass, had nights where I had nothing to eat and finally, I'd saved enough to go from the boarding house into a cheap place to live." He squirms in his seat, now looking at our joined hands.

"That's how I met Jared. We were both staying at this boarding house. He was worse off than me. Once I got my own place, I let him crash, and we bonded over our love of music. We both wanted to have a band, and we put a call out for auditions. That's how we met Eli and

Rich, our first drummer, and formed Trojan. We started off small, performing in dive bars. One night, Jimmy Ellis came into the joint and lucky for us, he wasn't so wasted that he couldn't recognize talent and sought us out. That led to our big break."

"Jimmy Ellis?" I repeat, sure that I heard wrong.

The man is a rock legend, albeit portrayed as a heavy partier and drug user. He's been in and out of rehab throughout his career.

"Yeah. He introduced us to a few key people in the industry, and as they say, the rest is history. Anyway, once we made it big and our name was being dropped all over the place, my parents reached out through Bianca."

"Bianca?"

"Yeah. She grew up with Jared. They'd parted ways but ran into each other at some party. She was also in the business, and became our manager."

"She's almost a member of the band."

"She is. Sometimes she can be hard to take, but her heart's in the right place. She's got our backs no matter what. Anyway, my parents apologized and were all over me. At the time, I never questioned it. They're my parents, and I'd missed them. A lot.

"But not long after, the money I sent monthly wasn't enough. They started asking for more. Again, at first, I gave it without hesitation. They'd taken care of me all my life, and it was my turn to take care of them. But in the past five years, it's been bad. They're all about the money and what I can do for them. I feel like a bank account."

The pain in his voice is a shot to my heart. It's hard to believe parents could do that to their child. I brush away his hair; sadness invades his beautiful face, and I lean into him.

"Did you ever talk to them? Ask them why?"

"All the time, and they tell me it's all in my head. They have no clue what I'm talking about. But it's always about the money. Even now, they don't want me to quit because they fear my money will dry up. I couldn't stay there with them. I've given them money for a hotel and told them to be gone before I get back."

I gently kiss the underside of his jaw and wrap my arm around him. He willingly sinks into me, his shoulder resting on my head.

"I'm so sorry."

His angry outbursts make more sense now. Despite his playful persona or his sometimes hard-ass demeanor, he's a caring man. I can only imagine how he's coping with the loss of his parents' unconditional love or the fact that they won't acknowledge the change or give him any answers.

"It's just..." He glances away, then back to me. "I miss them. Who they used to be, and I..."

He holds me tight. His beard brushes against my neck as he kisses and licks along my neck and jaw. His mouth lands on mine, our kisses soft at first. I want to take away his pain, make this all better.

I can't fix it, but I can help him forget, if only for a while. I deepen our kiss, my tongue delving and sweeping through his mouth. His lips are hot, plump, and softer than you'd think. Our kisses are long and wet, our tongues dancing to the beat of our increasing desire.

Until he breaks away from my mouth, trailing kisses, licks and nips down my neck while he palms my breasts through my tank. "Fuck, I love these, so perfect." His breath tickles my skin.

I arch my back, giving him better access while his fingers dip beneath the neckline to pull the fabric below my breasts. He pinches and pulls at my nipples, sending shivers directly to my core.

Latching onto his shoulders, I clumsily yank at his shirt until he finally understands my need to feel his hard, bare chest under my fingertips. He pulls his shirt over his head, and as soon as he's free of the fabric, he dives back in. His hot, wet mouth covers my hardening nipple, sucking and nipping at the sensitive bud.

A loud, sharp knocking on the door causes us to jump and break apart. His shirt is strewn on the floor, my breasts are spilling out of my tank, and our respective heads of hair are untamed.

"Don't answer it." Silas quickly regains his focus and goes back to worshipping my breasts.

I want to give in and ignore whoever it is, but they are persistent.

As I'm internally debating whether I end our make-out session or take Silas to bed, the lock turns, and the door opens, shocking us both.

25

TWISTS
PANSY

*S*ilas springs into action and presses my chest against him to shield me from wandering eyes.

Daisy, my sister, stands at the door in a well-fitted yellow sundress and red espadrilles with wedge heels, with two large suitcases at her feet. Beside her is my landlord, Dick – the name suits him – who is amused at what they walked in on.

Forgetting my tank is pulled down, I attempt to step from behind Silas, but his grip tightens on my hip, keeping me where I am. He growls, my name slipping past his lips like a curse.

Despite his caveman moves, I'm grateful and shove my boobs back into my top before coming to stand beside him. Silas waists until I'm decent to put on his shirt.

"Daisy. What are you doing here?"

"Nice to see you, too, Pansy," she says with a huge dose of attitude.

We haven't seen each other in the five years since my mother died. A sharp pang rips through my heart when I think of that day. Ivy and Daisy picking over mom's things like vultures, while Poppy and I wanted to be anywhere but there. Since then, Daisy and I have emailed and texted occasionally, but nothing significant. Why on earth is she here?

"Holy shit, you're Silas Palmer!" Daisy squeals, coming fully into my place.

I snort and roll my eyes; everyone looks to me, and an embarrassed heat creeps up my neck. Silas tucks me into his side and gazes back at Daisy. Dick still stands mutely at the door, his sallow complexion flush as he stares at me as if he's seen my birthday suit. I suppose I did give him an eyeful.

Daisy's gaze is glued to Silas, and she hesitates for a brief second before throwing herself at him. Arms and legs are clinging to him like a monkey. An ugly feeling twists in my belly, my hands curling into fists.

Silas pries her arms off and steps away from her, sliding back to my side, arm around my waist. Daisy zeroes in on the gesture, her eyes flying to meet mine with arched brows and her mouth slightly parted.

"What are you doing here?" I ask again.

"Sheesh, since when did you become such a bitch?" Daisy snaps, plopping herself onto the couch where we just made out.

"Daisy." Silas's tone is a warning. This is all new to me, someone defending me without question.

Daisy clamps her mouth shut with Silas's hard glare on her. Satisfied that she got the memo, he turns and says to Dick, "You can leave."

My landlord's beady eyes squint in what I'm sure he thinks are his bedroom eyes. Right at me. It's creeping me out. Dick is easily in his late fifties with a beer gut that hangs low over his belt, and a stringy comb-over that barely covers his balding head.

"Oh, yeah," he mumbles, his doughy jowl jiggling as he nods and pulls the key from the lock.

Silas grasps Dick's shoulder, and from the older man's wince, I'd say it's hard. "And next time, unless a putrid smell or smoke is coming from under the door, you don't come into this place uninvited. Got it?"

"I was just doing my job. She said," he waves in Daisy's direction, "she was worried about her sister."

"Putrid smell or smoke. Got it?" Silas repeats. Dick screws up his face, mumbling under his breath, and leaves.

Sitting across from my sister, I try again. "Daisy, last I heard you were in Croatia or Greece or something like that. What happened?"

Daisy coming back to the US is unusual. She swore she never would, preferring the jet-setting life.

"I missed you. Missed home."

Raising my eyebrows skeptically, I study her. Her eyes dart between us as Daisy sinks her teeth into her bottom lip.

Taking his hand, we walk to the front door, and I lean in to whisper, "Silas, you stay here and sleep. I need to talk to my sister."

He frowns, a gruff exhale passing his tight lips. "Nah, I'll go home. You guys talk. But I need to see you soon."

Daisy's thrown a wrench into any plans of talking, knowing she'll demand all my time. That's what she does. If she isn't the center of attention, then she creates a reason to be.

"We'll figure something out."

Cupping my face, he lowers his voice. "I'm back in the studio tomorrow, laying down a few demo tracks..."

"Hey, it's only temporary. Go be a sexy rock star," I tease, smacking his hard butt.

Like a twister, he whirls around, hauling me against his hard chest and nuzzling his face into my neck. His warm, wet tongue licks at my flesh.

"Damn, you taste good. I'd planned on eating all of you."

"I can hear you!" Daisy shrieks, making gagging sounds from ten feet away.

"Then leave," Silas fires before nipping at my neck again. I squirm in his hold, a hot ache growing between my thighs.

In one swift move, she pushes to standing with her hands on her hips and huffs. Taking three steps to the partition that separates my bed from everything else, she halts when she discovers there's nothing beyond that.

She spins on her heel and her gaze lands on us; exasperated, she asks, "How do you live in this hovel?"

"You don't have to stay here." Silas is unrelenting in keeping Daisy in her place, and it's now my turn to bury my face in his neck, stifling my laughter.

"Call me later," he says before taking my face in his hands and planting a slow, sweet kiss on me; then he's gone.

Daisy is transfixed, her eyes glued to where Silas just stood. "What the hell, Pansy? Why didn't you tell me that you were sleeping with Silas fucking Palmer?"

"You say that like we share everything." I sit back down beside her. "C'mon Daisy, why are you surprised that you don't know anything about me?"

Knitting her brow, she crosses her arms and crinkles her nose, not pleased with my blunt truthfulness.

"It doesn't have to be that way. Can I stay with you for a bit and we could reconnect?" She's meek with the question, yet assessing my home as if it's livable.

"Not that you're not welcome..." It takes everything within me to say and mean it. She's my sister, I do love her, but she makes it so darn hard to like her, sometimes. "How did you find me?" As I ask, the answer comes to me.

"I called Ivy, and she gave me your address." She shrugs like there's nothing unusual about it.

"Why me? Why not Ivy? Or a five-star luxury hotel? My life, this," I wave my hand around my tiny but cozy apartment, "is not up to your standards."

"I can't... I don't want to go to Ivy's, and I'd rather not spend money on a hotel. Besides, as difficult as this is for you to believe, I did want to see you. It's been five years."

"I know."

"Just after Mom died." She shifts to face me fully. "And last time I heard from you... gosh, I don't know how long ago that was? Ivy told me about your escapade and jail time."

Her wry grin matches the glint in her eye, and she slings her arm around my shoulder.

"Yeah, don't remind me." I chuckle.

"The little adventurist. You always did know how to have a good time."

We sit in silence. Daisy's unusually quiet and restless, shifting her position every few seconds. My hand lands on hers, fiddling with an imaginary thread or lint or something on her sundress.

"Are you gonna tell me what's going on?"

Turning her palm up, she folds her fingers over mine, and we share a look. One that only sisters can. Even if you're not close or have your differences, there's a level of understanding that exists between siblings that's born of all your shared experiences. We know each other, even if we don't like each other.

"I messed up and just need a place to lie low and figure stuff out. I don't want to get into it now. I'm not ready to, but when I am, I'll tell you. It's just that, I think I may be done with modeling and I'm not sure what that means. Where do I go from here?"

"I get that. I'm at a crossroad too. I'm trying to figure out what I want to do with my life." I brace for a nasty remark, but nothing comes. Instead, she holds my hand tighter and nods.

She is my sister, and all my life I have wanted to be close to her. To have her see me, and this may be the moment. Or it may not. I'm under no illusion that Daisy and I may never get along, but this is the first time she's come to me. I can't turn my back on her.

26

ADDICTED

*S*ilas

I finally sleep for sixteen hours straight and wake to discover my parents are still here, even though I told them to leave. I get Jorge to take them to a hotel, and I call the band to tell them I'm not coming in today. Eli and Gray are cool with it. Jared and Bianca are ticked.

Jared is upset because we were on a roll, and he's right. We were making serious progress, with several songs complete. Bianca is troubled about the money and time being wasted by our delays. It means the label will be breathing down her neck.

None of that matters to me. It should, but I need to see Pansy first. We ended things so abruptly because of Daisy's arrival. I just want to make sure she's okay.

I slip into Betty's through the side door and stand quietly against the wall, taking in the chaos. The quaint restaurant is packed, and it's not even lunch yet, though well past the morning rush. You'd think they were giving something away with the line out the door.

Pansy's working the small space, serving orders and clearing tables. She hasn't noticed me, nor do I expect her to. For one, it's way too busy. Two, I'm supposed to be with the band. And three, I doubt even she'd recognize me in my ball cap and sunglasses, clean-shaven with a new haircut.

Gone are my beard and long locks in favor of scruff and shorter, jaw-length hair. It was time for the beard to go and my hair is still long by some standards, namely my father's, but overall, I'm cleaner cut, less rocker.

I needed a change. I'm heading in a new direction, I've got the best girl in the universe and every day brings me closer to the future. With my parents showing up, it felt like something I needed to do, as if I'm shedding the past and moving forward.

Even with my new hair, I've still disguised myself somewhat because the band is hot right now with the record in the making. And since Pansy's been here, I've frequented the streets of Santa Monica more than I ever have before. If I want to keep my resident status a secret, maintaining my low profile is definitely needed.

As I look around, there's more than enough action to entertain me: the young couple locking lips in line, the Barbie look-alike adjusting her tits, or the goth chick smooching her chihuahua.

But even with all these distractions, I can't tear my gaze from Pansy. She hustles from behind the counter, a tray in hand, laden with food and coffee. She's wearing those damn fuck-me shorts. Yes, the same ones that stole my breath in the middle of the desert.

As much as I hate seeing her in those shorts, or I should say hate other guys laying eyes on her in them, she's heart-stopping. She is graceful and sensual in an unassuming way, with the subtle sway of her hips and gentle bounce of her perky tits. A few strands of her tresses have escaped her messy top knot and wildly frame her pretty face.

Blowing a long stray lock from her vision, she sets the tray down in front of an older guy who can't keep his eyes off her. While I share the compulsion, I hate it.

She smiles and says something to the dirty old man. I don't like her working here. He returns her smile, although his is more a leer, then she turns to leave.

If I weren't watching, I'd never have known, but the fucker sticks the tip of his shoe in her way. It's subtle, nearly imperceptible, but Pansy stumbles, losing her balance thanks to his move. It happens in slow motion.

The asshole latches onto her hips, thrusting her backward onto his lap, a smarmy grin spreading across his face. She shrieks in surprise, one hand flying to her mouth and the other to her chest as the bastard chuckles.

Without missing a beat, he wraps his arm tightly around her and whispers into her ear. Immediately, her cheeks redden, and she wriggles to get free, and me, like a grenade with the pin pulled, I'm ready to explode. I charge toward them, single-minded in my mission to kick the ever-loving shit out of this asshole.

Pansy's now out of his grasp and saying something to him. One hand on her hip, she points her finger at him, oblivious to the incoming missile.

He, in turn, raises his hands in surrender, eyes widening as he catches sight of me barreling toward him.

She glances behind to see what's got him shaking in his boots, and places her hand where my heart is, stopping me from going further.

"Silas." Her pitch is higher than usual, and her anxious expression morphs into a small smile, eyes brightening, then dimming as her features shift, yet again, into a tense frown.

"Pansy, please step out of the way. This asshole deliberately tripped you," I grind out, my eyes laser-focused at the douchebag behind her, shaking in his seat. He is about to get his face acquainted with his ass.

"Silas, I know." Her tone is softer, calmer as she rubs small, warm circles on my chest. Her other hand caresses my day-old stubble with a twinkle in her eye. My cock jerks, happy to have her hands on me. "Please let me handle this."

"Look, I was out of line, I'm sorry..." the asswipe has the nerve to say. I stab him with an icy glare, and he shuts the fuck up.

"I want to rearrange his face, or better yet, knock all his teeth out,"

I threaten loud enough for him to hear over the din of the crowd, my eyes never leaving his.

"And I'd let you if I didn't think I could handle it. Please..."

"Hey, come with me," Betty interjects out of nowhere, nabbing my bicep and tugging me away from the jackass.

Pansy mouths *thank you* to her employer and cuts back to me. This time our gazes lock, and I see how much she needs me to listen to her. To let her handle this, even though every fiber of my being wants to kick the shit out of him.

Betty drags me through the small, hot as hell kitchen and out the door to the rear of the building.

"Just what the hell do you think you're doing? Are you looking to cause a scene and have all of the LA media at my doorstep?" Betty may be only five feet tall and well over sixty, but right now, she might as well be a fire-breathing dragon. She's spitting nails, and they're aimed at me.

"Shit, Bets, I'm sorry."

Slumping onto a stack of wooden pallets, I rip the ball cap off my head and roughly comb my fingers through my hair. She's right. If I'd hit that guy, people would have had their phones out, and in no time at all, it'd be viral that Silas Palmer went ape-shit on some poor guy.

She relaxes her warrior stance; coming to me, she rests her small hand on my shoulder.

"It's not to say that jerk doesn't deserve an ass-kicking," she says, smirking. "I also saw what he did and was ready to come out and deal with it myself. But in case you missed it, that little lady in there can take care of herself."

We share a sardonic grin before I chuckle, nodding. "True. She's certainly put me in my place many times."

"I know you want to protect her. If it helps, I look out for my people. She's in good hands when she's here. I won't let anything happen to her."

I pull the spry woman into my side and gently squeeze her. She's a sweet woman, and it's comforting to know she's got Pansy's back.

"It does help. Thanks, Bets." I kiss the top of her white-haired head as Pansy comes out into the lot.

With her hands on her hips, she squints, watching as Betty stands and pats my hand.

"Go easy on him, his heart was in the right place," Betty says before leaving.

She's upset, but is it at me or the fuckwad inside? She brushes a few wisps of hair from her face and nears me until she's standing a foot from me. I just want her in my arms, but she doesn't budge.

Instead, her eyes take me in, from head to toe. She cocks her head to one side and narrows her eyes while her teeth sink into her lower lip. Fuck me; she's killing me. A light sparks her eyes and a slow, sexy grin strikes her mouth like the bright sun rising.

"Your hair and beard." She closes the gap to finger my locks. "I like it."

Her hands freely roam my scruff, and her touch is the greatest fucking high. As her long, slender fingers cup my cheeks, she steps in between my legs and her eyes are warm and hazy. She can't seem to stop running her hands along my cheeks and jaw like she's addicted to me as much as I am to her.

Her cherry lips lightly kiss the side of my mouth, her tongue darting out to flick my upper lip. My cock jerks like she just licked the tip, and I squeeze her ass, needing something to hold onto.

Her shorts, so tiny they should be illegal, allow for my fingertips to slide along the smooth underside of her luscious ass. Glorious.

"Hey, you," she murmurs against my lips before her tongue delves into my mouth.

My *hello* slides down her throat as I haul her flush against me. The stacked crates I'm perched on are low to the ground, bringing her chest to my eye-level. My hands slide from her ass to the back of her thighs, down to her calves. Her skin's ridiculously soft, only making me want to get her naked this instant.

She leans down to deepen our kiss with her hands still caressing my face, still roaming from jaw to chin, cheekbone to neck. She can't get enough of me, and this strange stirring grows within me, heating and swelling.

"I've missed you," she mumbles against my cheek before licking and biting at my jaw.

"Me, too," I manage to respond, in between kisses, strokes, and nibbles.

"Did you get to sleep?" she asks.

"Yeah." I yank her onto my lap, and she settles in like she's home and we continue kissing. We stay like that, getting reacquainted and making out, albeit PG, for I don't know how long. I think we'd still be there if it weren't for Betty interrupting to tell Pansy that she needs to get back to work.

"Hey, wait. Daisy's here to stay?"

"So it seems, but we'll see. She's high maintenance and living at my place is way below her standards."

"How is that going to work with only one bed?"

"I don't know. We'll see. It's barely been twenty-four hours, and we've already had our moments, but she is somewhat different. She seems to want to try at this sister thing. She also has stuff going on in her life, and I think she's looking for family support."

"Family support? Like financially?"

"No." Again she laughs. "She has more money than me. She wants someone in her corner."

"I thought Ivy was her go-to sister?"

"Usually she is, but there's more. I don't know what, but Daisy doesn't want to go to Ivy, so something tells me that whatever it is, Ivy won't approve."

"What? So you're the default sister? Because her fav won't support her, she's slumming with her baby sister?" I fail at hiding my vitriol.

"It's not like that. Or at least, I hope not. But we'll see."

"I just want you to be careful. Just because you're family, it doesn't mean you can trust her or that she's got your back." I speak from experience and shouldn't paint Daisy with the same brush, but from all I've heard, she could just be using Pansy. I won't let that happen.

"True, and I've got my eyes open, although I like to think that's not the case."

"Okay, but if you need anything or need my help getting rid of her, tell me. I will help you." My grip tightens on her. "Can I see you after your shift?"

"I promised Callie that I'd help her with setting up her website. How about tomorrow before my shift? But no sleeping at your house," she says with a smile.

"I can't. I'm having breakfast with my parents." She straightens, her eyes full and optimistic, but I quickly dash any hope. "It's the only way I got them to agree to leave."

"Pansy," Bunny hollers from the door. "Jagger, get your hands off my flower girl. She's got work to do."

27

FEAR

*P*ansy
Over the next few days, Daisy's predicament becomes abundantly clear. I didn't have to be a rocket scientist to figure it out. Keeping her secret was next to impossible in my small space. Another drawback of one bathroom and paper-thin walls.

Morning, noon, or night, her retching is audible from all corners of my apartment. The first few times, I try to help and knock on the door for her to let me in, but each time, she tells me to go away. Three days in, she breaks down and lets me in.

I use a knife and pick the lock to get it open; she says she can't move, and the task is rather easy. I find her on her knees over the toilet. Her usually shiny light blonde hair is dull, hanging like wet spaghetti around her face.

She heaves, and I rush to pull her hair to the sides, rubbing her back as she expels a watery bile. Once I think it's over, I wipe a cool damp cloth on the back of her neck and face.

"I think I'm done for now. I need to lie down."

She leans on me as I guide her to my bed and get her tucked in. Her forehead is damp with a light sheen, and she's pallid with dry lips.

I wet the cloth once more and place it on her forehead before going to the kitchen to get some ginger ale. Sticking the straw to her mouth, I make her take a few small sips.

"How far along are you?"

"About five weeks. I haven't been to a doctor but have an appointment next week."

"And the father, does he know?"

"Yes." She says it with such defeat that my heart aches without even knowing the situation.

"And?"

"He wants nothing to do with the baby. Or me. We'd been seeing each other for seven or eight months. It wasn't serious. He's a model, and a baby would cramp his style. I'm on my own."

Clutching her limp, cool hand in mine, I gently hold on as tears shine in her eyes and her lower lip quivers.

"Pansy, I'm so scared. I can't do this alone. I need you so much."

Daisy's plea or confession, depending on how you look at it, moves me and shocks me. I never dreamed of hearing anything resembling that from her. Ever. But even at this moment, I don't want to be her doormat. I have a life too, and while I'll help in any way I can, we need to get a few things straight.

"Why didn't you go to Ivy?" She winces. I'm not beating around the bush, I want answers. "I didn't mean it like that. You're welcome here, but Ivy's the doctor. She can do more for you."

With pursed lips and an eye roll, the Daisy I'm thoroughly acquainted with comes back. "She'd lecture me and make me suck salt for how stupid and irresponsible I was. She likes to kick you when you're down, and I don't need that."

I nod. It's sad but true. "Why me? Daisy, you're not alone, and I'll help, but I need to understand why you didn't go to one of your friends, someone you're closer to, or heck, you have money, you could do this on your own."

Daisy pushes up into a sitting position, resting the cloth on the bedside table. "You're not going to make this easy, are you?"

"No. You and I have always just tolerated each other, even when

Mom thought we should be best friends because we were the youngest." I'm not telling her anything she doesn't already know. "Why me?"

Taking my hand in hers, she squeezes until our eyes meet. "I'm a bitch and have taken my crap and insecurities out on you. I'm not proud of it, and I'm sorry. Pansy, the sad truth is, I don't have any friends."

"What?"

I run through all her emails and photos, one- or two-word texts about parties, jet-setting to one place or another, shopping, dancing, you name it. I'm confused.

"None of the models I hang with are truly my friends, and if I've gotten close to someone, it doesn't last. And yes, I could have gone to Ivy, but despite what you think, we aren't really that close. Ivy doesn't need anyone.

"Well, that's not true. She needs people to take charge of, but she doesn't seem to need or want a friend. She would scold me for the baby and make me feel like a failure for it, but she wouldn't be there for me. I need a friend."

It's a shock, like a jolt to my heart. She wants me as a friend? Sure, Ivy'd be judgmental and condescending about Daisy having a baby, but she's the matriarch. She'd make everything all right, yet Daisy came to me.

"And that's me? A friend?"

"Yes. I've always wanted to be your friend. You're funny, smart, and caring, but you also scare me." My eyes widen, as does my mouth, and Daisy giggles. "You should see your face right now."

"I just don't understand what you're saying. All our lives, I've felt like the screw-up, the baby who got away with everything, and now you're telling me something that I just never thought I'd hear."

"I hid my true feelings really well."

"'Why?"

"Because I'm nothing like you. Letting my feelings out doesn't come easily to me, I fear rejection, and..."

"Go on," I say encouragingly.

"You always followed your heart and embraced life without any fear, or if you were afraid, you pushed through it no matter who was in your corner or not. I kept you away for fear of finding out that we couldn't be friends, that we wouldn't get along. Instead, it was what I wanted all along. Like I said, I'm a bitch, and I'm sorry."

She pulls me in for a hug, and I'm stunned. "Does this mean you don't like modeling?"

"No, I do. I was fortunate to find something that I do love, and I'm good at, but this pregnancy has forced me to reevaluate the way I've been living my life. I need a friend, Pansy, and that's why I came to you."

Her smile is watery, but it reaches her eyes, and I hug her again. My emotions are all turned upside-down.

"I'm here for you. You're not alone."

"Thank you. And I promise I'll get my act together. In fact, I've just had a call from my agent about a bikini shoot in Europe. I have to give them an answer quickly because their original model backed out, and while I hadn't counted on doing any more, I might take it. One final gig. I haven't told anyone about my pregnancy yet. They all think I fled because Costa and I broke up. That I'm heartbroken."

"And are you?"

"No. Costa and I were only friends with benefits. He made things less lonely, but we weren't serious. I wish he wanted to be a part of the baby's life, for the child's sake, but maybe it's better this way."

"Can I ask why you're having the baby when it will disrupt your life? And before you answer, know that I support your decision. I just want to understand."

"I can't really answer that or explain it. All I know is once I found out, there really wasn't any other choice. I was happy to know that I'd have a chance to give a child the love and support Mom and Dad did for us."

"Daze, I totally understand that."

I'm surprised by her revelation and also elated. It goes to show; things aren't necessarily how you see them. I feel more confident and hopeful about my future than ever before.

28

WORTHLESS

Silas

I'm wired and anxious to have breakfast with my parents. I would prefer not to see them, but it's the only way they agreed to leave. Their flight's today. I'm up, dressed, and on my way to the city long before I have to be there. I just want to get this over with.

When I arrive at La Mondrian -- only the best for Alice and Chuck Palmer -- I bide my time by the pool, drinking coffee. I'm not going to their room any earlier than I have to. The time goes by too fast and too slow, but like all things, the inevitable comes, and it's time to go up.

Mom answers the door wearing a crisp linen skirt and blouse. Her hair's in her usual ponytail, her makeup light, but her fresh look is complete with a simple string of pearls.

"Silas, honey." She kisses me on the cheek and gives me a long hug.

I'm somewhat taken aback because it almost feels sincere. I don't know if it's me and my wishing for that to be the case, or if it really is. Either way, it doesn't matter. She kills my sentimental thoughts as soon as she starts talking.

"Silas, have you considered what quitting the band means?"

She pours us coffee and motions for me to sit with her. Reluctantly, I obey.

"Yes, Mom, I have."

"Honey, I don't know how to say this, but you need to know that even with you doing this, we can't... um, we can't..." Her eyes flick to the doorway that leads to where the bed and bathroom are. It's like she's seeking reinforcements. My dad.

"Just say it, Mom." My exasperation is strong and clear in my tone.

"What your mother is trying to say is that we can't take a reduction in the money you send us even if you quit the band." My father strolls into the room like he rules the world, his hands busy knotting his tie. "It's simply not an option."

Our gazes lock, his hard eyes challenging me, almost wishing that I'll take him on.

"Excuse me?"

"You heard me, son." His tone is somewhat softer, especially on the word *son*, but the hard glint is still in his eyes.

"Well, I haven't even got there yet. I need to talk to my financial advisor to figure things out. It all depends on what I plan on doing next."

I've never begrudged them anything, and even now, when my money is all they seem to care about, I still don't want to leave them high and dry. They wouldn't be destitute, or at least, I don't think so, but either way, they are my parents.

Even with all of this, it still feels wrong, and it hurts like a motherfucker to have them dictate to me what I can and can't do with my money. No matter how many times I go over our past, I don't know how we got here.

"Silas, you don't..."

"Chuck," my mother interjects. A scowl covers his face, and she comes to his side, tugging on his arm. "We should eat or else we're going to be late for the airport."

He mutters under his breath, but relents and sits to eat. Our meal is rife with unspoken words, and we all pick at our food, hardly eating anything. Our appetites are lost to the thick tension in the air.

Mom dabs at the corner of her mouth with the napkin and puts on a tight smile. "Well, we best be going or else we're going to miss our flight."

"Yes, let's go," my father responds tersely, his eyes finding mine. "We'll continue this conversation another time."

Not a chance.

"Have a safe flight," I say, heading to the door.

"But wait, aren't you driving us?" Mom is quick to ask, her worrisome nature rising to the surface.

"No, I figured it would be best to have a driver take you. The limo is downstairs waiting for you." I don't look back as I walk out the door.

My chest aches like I've got an elephant sitting on it and breathing is hard. Fuck, why does this have to hurt so much? Anger runs like hot lava through my veins, and the urge to hit something is overwhelming.

Lost, fearing I'll lose control, and with nowhere to go, I drive for a while along the coast, trying to find some peace or balance or whatever the fuck is going to help. The one thing I want right now, the one person, isn't available. Pansy.

It's then that I find myself doing the most unexpected thing of all. Pulling to the side of the road, I call Dr. Wexford, my therapist. I haven't spoken to her in almost a year, and I'm surprised when she answers, and even more so when she tells me that she has time for me.

She's waiting for me on the front step of her beach house. She's a pretty woman in her early forties with bangs and long dark hair that she wears tied in a low ponytail. Her long, flowing dress and her willowy figure sway with the breeze.

"Silas, it's so good to see you," she greets me with a warm smile and handshake.

"Dr. Wexford, thank you for seeing me, it was... ah... spur of the moment."

"Sometimes, that's the best way." She turns, and I follow her up the steps to her office above the garage. "It just so happens my usual appointment is on vacation, so I was free. I'm so glad that I was. It's been a long time. How are you doing?"

Her office hasn't changed since I was last there. It's nothing like a doctor's office, but more like a living room, with warm colors, comfortable furniture, a fountain, plants, and beautiful art. Behind her desk is a picture window overlooking the Pacific Ocean. I always feel calm and at peace in her space, even when I dreaded coming.

Sitting in an armchair, I glance her way, and she smiles encouragingly.

"I'm good. No, for the most part, I'm great. I met someone, and she's changed my life in so many ways."

"I can tell by the way you speak about her. Tell me more?" She crosses her legs in the overstuffed chair.

She listens, asking few but pertinent questions as I tell her all about Pansy. How we met, how things are now, and that I want her to live with me.

"She sounds like a remarkable young woman. I hope to meet her someday." I nod and smile, feeling a bit self-conscious about having spilled my heart and soul to her, although she knows all there is to know about me. "What's the but?"

"Pardon?" I furrow my brow, puzzled.

"I'm sensing that something is bothering you. Something prompted you to call me. And I'm glad you did. It can't be that Pansy is not living with you, so tell me, what is it?"

Her soft, lyrical voice weakens me, and like water gushing from a breached dam, all my hurt, disappointment, and anger concerning my parents spills out of me.

Dr. Wexford knows the history with my parents, and the current state hasn't changed since the last time I saw her. In fact, we spent most of our time focused on my mother and father. She also knew about my unhappiness with the band and wanting a change, but she felt a lot of my anger was rooted in my relationship with my parents. Or lack thereof.

"How did it make you feel when your father told you that lowering or stopping the deposits wasn't an option?"

I'd forgotten how her simple questions, almost pointless because the answers are so obvious that a response isn't needed, are always the hardest to answer. She gets to the crux of things simply and straightforwardly.

My response is on the tip of my tongue, yet my throat tightens, and my heart thunders against my rib cage. Fuck, saying it out loud isn't easy.

"It pisses me off," I grind out, my jaw clenching so tight it makes my head throbs. "Hurts. Like I'm worthless."

"Worthless? How so?" Again, she's curious at my choice of word, yet I'd bet she already has the answer.

"I don't matter." My voice cracks and I clear my throat, flicking my eyes to the floor.

Fuck, why did I come here? Because I want to talk about this. Because I want to put an end to this burning, all-consuming anger inside of me.

"Tell me more," she prompts, her voice soft and soothing.

"My money is all they see and not their son." I swallow hard and clasp my hands together with my head hung low.

The ugly, gut-wrenching feeling sits low in my belly. Oppressive and suffocating. Then the anger comes and burns as it washes over me.

"Talk to me, Silas."

"Why the fuck am I ashamed?" My voice is steely cold and my fists so tight that my knuckles are white and the veins in my forearms are pulsing and bulging. "I don't get it."

"What don't you get?"

I'm starting to get tired of her questions, but I catch myself and recognize what it is that I'm doing. It's my knee-jerk reaction to redirect my anger at whoever is in my vicinity. Dr. Wexford always said the first step was to acknowledge the anger and the need to lash out. Don't give in to it, I am in control, but recognize it because then I can choose.

"What happened to them? Between us? When did I become just a bank to them and nothing more? They don't care about my music or the band. They haven't asked once why I want to quit."

"If your parents were here right now, what would you say to them?"

Lifting my head, I stare into her dark eyes that hold only patience and compassion.

"What? I don't know."

"You don't know what you'd say to them? Really?" she pushes.

"I'd say nothing. That's what I always do." Defeat floods my voice, and it disgusts me.

"Okay. I've got some homework for you. Are you doing the exercises I'd given you to do?"

"Sometimes, not every day like you told me. Only when I feel on edge."

Nodding, like she expected that answer, she says, "All right. I want you to do the exercises daily and also when you need it. And I want you to think about what you'd say to your parents. No holding back. Write it down and bring it next time you come. I'd like to see you next week."

"Okay."

We say our goodbyes, and as I walk to my car, I'm caught up in what I already know. Confronting them about their behavior is what strangles me. It stifles my air, redirecting and breathing life into my anger.

I know what I want to say, but fear has me by the balls. It could change everything. It could end things.

And as much as this hurts, as much as I want this to stop, I don't know if I can ever say what I want to them for fear of losing them forever.

29

DISDAIN

*P*ansy

"Hey, Pansy," Daisy says, walking into my place with two shopping bags.

We went to the doctor the other day and got a prescription for her nausea. The doctor says it will take a while to kick in, but she should start to feel better soon.

Whether it's a placebo and just knowing it will get better is helping or if it's actually working, she seems to be handling the nausea and has decided to go on the final modeling shoot to Europe before her belly pops. After that, she will tell them that she's pregnant and then everything will change for her.

We've talked about getting a place together once she's back, and while the idea is appealing, I'm also considering Silas's. But I haven't voiced my desire to anyone. Our lives are hectic, and I do miss him, a lot. Living together would make things easier, and in my mind, I've managed to rationalize that it wouldn't be a hand-out if I contributed. Although I'm sure Silas wouldn't accept it.

"Hey. Great timing, dinner is ready." I cut the frittata down the middle, placing one half on her plate and the other on mine.

"Wow, this smells good. I'm starving." She plops into the chair and begins to eat.

"Silas is having a barbecue tomorrow and wants you to come. He's also invited Vinny," I say.

"Great. What's the occasion?"

"There's no special reason. He just wants to hang out, and he wants to get to know you and Vinny better."

Daisy has met Vinny and even come with him to take me to and from class. She is genuinely supportive of my pursuing marine biology and is interested in learning more. Her support is still all new to me, and at times, I still question if it's real.

"All right, sounds good. Did you ask him if he'll take me to the airport?"

"Yup, he will, and if for some reason it doesn't work out, Jorge will."

"Great, thanks." Daisy shovels the last bite into her mouth and eyes the food still on my plate.

Before she can ask me for a bite, which is her new thing, there's a knock at the door. Despite feeling queasy, Daisy's hungry most of the time. She bounces from the table and swings open the door.

Because my place is basically one big room, I've got a clear view of our uninvited guest. Ivy, my eldest sister, stands in a cream linen suit. Her open-toed kitten heels are an ocean blue and her strawberry blond hair falls past her shoulders, longer than the last time I saw her.

She's immaculately put together, every bit the neuro-surgeon you would want to manage your health.

"Ivy," Daisy and I say in unison. Our tones are both a mixture of surprise and dread.

"Hello Daisy, Pansy." She steps into my place, wheeling her silver Tumi carry-on behind her. Leaning in to air-kiss Daisy, before she does the same for me, she then stops in what is the center of my small apartment.

"You live here?" Her voice drips with disdain, and shame threatens to drown me.

Digging deep, I fight my usual pattern of slinking into the background while Ivy spews her crap. This is my place, my life, and she can't just walk in and shit all over it.

"If you don't like it, you know where the door is."

"What are you doing here?" Daisy asks what I'm thinking.

Ivy takes another cursory glance around the room, her features twisting like she smells shit, before resting on me. Having lost my appetite, I push away my plate and stand, folding my arms over my middle.

"That was rude of me. It's quaint." Her compliment is a stretch and a struggle.

"What are you doing here?" I ask.

"I wanted to visit, and I knew Daisy was here, so I thought now was as good a time as any."

"How did you know I was here?" Daisy asks.

"Come on, Daisy, you're smarter than that. Did you really think that I wouldn't figure out why you wanted Pansy's address? I didn't fall for your 'I want to send her a package,' and when I called your agent, and he told me that you left weeks ago, I knew you were here."

"And? Why is what I do any of your concern?" Daisy sits on the couch and crosses her legs.

"I've been meaning to come visit Pansy, see how she's doing, and when I figured out you were here too... we haven't seen each other in five years. Don't you both think it's been long enough?"

There's a hint of vulnerability in her tone, and I'm taken back. Ivy is a fortress, and stoic is the only way I know her, so to hear something else, something needing in her tone, softens me a bit.

"It is good to see you."

"And you too, both of you. Although, Daisy, you look thinner and a touch peaked. Are you not well?"

"I'm fine." Daisy sits ramrod straight, and her eyes lock with mine. A plea for my help mushrooms in her deep blue eyes.

"It seems you don't have enough space," Ivy says out of nowhere, glancing behind the screen to where my bed is. "I didn't plan on staying in a hotel, but it looks like I'll have to make arrangements."

"Sorry, if you'd told me you were planning to visit, I would have told you that. There are quite a few lovely places to stay, pass me your phone, and I'll show you."

She hands over her phone, and within forty minutes, we have her booked in a luxury hotel not too far from here. Once that's out of the way, Daisy makes some tea and the three of us sit quietly, and awkwardly, around my tiny living space.

"Daisy, you live here too?" Ivy asks.

"Yes. Pansy and I share the bed. It's cozy." Her joke has a tinge of sarcasm, but it is not directed at me.

"Why are you here?" Ivy directs her question at Daisy, who now stiffens and darts her gaze to me. Ivy is shrewd and catches our brief shared look. "What aren't you telling me?"

I nibble on my lip and implore Daisy to tell Ivy with my stare. Daisy squirms, crossing and uncrossing her legs, while Ivy does her toe-tapping thing that she is so good at.

"I'm pregnant," Daisy blurts.

Ivy jumps to her feet and glares at Daisy. "Seriously? How could you? This is the type of thing I expect from Pansy, not you." That stings, and I clench my fists at her cruel comment. "You're a model for Christ's sake, you do realize you've messed up your career?"

Her nose crinkles before she sticks it in the air and places her long, finely manicured hands on her hips. Daisy's eyes shine with unshed tears, and I'm ticked. Usually, I would refuse to get involved. This is between them, and I don't want any part of this, but that was the old me.

"Ivy, she could still model after the baby is born. Her career isn't over if she doesn't want it to be."

Ivy scoffs, rolling her eyes at me as if I've just wasted my breath with nonsense. My chest pangs at her dismissive nature, but I know that it isn't me per se, it's just the way she is. She is always right, no matter what.

"And the father? Do you even know who the father is? Will he help?" Ivy shoots her questions as if she's at a firing range. Round after round, hoping for a bullseye.

"Yes, and no," Daisy says, now standing and squaring off with Ivy. "And my life isn't ruined. I want the baby. I'm keeping it. This is my life and my choice. I didn't come to you with this because I knew this would be your reaction. Your help and advice are not needed. Thank you very much."

"I'm only looking out for you," Ivy says. "You think I want you to ruin your life? Come stay with me, and I'll make sure you have the best OB there is."

"I'm staying here."

"Look around you." Ivy waves her hand around the space and at me. "Do you really think you're going to get the help and support you need? Don't be foolish. Pansy can barely take care of herself."

"Ivy, that's enough!" I shout, the heat rising from my chest into my neck and face. "If you can't be supportive and you don't have anything nice to say about Daisy or me, you can leave."

My finger points to the door, and I'm shaking. Ivy's eyebrows rise, her eyes wide and mouth agape as she studies me. Smoothing her hands down the sides of her waist, she stands tall and relaxes her features.

"Fine. I really am only trying to take care of you."

"Your kind of take care means to take charge," Daisy says.

Ivy sniffs, her finger wiping at an invisible tear at the corner of her eye. "What about you, Pansy? What's new with you?"

Slumping into the chair, I dig deep for the last bit of patience I might have. I will give this one last try, and proceed to tell Ivy about what I have been up to. Surprisingly, she keeps her mouth shut for most of it, and even perks up when I tell her about marine biology. I dare say I think I might have her approval with that choice, but the funny thing is, I no longer want it or need it.

"That's wonderful," Ivy says as I finish up about my diving course and looking into registering at UCLA.

"And she's dating a rock star," Daisy adds.

"Daisy."

My irritation's evident in my voice as I scold her for mentioning

Silas. He isn't a secret, but I deliberately left him out, knowing Ivy would have a problem with it.

"Sorry." Daisy's hand covers her mouth, and her cheeks reddened at her faux pas.

"A rock star?" Ivy arches a brow. "Care to elaborate?"

"Just what Daisy said -- I'm dating a rock star, and I'm crazy about him." I shrug, not caring what Ivy has to say. "Actually, you've met him. At the police station."

Her eyes darken with understanding. "I see."

"If you want, you can get to know him better tomorrow. We're going to his house for a barbecue."

The invitation is the nice thing to do, but I cringe on the inside at the thought of Ivy and Silas talking. Silas isn't a fan, and I highly doubt Ivy will be of him.

"I'd love to," is all she says on the topic of Silas.

We spend another hour with Ivy before she decides to check in at her hotel. We make plans for the following day and Daisy and I spend the evening freaking out at the arrival of our older sister. We both pray her visit is short, knowing that it will be anything but sweet.

30

LUST

*S*ilas

"Wanna go for a swim?" I pop my head in the kitchen where Pansy and Lucia are making tortillas.

I picked her up after her shift at Betty's. While Pansy's sisters are joining us later, as is Vinny, for about an hour I have her all to myself.

Pansy turns, and I grin at the smudge of something white on her face. Unable to keep my hands to myself, I stroll over and wipe her cheek.

"Sure. Let me just wash off and get changed."

Boy and I follow her through the house, and she glances back at me every few feet with a puzzled look on her face.

"What are you doing?"

She rounds the corner into her old room, and I point to the bed, where there's a wrapped box with a blue ribbon.

"For me?" Her eyes are wide, and her smile's just as big.

"Yup, open it." I hand her the box and eagerly watch as she rips away the paper and removes the lid.

She pulls out the swimsuit, wrinkling her nose and looking at me.

"You bought me a bikini?" I nod. "Why?"

"I didn't go looking for it, but I saw it in a shop window and immediately thought of you."

It's unique, just like Pansy. It's mainly hot pink with a boho-gypsy print of yellow, blue, green, and burgundy. I can't wait to see her in it.

"You don't like my swimsuit?"

She's trying for indignation, but the sides of her mouth twitch and she bites her lip to stifle the smile.

"I love your swimsuit. I love you in anything. As I said, I saw it and thought of you. Put it on."

"This reminds me of a time when we were kids, and my parents bought each of us a swimsuit for our trip to Texas. Mine was this frilly pink bikini, and I hated it."

"You did?" I arch an eyebrow as I fear I made the wrong move.

She nods, holding the suit in one hand. "Yes. The bikini was so unlike the one-piece swimsuits that the women would wear on the TV shows I'd watch with my father. I wanted to be taken seriously. Being in the water was fun, but it was also an adventure and a chance to learn something new. My dad was always teaching me about sea life, the plants, and animals."

She's beaming again. Every time she talks about the sea, about her father, she glows. Unexpectedly, she kisses me on the cheek and thanks me for the gift before going to the bathroom to change. In what feels like fifteen hours, but is more like fifteen minutes, she finally re-enters the room.

My breath leaves me on a shuddering exhale, hunger and unleashed lust barreling through my chest en route to my crotch. *Fuck me.* I have a hard time as it is keeping my eyes off her, but in that swimsuit, I can't tear my gaze away. Hot and stunning.

At first, she's shy, clasping and unclasping her hands in front of her, in between fidgeting and adjusting her bikini top, which is perfect as it is.

"I fucking knew it," I assert.

"What?" Her sass returns as she cocks her hip to one side and places her hands on her waist.

"You're sexy as hell."

She blushes, waving her hand dismissively as she dons my shirt, the one she borrowed days ago and now seems to live in.

Taking my hand, she pulls me to the sliding door. "Thank you; I love it."

"You do? Even if it's a bikini and it may be hard to explore in or be taken seriously in?"

"Yes. You totally knew this was me."

I nod with a smirk and a wink before checking to make sure Boy's right behind us. We find a spot not too far from the house to lay out the bamboo mat and dump our things, then decide to walk for a bit; Boy is eager to run before going into the water.

Once back, we're hot and ready to get wet. I watch Pansy's fine form bending to pat Boy. The dog wags her tail furiously, her tongue lolling to the side in sheer pleasure. Pansy's lyrical laugh flits through the air, and I enjoy the breathtaking view, warmth spreading throughout me.

She glances over her shoulder, calling for me to join her. The wind whips her hair all over the place as I greedily drink her in. The bikini sculpts every swell and curve, her long legs gleam in the sunlight, and she tips her head back to face the sky. With closed eyes, her mouth bends into a smile as she basks in the sun.

My knees buckle with intense desire scorching down my spine to my painfully throbbing cock. On impulse, I run to her, my hands grabbing her waist and spinning to face her.

In one fell swoop, I pick her up, her shriek ringing through the air as she wraps her legs around my middle. With her in my arms, I dive into the cold, salty water taking us under. We break the surface with Pansy sputtering and laughing.

"Silas, what the hell?" She coughs while grinning at me.

I cop a gratuitous feel of her ass while securing her to me. My lengthening dick grazes her core, and I groan while her breath catches, pupils widening like saucers as she parts her lips.

"Silas." Her voice is sultry as she bucks against me.

"Pansy." My tone has an edge, not knowing if I can control myself if she keeps gliding along my dick.

It doesn't matter that we both have clothes on or that we're in the ocean, the barrier is insignificant if I want inside her. And I do.

"I..." She sucks in a breath, her lips parting wider as her tongue darts out to lick her bottom lip.

My lips descend on hers, my blistering hot tongue diving into her mouth, wanting her taste. She's the ocean, the sky, and everything in between.

Our tongues duel as my hand travels from her waist to her chest. My fingers pinch one tight, eager nipple through the fabric and she moans into my mouth, pushing her breast further into my palm.

Our kiss is urgent as her fingers curl into my ass, her sex sliding over my rock-hard cock, frantic and tormenting. I wedge my hand between us and dip my hand into the front of her bikini bottoms; my fingers run the length of her slick pussy. She's so ready for me. Pansy tips her head back, exposing the sensuous arc of her neck, and sighs my name.

"Pansy," I grate, anxious to keep my control.

With the call of her name, she lifts her head and with a determination I haven't seen before, her lips land on mine and her fingers weave into my hair. Her kisses are fervent like it's life or death.

Boy swims around us, barking excitedly, wanting in on the action. With my hand still in her pants, Pansy grudgingly breaks the kiss.

"Silas, what if my sisters arrive and see us?" Her pretty mouth frowns.

I smile at her despite not wanting to end this, because I understand. She kisses the side of my neck, her mouth burning my skin in the best way imaginable, lighting a fire within me. I force my hand out of her bikini.

She writhes once more against my erection, and I groan, steadying her hips to stop the painfully tantalizing motion.

"Okay, fine."

With one more kiss, I release my hold, and her soft, sweet body slides down mine. Life has gotten in the way and made our time even more precious. It always does. The band demands my time. Her work, and now her sisters, are taking up her time. Soon it will also be school, and I'll slip down her list of priorities.

I meant what I said; I'll cheer her on and make sure she stays true to her dreams, even if that means I come last. All I want is to be *on* her list. To be among the things she wants, that matter to her.

By the time we're showered and changed, everyone has arrived, and Pansy heads over to talk to her sisters.

"You've got a beautiful place," Vinny says.

"Thanks. Can I get you a drink?"

"Nah, I'm good." He holds up his beer.

"So, what do you do when you're not teaching?" I ask.

"I love to teach, but I also miss the water and the research, so I help out my colleagues and others in the sector when I can. In fact, I've applied for a sabbatical for this year to join a research trip to South America."

"Really? Sounds interesting. Does Pansy know you might not be teaching this year? You're one of the reasons she wants to go to UCLA." I try to move past the twinge in my chest at knowing Vinny is important to her.

Vinny cocks his head to the side, brown eyes studying me. I'm not sure what I said, but he looks at me like I've insulted him.

"You don't think Pansy is serious about her studies?" he asks.

"That isn't what I said or meant." I cross my arms, then immediately relax my stance, unfolding my arms. My body language is defensive and not what I intend. "She is very serious, but she admires and respects you. I think she sees you as a mentor and I wonder if she knows your plans."

Vinny nods, his features relaxing as his lips curve into a smile. "That's nice to hear. And yes, she does know. She was a bit disappointed, but I'm not the reason she's pursuing this. And it's not like I won't teach there again, I'll be back. Can you keep a secret?" He glances around to see who is near.

"Sure." I lean in, eager for what he has to say.

"The college approved my sabbatical. I leave in two weeks for Uruguay to study the dead zone."

I have no clue what that means, but his eyes gleam with happiness. "Wow, that's great. Pansy doesn't know?"

"No, not yet. I'm going to ask her to join the team. It'll be about six to eight months, and I have approval for two assistants. One will help with the data, cleaning gear, and other stuff. It's not glamorous, but you don't need all the formal training, and I had Pansy in mind for the position. She would learn a lot."

"Wow, that's great." I parrot my previous comment as something heavy and uncomfortable twists in my gut. She would be gone for six months or more. I already miss her.

"Do you think she'll come?"

"I don't see why not. It sounds like a great opportunity."

My smile is forced, and swallowing becomes difficult. The possibility of losing her rears its head like a cobra ready to strike. I won't stop her if she wants to go. Damn, I'll encourage her every step of the way, even if it means losing her.

We have a great lunch with fish tacos, chicken tostadas, and Lucia's delicious margaritas. Once the table is cleared, Pansy, Daisy, and Vinny opt to walk Boy, while I have to take a call from my lawyer.

I come back onto the deck to find Ivy. I nod to her and start for the stairs down to the beach when she approaches me.

"Silas, wait, may I have a word?"

"Sure."

I lie. I would rather have a root canal, but I will try for Pansy. Ivy and I had a few words months ago in that desert police station, and it didn't take me long to determine that I didn't like her.

"Pansy finally has her act together." Her nasal voice is irritating and her tone condescending.

Where Pansy is warm and inviting, Ivy is cold and standoffish. Besides their flowery names and the tinge of red in their hair, I find it hard to believe they're sisters.

"She's always had her act together if you ask me."

She waves her hand at me like I'm a nuisance. "Hardly. But marine biology is a great profession, although it doesn't necessarily pay well, depending on where she decides to focus. And knowing

Pansy, she'll choose the lowest income." She sits and runs her hands down her skirt, smoothing out the fabric. "Don't mess this up. Stay out of her way."

"Pardon?" My tone is sharp like the edge of a knife and Ivy takes note, arching a brow and pursing her red lips.

"Don't get all offended. You know what I mean. This is a fling for you, but Pansy gets easily caught up in things, and from what I can tell, she really likes you. Don't string her along, she's a master at self-sabotage. And a pretty boy like you comes with a huge caution sign that will have Pansy running straight toward you."

Folding my arms over my chest, I clench my jaw to prevent myself from telling Ivy to go to hell. While I'd like nothing better than to tell this chick off, I'm working on my temper, and alienating Pansy's sister, no matter how much she deserves it, is not a wise move.

"This is not a game to me. Pansy is not a fling. Your sister means a lot to me. I've never been this serious about a woman before, and I don't intend on messing anything up for her."

Vinny's news flashes in my mind, and my resolution to support and encourage her to go on the trip solidifies. I meant what I said, her happiness and dreams come first.

"I don't think you understand..."

"Yes, I do. But you don't understand that I will support your sister in any way I can. Her dreams matter to me, and I don't intend to get in the way or mess anything up."

"Ivy," Pansy says from the top of the staircase.

Our eyes lock, and Ivy swivels her head to face her sister. Pansy only has eyes for me. Concern and compassion coat her features and I smile, letting her know it's okay.

"What?" Ivy stands, her back to me, hands on her hips. "I'm only looking out for you."

She marches into the house before Pansy can respond, leaving us alone.

"Sorry." Pansy is at my side, her hands around my waist, as she lightly pecks my bare chest.

"Don't apologize for her. Besides, I'm a big boy, I can handle Ivy."

"A big boy, huh?" She waggles her eyebrows and smirks.

"And you know it."

"I sure do." We kiss, soft and brief. "I can't wait until she leaves."

"Hey, don't let her get to you. I know this may sound weird, but she was just looking out for you. Her delivery and attitude is abysmal, but I do think she cares about you in her own warped way.'"

Pansy chuckles, furrowing her brow before resting her head on my shoulder. "Yeah, but I think her need is more about her than me."

"That may be true." I squeeze her side. "Let's join the others." Taking her hand, I lead her down the stairs onto the beach, knowing it will help with putting Ivy behind her.

31

BLOOM

*P*ansy

It's well past seven in the evening when I'm finally done with work. My feet ache, and my hair and clothes reek of grease and sweat. I need a shower. But first, food. I'm starving. Heading to the office to gather my things, I stick my head in the kitchen. Bunny is chopping onions and whistling to Coltrane.

"Hey, Bunny, can I have a veggie omelet?"

He glances up from his task, his pearly whites beaming at me as he winks and nods. "Anything for you, flower girl," he rumbles in his gravelly baritone.

"Thank you!"

Once I've freshened up, feeling more human, I check my phone and see there's a text sent an hour ago.

Silas: *Are you working tonight?*

I quickly reply.

Me: *Just got off. I'm going to eat here with Ivy, and then home. How late are you working?*

By the time I get out front, Callie's coming from the kitchen with my dinner. I sit at the table Ivy has occupied for the last hour. She just showed up and had dinner while I finished my shift. So far, all has been good. She hasn't made one derogatory comment and was even civil to Betty and Callie.

"I wish I was off. We could all grab a bite or go for drinks." Callie pouts.

"I'm too tired." I shovel the hot omelet into my mouth.

"Slow down. You're going to burn your tongue or choke with the way you're inhaling that." Ivy scrunches her nose and rears back a bit, like I might throw up on her.

I laugh and blush. She's right. "Sorry. I didn't eat anything on break."

"You really should snack regularly. Just slow down, it's not going anywhere," Ivy says.

Callie laughs, nodding in agreement while leaving to greet the couple that's just come in. My phone vibrates with another text.

Silas: *I'm done in an hour. Want to stay at my place?*

Me: *Can't. Sister time* 😢

Silas: *Boy misses you.*

Me: *Just Boy?*

Silas: *Lucia and Jorge too.*

Me: *No one else?*

Silas: *I ALWAYS miss you. Let me come pick you up. I'm leaving now.*

Me: *Can't wait to see you. xo*

Silas: *Me too.*

"Hey, Pansy, how are you?" Vinny stands over me.

"Vinny! Did we make plans? I'm a wasteland right now." I tap my head and laugh.

"No, no. Hi, Ivy," he says, and she returns the greeting. "I wanted to drop by and share some news."

"What's up?" He takes the seat beside me.

"The college approved my sabbatical to join the research team!"

"Oh my God, that's amazing!" I jump up and swing my arms around him.

Chuckling, he tightens his hold. He's been working on this for some time now, and this is huge.

"Yeah, it really is." We break apart. "But, it gets better."

"What?"

"I want you to be one of my assistants."

"What?" My eyes widen, incredulous.

"That's fantastic," Ivy says.

"I've got a spot for someone to help with the research, and there's lots to do. An extra pair of hands and a brilliant mind would really help."

"But I don't know anything. I'd just get in the way."

He grins. "No, you wouldn't. You'd learn a lot, and this will help you figure out if you want to do research."

"I don't know what to say."

"Say yes, you silly girl," Ivy adds.

Vinny and I ignore her. "Pansy, it's been a while since I've come across someone this enthusiastic about my profession, even after knowing how much work is involved." Taking both of my hands in his, the corners of his eyes crinkle with a smile. "You remind me of me. I want to feed this passion."

Ivy starts rattling off questions, all of which Vinny graciously answers while I stare at my empty plate, trying to process it all. What would it mean for school? I thought I'd start in the fall, but September is only a few months away. I don't even know if there's space for me in the program with it being so late in the year.

"I couldn't start school this year," I say randomly.

"Yeah. You could start next year. But this opportunity would put you ahead of many of the students. And it'll help in finding a job."

"You have to do this," Ivy says as the door chimes.

Silas walks in, and I can no longer contain my excitement. I launch myself at him, and he welcomes me with open arms. He twirls me around and chuckles as he sets my feet on the ground.

"Now, that's what I call a hello."

"Silas, I'm so glad you're here."

My lips cover his in a long, deep kiss. His hands grip me tightly, and even though he has no clue what's got me so exhilarated, he's all in. As I end the kiss, it hits me. I can't tell him that I'm going to be away for close to six months right here, in front of these people. Then

the thought of Ivy slams into my other thoughts. She could easily
blurt this out without any consideration.

"You feel so good," he murmurs into my neck. "I'd like to think
seeing me has you so happy, but I'm not that much of an egotistical
ass. What's up?"

"Well, Mister Ego, it is you." It's not a total lie, and I bite the inside
of my mouth as punishment for bending the truth.

"Tell him," Ivy pipes up from behind me, and I twirl to shoot her
a glare.

"Tell me what?" Silas now has confirmation that there is something more going on.

"It's nothing. I'll tell you later. Let's get out of here." Turning to
Vinny and doing something rude, but necessary, I ask, "Would you
mind driving Ivy to her hotel?"

"Pansy!" Ivy protests at the same time Vinny agrees.

Fortunately, Silas forgets the last few minutes once he knows I'm
coming home with him. We quickly say goodbye with my promise to
call Vinny.

I don't mention the trip that night, and Silas doesn't ask. There
are Silas and Daisy to consider, and as amazing as it sounds, maybe
now isn't the right time?

&

*T*he next few days fly by, and before I know it, Ivy is leaving,
and I'm driving her to the airport. Silas is at the studio, and I
could have asked Jorge to drive or take us, but I didn't want to subject
anyone else to the torture. Daisy begged off joining us, claiming she had
some last-minute shopping to do before her flight to Europe. Yeah, right.

"Pansy, you need to go on that research assignment with Vinny,"
Ivy says, breaking the silence.

"Ivy, I haven't decided yet. I think I want to start school. It's a long
road ahead, and if I want my Masters and Ph.D., I've got many years
of school."

"It's Silas, isn't it?"

We're nearing LAX, and I quickly give myself a pep talk, that I can make it until then. Only a few more minutes.

"No, it's not just Silas. I have a life here. I'm not sure if now is the right time."

"Is it Daisy too? If it is, know that I'll be here for her. She won't be alone."

I can only imagine how happy Daisy will be to know that. It's mean to think, but it's the last thing Daisy wants. I pull up to the curb and put the car in park.

"Pansy, don't throw your life away for some man," Ivy says before getting out of the car.

I pop the trunk and join her at the back of the car. Once she has her bag and I've closed the trunk, she studies me long and hard. Taking her hands in mine, I use the opportunity to say what I mean once and for all. To show Ivy, even if she doesn't want to know who I am or to accept it.

"Ivy, the thing is, it's my life to do with as I please. I appreciate your concern, but I don't need a mother. I had one, an amazing one, and she taught me to follow my heart and trust in myself. I know what I'm doing. It may not be what you would do or what you would want for me, but again, it's my life. Thanks for visiting and I'll call you soon."

This time, the tears are real. Water gleams in her eyes, and she gives me a thin smile. "Okay." Her face is still tight, but I can tell she's trying to meet me halfway. "And you're right; Mom did instill in us to follow our hearts. I won't stand in the way. That's been my intention. I suppose I was mothering and could be overbearing. I'll try to keep my nose out of things that don't concern me."

I laugh and gently squeeze her fingers. "That would be appreciated."

This time we both laugh before we embrace. I watch as she heads into the terminal.

Once I leave the airport, I head for the studio. Silas has asked me to come numerous times, and I've never taken him up on it. I want to see him now. I text him that I'm on my way.

I push through the doors into the modern, yet cold reception space of the record label's office, with white walls and floors, lots of glass and metal. The tall, lean guy behind the desk calls out a greeting in between sucking on a lollipop. Brushing his brown hair from his eyes, he smiles, removing the candy from his mouth with a pop.

"May I help you?"

Standing with his arms resting on the desk, he leans toward me as I near him.

"I'm here to see Trojan. Bianca Ramirez is expecting me."

"And your name is?" His lips slide into a flirty grin.

"Pansy."

"What a beautiful name. Like the flower?" Here we go again. Always my name. He steps from behind the desk.

"Yes." I return his smile with a faint one of my own. Not wanting to encourage him, but also not wanting to be rude.

"I'm Brandon." He offers his hand, and before I can fully extend mine, his large hand wraps around my fingers. His clasp is strong, warm, and a touch clammy.

"Hi," I reply. He's not just flirting; he's serious.

There's an awkward silence while I try to free my hand from his grasp, but he doesn't get the picture.

"Go out with me?" He inches closer.

He's cute in a nerdy, wannabe-rocker kind of way. His forward-ness is creeping me out. Before I can yank my hand from his, needing to put some distance between us, a tsking comes from behind me.

"Drop her hand, Brandon. Get back to work."

It's Bianca. Her tone is terse and cold. His eyes flit to the gorgeous Latina, and immediately, his grin widens, and his eyes twinkle.

"Aww, Bianca, don't be jealous. You'll always have a special place in my heart. I was just getting to know Pansy."

"What you need to know is that Pansy is Silas's girl."

Before Bianca can finish, Brandon drops my hand like he's been burned and scurries behind the desk.

"Shit," he mutters under his breath, glancing at us apologetically. "Pansy, I'm sorry. I didn't know. I was completely out of line."

Bianca doesn't give me a chance to respond, putting her arm around my shoulder and steering me down a hallway.

"Bianca, don't say anything. I didn't know!" Brandon shouts after us, and Bianca snickers.

We enter a circular room with dim lighting. It's like a mini-amphitheater with several rows of bench seating, leading down to a large pit. Everything is black. In the pit, the guys are spread out in various poses, each of them concentrating on something.

Silas is furiously scribbling on what looks like sheet music. His golden hair is wonderfully disheveled and dark blond, day-old scruff sprinkles his chiseled jaw.

"Look who I found!" Bianca breaks the silence as we walk down to the center.

Raising their heads, each of them offers a welcome. Silas's lips split into a wide smile, and he pushes off the bench to meet me.

Jared catches my eye, and he too smiles; it's small but genuine. Since his apology at Silas's, things have been good between us. He's been nothing but a gentleman if you can call it that, which is bizarre given he's rough and raw with his eyeliner, tattoos, and leather.

"Hey, you." Silas wraps me in his arms, burrowing his face into my neck and inhaling me. Butterflies flutter in my belly, and my heart does a strange pitter-patter. I wonder if I'll ever get used to his touch. I hope not.

"Hi," I whisper for only him to hear, my fingers digging into his taut shoulders.

"Okay, you two, let's get back to work." Bianca's no-nonsense tone cuts through the air and Silas releases a low growl, igniting tingles within me.

She's standing right beside us with a few papers in her hand. "Sign these, please."

I watch as Silas barely glances at the papers put in front of him.

His eyes are on me, every chance he gets. His gaze only veers down to the document when Bianca taps her finger at the next place he has to sign.

"Okay, thanks." Bianca gathers them up and walks away.

"We were just about to do a run through of 'Bloom.'" Silas sits on the piano bench. "Want to hear it?"

"Is that the song you've been working on?" I ask, and he nods. "I'd love to."

He pats the space beside him before adjusting the mic and warming up his fingers. It's strange because my throat is dry and I have difficulty swallowing. I don't know why. It's not like we haven't done this before.

I've sat with him many times while he plays. It's one of my favorite things to do. But this is different. We're not alone, despite the hunger in his eyes that makes me feel like it's just us.

I sit beside him, thigh-to-thigh, and the heat rolling off him warms me. My cheeks flush, and I clench my thighs together as I imagine his long fingers caressing my flesh the way he does the ivory.

He glances eagerly at the guys while his fingers glide sensually along the keys as if speaking to them, priming the instrument to become one with him.

After a few chords, soft and melodic, the tempo increases and Silas begins to sing. His deep, smooth voice caresses each exquisite word before releasing it into the world.

"Bloom" is a ballad and so different from what the band usually produces, more in the vein of "Only," the song I adore.

Each note played and each word sung lures me in. I'm mesmerized as he sings about a near miss with a car, cursing happenstance until a kiss under the night sky like a bursting star, colliding lips, crashing souls changed everything. A bright flower in a bed of loss, the bloom to the fading light.

I'm biased, but the song is beautiful and captivating. It's not only the lyrics or the haunting melody that's pulling me in; it's Silas and our story. The way he's staring at me as he retells our meeting like it was magical and life-altering.

The song comes to an end, the guys stop playing, but Silas continues with another round of the chorus. Just him and the piano. My eyes glisten, and if I wasn't already falling, I fall right then and there.

"That was amazing. Beautiful," I say.

"Fuck! Let's try that again," Jared's voice booms from the other side of the circle. "That sucked, I think we need to change the line about the dark or maybe the tempo." Jared pulls at his long locks, putting half of it in a ponytail.

Silas doesn't say a word. His gaze is intent on me and mine on him.

"There's nothing wrong with the line," Eli says, smirking. "You just keep fucking it up. You gotta go down an octave, and it'll work."

"What's the matter Jared, you can't find your balls?" Gray asks.

The guys chuckle, except Jared. "Fuck you."

Clearing his throat and with a wink for me, Silas joins in, "Hey, Jared's balls may be the problem. Pansy did a number on them."

Silas shoots me a sexy grin before joining the other two guys in laughter.

Jared's face flushes, and he winks at me, shaking his head. "Yeah, she sure did."

Watching the guys create and jam while keeping it light is a glimpse at another side of Silas. They may have their rocky moments, and things won't always be smooth, but their joking, laughing, and a shared love of the music says so much more about them.

They're a family, and Silas isn't the hothead that I've seen on occasion. He's the goofy one. He gets the guys laughing at their mistakes and takes the edge off when one of them gets frustrated.

It's sad that he wants out, to end all this, but it's not the guys he's quitting, it's the lifestyle. I only hope that the end of Trojan isn't the end of their friendship. Silas needs all the support he can get.

Now that I've met his parents, I realize his anger goes deep, and it's still raw. He lashes out when stressed and overwhelmed, but the main threat is his parents.

32

SMARTASS

*P*ansy

"Hey, Pansy," Daisy says as I shut the door behind me.

Her suitcase is on the kitchen table, and she's packing. She leaves for Spain in two days and will be gone for a month.

"Hi, there -- you ready to go to Silas's? He's going to be here in about an hour."

"Yup. So, Ivy called while you were at yoga."

"Uh huh." I grab my towel and head for the bathroom to take a shower.

"She called to ask if you were going on the research assignment with Vinny. Of course, I had to tell her that I didn't know anything about it. When were you going to tell me?"

With an exasperated sigh, I twirl to face my sister. I haven't heard from Ivy since she left but figures she would call Daisy.

"I didn't say anything because I'm not going. Nothing to tell. End of story."

"Oh really? That's not what Ivy and Vinny say."

"Seriously, since when do you take Ivy's side? And when did you speak with Vinny?" I throw down my clothes and near Daisy, not at all impressed with her sleuthing abilities.

"Pansy, he told me about his offer. That you have a chance to come along, but you said no."

"Now isn't a good time."

"What are you talking about? It's the perfect time. You're not in school."

We stare at each other, neither backing down nor saying a word.

"The baby? Me? Silas? Those aren't reasons for not going."

I had turned Vinny down, and even though he was disappointed, he said he understood.

"I don't want to talk about this."

"No." Daisy firmly holds my hand when I attempt to turn toward the bathroom. "We're doing this, now. Pansy, when I said I need you, that's true, but I can be without you for a few months. Heck, I'll be away for four weeks."

"It's six months, Daisy. You'll be close to your due date or may have even had the baby by the time I come back."

"Oh." Her shoulders slump, and she releases me. Her fingertips now drum on the table top. "It doesn't matter. You'll be here once the baby is born. I can do this. Besides, I won't be alone. I'm sure Callie will help, and there's Silas and the band." She names them all like she's hoping it's true.

"Don't count on Callie. She's wonderful, but she's a free spirit." I chuckle. "She might not be here tomorrow, let alone six months from now. Silas would help for sure, but..." Darting my gaze away from her, I sigh.

"You don't want to leave him either, do you?"

"He needs me." What I don't say is that I need him, too. "He's going through a lot right now with the band, the album, his parents. I don't want him to think I'm abandoning him, especially now."

Daisy shakes her head at me. "You're wrong. If Silas loves you, he'd want you to follow your dream."

"Daisy, he doesn't know, and you're not going to tell him." My tone is as hard as the scowl darkening her face. "Not everyone gets to live their dream. I set out to find mine, and I got lucky because I found way more than that. I discovered something greater and bigger than I ever dared dream."

"What?" Daisy's voice is softer, and she's no longer glaring at me.

"I found love; I found Silas. I found that feeling of family that I had with Mom and Dad, and I won't turn my back on him when he needs me too."

Daisy isn't satisfied with my answer, waving me off with her hand as she takes the dishes to the sink. That's okay. She's never been in love, so I don't expect her to get it.

Later that evening, Silas picks us up and takes us to his place. Bianca and the band are there, hanging out on the deck overlooking the beach. Daisy doesn't stay long before calling it a night. She's tired.

"Daze, you want anything?" Jared calls from where he's leaning on the balcony railing.

"No thanks. I'm good. Night, guys," Daisy replies and slips through the sliding glass door.

Bianca snorts and rolls her eyes at him. "Gawd, do you ever stop thinking with your dick?" she asks.

"Fuck, B, I was only being a friend. She's pregnant. I was offering to help if she needed it," Jared says defensively.

"Easy, guys," Silas chimes in as I watch all three of them, keenly aware of the thick undercurrent of dark secrets swirling around them. "Drop it, B."

"Silas, you know just as well as I do that Jared never does anything out of the goodness of his heart. He doesn't have one." She bounds down the stairs to the beach, not stopping for either Eli's or Silas's calls.

"Yeah, go! Good riddance," Jared yells, knocking back his entire drink.

"Shit," Silas mumbles and lightly kisses my neck. "I've got to go talk to her."

I nod, and Silas leaves, while Jared heads for the bar. He pours a quarter of the vodka bottle into his glass and proceeds to drink it like water.

I wince at how the alcohol must burn going down in gulps like that. Gray and Eli join Jared, and Gray takes the vodka bottle while Eli steers him to a far corner.

As they talk in whispered tones, I move farther away, giving them privacy. At the balcony, I see the silhouettes of Silas and Bianca on the beach.

He's hugging her, and she's shaking, maybe crying? I turn my back to the ocean and away from their private moment. Even though Silas and I are together, it feels wrong to watch.

Boy saunters over to me and rubs her body along my calf. "Hi, beautiful baby. Who's a good girl?"

Rubbing her soft, thick fur is soothing, and only when I hear Silas coming up the stairs does unease slide in at the tone in his voice.

"It wasn't part of the agreement, Bianca," Silas says as they reach the landing.

"I know, but it's good publicity, and they aren't really asking. It'll create some buzz for the album, build to when people find out it's your last. They'll go crazy."

"This is just a PR stunt, and I made it clear, Otto made it clear, I'm not doing this shit. I agreed to the one concert, and that's it."

Silas runs his fingers through his hair, glowering at her.

"What's going on?" Gray asks, and I follow him as he nears them.

"Would you please talk to him? The record label is having a party for some of their big artists, and they want Trojan there. Silas is refusing to go."

Gray shrugs. "He's right. It isn't in the contract. We don't have to go. I don't care either way."

"Thank you," Bianca says, thinking he's on her side.

"Bianca, if Silas is in, so am I. And if he's not, neither am I," Gray finishes.

"Seriously, Gray?"

"Me too," Eli adds.

"Fuck, make that three. I'm sick and tired of those things," Jared says, his hands on either side of his head like he is holding it together. He doesn't look so good.

"You guys are killing me! It's one lousy party. C'mon," Bianca begs.

"Will it be good for the band?" I ask.

"Yes," Bianca answers. "It'll be good for all the guys."

"Can I go?"

"Pansy." Silas slides his hand around my waist, tucking me into his side like he usually does. "I don't want to go."

"Yes, of course, you can go," Bianca says.

"Let's do it, then," I say. "I've never been to a record label party; it could be fun. Besides, I have a few fancy dresses that Daisy gave me that I'll never wear otherwise."

"Are you sure you want to go?" Silas asks.

Nodding at him, Bianca crosses both her fingers and smiles at me as Silas looks to each of the guys. They each shrug like it doesn't matter to them either way.

"Fine, we'll go," Silas says, and Bianca jumps while clapping her hands.

"Thank you, Pansy!" She squeezes my arms and heads back down the stairs to make a call.

Silas ushers me toward the house, telling the guys to let themselves out.

"Night," I holler to the guys as Silas closes the glass door behind us. "That was rude. Are you going to be rude to me?" I quip, letting him pull me further into the room.

"You bet. Rude and downright filthy."

He stops to bring my back against his chest. His hard erection digs into the crease of my ass.

"I see."

"You're going to be more than seeing. You'll be feeling pretty soon, too." His mouth lands on my shoulder as he nips at my flesh and kisses. "Thank you."

"For what?" I ask while he shuts his bedroom door.

"For the whole party thing. Bianca knows what the deal is, yet she does their dirty work all the time." Now, he stands right before me and leans in for another kiss.

"Everything okay with Bianca?"

"Yeah." His mouth brushes the corner of my mouth. "It's all good.

Jared and B have this love-hate relationship. The fighting never lasts long. Let's not talk about them. Where were we?"

His sexy grin comes out to play, and he winks with a light squeeze to my hips. Rolling my eyes with an unattractive snort, I laugh. "Yes. Let me just change."

With a light peck on his cheek, I turn to grab some clothes, and he exhales a "thank fuck" that has me turning around to face him.

"Is that all you care about? Getting laid."

"No. Getting laid by *you*."

"Silas Palmer, you have a one-track mind."

"And you love it." He swats my ass as I walk by with a tank and sleep shorts.

"Nah, I like my men complex. Awesome in bed is definitely important, but there's also got to be depth behind the pretty face and gorgeous body."

"Are you saying all I've got going on are my looks?"

Quirking an eyebrow, I stop at the threshold to the bathroom to face him. "Well, if the shoe fits."

"Smartass," he says, striding toward me.

Wild anticipation courses through my veins as he leads me to the bed, sitting me on the edge of the mattress with him standing in front of me.

Bending over, he kisses me, long and hard, and my fingers smooth over the solid expanse of his stomach. Once we break our kiss, I continue my meal, my mouth tasting every line and curve of his abs. Salty, earthy, and masculine. *Silas*.

My lips trail kisses over every line and dip, while my fingers undo his button and zipper, pulling out his semi-hard cock. He hisses and tugs at my hair, the sharp pull-like a command, and my core clenches.

"Let's put that mouth of yours to good use." He guides the back of my head toward his growing erection.

I jerk back, my eyes and mouth wide, while his hand stills and confusion clouds his expression.

"You did not just say that, did you?"

A sexy grin blooms across his face, his eyes shimmer, not a care in his features. "Pansy, I was kidding."

"Really?" I let him go and stand.

He groans in regret. "It was a joke! Obviously, a bad one, come back!"

His strong hands hoist me up and around to face him, and my surprised laughter floats between us. The tension in his body vanishes when he realizes I'm not upset at all.

"Perhaps we should put *your* mouth to good use," I tease, my finger lightly tracing his full, sexy lips.

With a nip at my fingers, his wet tongue wraps around my digits and pulls them into his mouth, only serving to stoke the formidable desire within my core.

"My pleasure." His smooth, sultry voice sends shivers down my spine.

Tossing me onto the bed, he peels away my clothes, taking my underwear with my shorts, and with a flick of the wrist, my bra is discarded too.

His hot mouth covers my sex, his tongue, oh my, his tongue licks and sucks voraciously. His mouth is positioned for the best suction and deepest penetration with his tongue alternating between thrusting into me and lapping at my clit.

"Fuck, Silas."

Clutching his hair, I whimper and moan for him, for more, for this to never end. All I want to do is grind against his face, but his hold is strong, guiding me where he wants me.

Heat prickles along my chest and neck as my release builds to a roaring bonfire. The flames are rising, licking, and threatening to consume us both.

He's rough and unapologetic in how greedily he feasts on me. It's both breath-stealing and mind-blowing.

"No, don't stop.... Stop... Fuck."

If I weren't on the receiving end of this glorious act, I'd think he was enjoying this more than me by his sounds of pleasure vibrating through my sex. His lips latch onto my clit, sucking on my bundle of nerves, and I'm barely hanging on.

My fingers twist in his hair, and just when I think that I can't take any more, he inserts one finger, then another, pumping into me. With a final thrust, he pushes me over the edge into oblivion, and I shatter into a million fragments of bliss.

33

APPREHENSION

*S*ilas

Pansy's gone when I wake up the next morning. She had the opening shift at Betty's. Once showered and shaved, I find Daisy in the kitchen, sitting at the table with Boy at her feet.

"Morning," she says. "Do you mind giving me a ride to Pansy's?"

"No problem. I'm leaving in about twenty if you need to put your things together."

"I'm ready, and I even had time for a dip in the pool. I love it here."

Sipping at my hot coffee, I grin. I could take the bait and team up to get Pansy here, but I won't. As much as Daisy is growing on me, she's also always looking out for number one.

"You're welcome to stay any time Pansy is here."

"What about if she wasn't?"

"Come again?" My tone has a hard edge to it, worried she's insinuating something else although she's not trying to be flirty.

"You don't know, do you?" She stands and slips her sunglasses on as she gathers her bag from the table.

"What don't I know?" Apprehension slithers up my spine and coils in my belly.

"She asked me not to tell you and I shouldn't, but you have a right to know."

"Know what?" I'm losing patience with her cat and mouse game.

Daisy stares at me behind her aviator glasses, and while I can't see her eyes, I can feel her glower on me. I'm not an egomaniac, but she can't stand that her sister is with someone famous and she takes that shit out on me. I'm good with that. I'd rather it be me than Pansy. I can take it, and I don't care -- as long as she's good to Pansy, she and I are good.

"Pansy was invited on Vinny's research assignment." I nod and Daisy cocks her head, wearing a quizzical expression. "If you know, why haven't you said anything to her?"

"I'm waiting for her to tell me. It's her news."

"And?" Her light eyebrows peak over the tops of her glasses.

"And what?" I'm confused.

"What are you going to say? She'll be away for about six months, if not more, and she doesn't want to leave us. That's what is holding her back from making a decision. I've told her that she should go. We'll be fine, but she won't listen."

That familiar knot forms in my stomach at the thought of her absence, and it multiplies at the idea of her passing up a once in a lifetime opportunity. I've been waiting for her to mention it to me, and I'm perplexed at why she hasn't, as well as annoyed that she might not go.

"She'll tell me, soon, I'm sure. And I will support her decision to go."

"Thank you. I knew you'd be supportive."

"You did?" I eye her skeptically.

With a huff, she lifts her glasses to look me in the eye. "Silas, I may give you a hard time, but I know you love my sister."

After dropping Daisy off, I head to Dr. Wexford for my appointment before the studio.

"Silas, I must say, I'm impressed with the progress you've made in such a short time," says Dr. Wexford.

She sits casually, legs crossed as usual with a cup of tea clasped in her hands. Today her long hair is back in a tight, neat bun, but she's in her usual free-flowing skirt.

I've been seeing her weekly and completed every homework assignment she's given me, even the brutal ones. The ones where I'd rather climb Mt. Everest barefoot, but it means going deep and facing the truth, or my flaws or faults.

To date, the hardest was writing down what I'd say to my parents. I mean, really say. The truth, no holds barred. I hope I never have to say it to them because it will likely be the end of our relationship if I do.

"Thanks. Yeah, this time is different."

"Different how?" she asks.

"Pansy."

She crinkles her brow and twists her mouth in contemplation. "How so?"

"Before you go thinking that I'm doing this *for* Pansy, I'm not. It's for me. What I mean is, she grounds me."

Her face relaxes, then she sips her tea and nods. "Go on."

Normally, her prompting me to open myself up more, bare all my inner thoughts and fears, would have me clenching my jaw and keeping silent. Or I might make some sarcastic quip, but this time, none of that even crosses my mind.

"It's hard to explain. I suppose she's shown me, or maybe just reminded me how good relationships can be. How it doesn't have to be hard or contentious and if it isn't easy or natural, then maybe a change is needed."

"I'm glad to hear this, Silas. It sounds like you've given this a lot of thought. So, what's bothering you?"

I don't know how she does it, but she has this uncanny ability to get to the heart of the matter every time.

"Pansy has a huge opportunity that will bring her closer to her dream, and she hasn't told me about it. I mean, she will tell me...I hope she will." I choke on the words, vulnerable in sharing my doubts.

"Do you know why she hasn't said anything?"

"I think it's because it'd mean we'd be apart for about six months. And her sister is pregnant with no father in the picture. Pansy's a nurturer, and I doubt she could easily leave us if she thinks we need her."

"And do you?"

"Need her?" I ask, and the doctor nods. With a hard swallow, I nod. "Yeah, I do. But I won't be the reason she doesn't go. It's only temporary, and no matter what, I'll make her see that she must go."

❧

A crowded LAX is nothing unusual, as we navigate our way through the people to the luggage drop off. Daisy is leaving for her modeling gig, and neither Pansy nor I have mentioned Vinny's trip. We'll be doing this soon enough, except it'll be Pansy leaving. If, or when, she tells me about it. It's a waiting game, although I don't think Pansy knows she's playing it.

I want to say something, but the selfish part of me wants to believe, to see if she will tell me. I fear if she doesn't say anything, then it means she doesn't have as much confidence in us as I do, or that she's already made her mind up without talking to me about it.

"Here's the last of it." I deposit Daisy's third and final suitcase on the conveyor belt. "Do you think you have enough?" My sarcastic remark matches Daisy's eye roll, and Pansy laughs.

"Whatevs," she says, dismissing me with a hand wave. "So, this is it."

Daisy turns to face Pansy, and her eyes shimmer with unshed tears. She quickly looks to the left, then the right, at all the activity going on in the airport.

"Have fun, but take it easy. Listen to your body and if you're tired, don't push it." Pansy sounds concerned and loving.

"All right, Mom." Daisy pulls her in for a long, hard hug.

"Remember. You're not alone in this. I'm here and only a phone call away," Pansy reminds her.

"*We're* here," I add, slipping my hand in Pansy's and squeezing.

"Guys, I'm going to miss you, but I'm also going to enjoy this final modeling gig. I didn't get to enjoy my last catwalk. At the time, I had no clue it was going to be my last."

"It might not be. If modeling is a dream, don't give up," Pansy says.

"Nah, my dreams are changing."

"Daze, be good and take care of yourself. If you need anything, call," I say.

The sisters hug one last time, and Daisy nods, a watery smile on her face, before turning her back to us. We stand hand-in-hand as she disappears through the doors to customs.

With my arms around Pansy, we head to the car. "You okay?"

"Yeah. It's odd timing and strange to say, but I feel like I've found my sister. That I have back part of my family. Here she is leaving, and I feel closer to her than I ever have before."

"I get it. You two have made a lot of headway in a short amount of time."

"I'll miss her, but she'll be fine, and when she gets back, she'll be thrilled to see where we're living."

At first, her words don't sink in, but when they do, I stumble over my feet and stop. "Where are you living?" I ask, needing to clarify before I jump to conclusions.

Her lips faintly curve up, her eyes sparkling. "With you."

My lips split into a smile as I lift her into the air. "Hallelujah!"

She squeals digging her fingers into my shoulders while I twirl her around. Her moving in will be short-lived because she'll be leaving soon, but she's coming back to me. To my place, our home.

"I'm glad you like that idea considering I didn't ask."

"Babe, you never have to ask. If I'd had it my way, you'd never have moved out."

I reluctantly loosen my grip, and her body slides down mine. I stop her descent as our lips line up, and I lean in to kiss her.

The drive back is glorious. The top is down on my convertible, and the thought of her moving in has me appreciating the shining sun, blue skies, and the warm, salty wind throwing her hair around. We talk about how quickly she can bring her stuff to my place, and I'll arrange for the little furniture she has to go in storage. I want to do it now, steal as many minutes as I can with her, but she shuts the idea down.

"I can't move in tonight; we have the record label party."

I groan. "Fine. You sure you don't want to skip it?"

"No way!"

"Can't blame me for trying. I've got something to tell you, too." I squeeze her knee and rest my hand on her bare thigh. Realizing I haven't told her everything either, and if I disclose, she may too.

I pull her hair out of her face, and a small smile plays at the corner of her lips. "What? It sounds intriguing and ominous."

"Nothing ominous. I wanted to tell you sooner, but I just never knew how to bring it up."

"Tell me. The suspense is killing me."

I chuckle, glancing at her, looking back at me. Her eyes shine, a smile playing on her lips, and her cheeks rosy.

"I'm seeing my therapist again about my anger, and it's going well. This time is better." It feels good to confide in her.

"Silas, that's amazing!" Leaning over the console, she kisses me on the cheek. "I'm so glad you're going and that you're feeling good about it."

"Yeah. I'm seeing the same doctor I saw before the tour."

"I don't want to push, and only tell me what you're comfortable talking about...what prompted you to go back?"

"My parents showing up."

Admitting it is both relieving and difficult. Pansy and I have talked about my parents, but it's still not something I like to do. She never pushes or brings them up.

"And it's helping?"

"Yeah. She's helping me deal with the helplessness before it gets to anger." I glance away from the road and her. I can't help but feel weak at my admission.

"Hey." Her hand rests on my shoulder, and I turn back to the road. "I get it, and it's normal to feel that way. They're your parents."

I realize my mistake when she slips into silence. With her forehead wrinkled and her twisting her lips, she is deep in thought, and I wonder if revealing my true feelings about the root of my anger pushed her to stay?

34

BALLISTIC

*S*ilas

The ride to the damn record label party is too short. Before I know it, we're here. First Bianca climbs out of the car, and then the guys and Pansy. People spill out of the large white double doors at the front of the house, onto the lawn. The music is loud. As we make our way inside, it is just as busy as outside, with every room almost shoulder-to-shoulder with people laughing, dancing, and talking.

And there's a shit-ton of booze, among other recreational drugs. None of it is good for Jared. He's gotten himself into trouble one too many times at shindigs like this, and we made him promise to go easy on the liquor, but who knows if he will.

Since we've been writing and recording the album, he's been trying to cut back on the shit and clean up his act. And while he has the best of intentions, we need to keep an eye on him. The man has no willpower. Tonight, Gray drew the short straw, and he's Jared's shadow.

With Jared covered, I tried to talk Pansy into not going. I promised to make it worth her while, we'd make out all night long, but she wouldn't budge.

She wanted to show off her smoking hot dress, and hot damn, smoking it is. My cock has been rock hard since my first glimpse of her in the elegant magenta shift dress.

The dress falls to mid-thigh with a low V neck and long bell sleeves. She's stunning with her silky hair, glowing skin, and the blinding brilliance of her hazel eyes.

And her four-inch black heels make her legs run on forever. Sexy legs I can't wait to have wrapped around my face. With that, I try again to persuade her to leave.

"How long do we have to stay?" I whisper, taking the opportunity to lick the shell of her ear.

With a shudder, her fingers dig into the arm of my suit as she releases my name like a breathy moan.

"Don't do that again."

"Why not? Don't tell me you don't like it."

"That's the problem. I like it too much. I think I just came."

My eyes smolder, my grip tightening on her hip as my fingers dance along the swell of her ass.

"Fuck, you can't say things like that and expect me not to want to fuck you right here in front of all these people."

"Silas!" Her eyes widen, pupils dilating, lips turned up, and cheeks pink. "Stop it, or else I might just let you."

I groan, ready to haul her into the nearest closet and fuck her senseless when we're interrupted.

"Silas, good to see you!" Gerald Pilsen, an executive with the record company, slaps my shoulder. "And who is this vision of loveliness?"

"Gerald, this is Pansy Dobson, and Pansy, this is Gerald Pilsen."

"Pleasure to meet you, Ms. Dobson," Gerald says, and then proceeds to show how much of a blowhard he is by rattling off his title and career history like it's proof that he has a gigantic cock.

"And you," Pansy says, shaking his hand.

"What are you doing with this bum? You like rock stars, do you?" Not waiting for her response, obviously on a roll and oblivious to how uncomfortable he's making her, he continues, "If you tire of him, come find me. I'll rock your world."

Stepping partially in front of Pansy, I glare at Gerald. "That's enough, buddy. Go find your own date; she's with me."

"Ah, relax, we're just having fun. Is she going on tour with you or is she just pussy of the day?"

"Excuse me?" I scowl, clenching my fists to stop myself from hitting him.

Pansy steps closer to me and narrows her eyes at him. I've never liked this guy, and I'm especially grateful that my days of having to deal with him are numbered.

"I want to know if I can look her up when you're on the road. How serious is it?"

I raise my arm, and Pansy's fingers dig into my shoulders, prepared to hold me back should I want to kill this guy. Her touch pulls me from crossing that line into the darkness of my anger.

Rather than take him out, as tempting as it is, I focus on his puzzling comment.

"Tour? What are you talking about?"

"Trojan's farewell tour."

"Gerald, I told you not to say anything," Bianca says as she joins the conversation.

"There's not going to be a tour," I grit out. "It's not part of the deal."

Bianca lays a hand on my forearm and wedges herself between Gerald and me. "Would you please give us a moment?" She directs the question at him.

"Fine, but this isn't over. Not by a long shot." His cocksure attitude is hard to miss. Glancing at me, he adds, "There will be a tour."

"No fucking way."

The asshole chuckles while walking away.

"Bianca, what the fuck?"

"Silas." Pansy's hold tightens.

"I'm sorry. He called this morning about doing a world tour. I'd told him it was likely a no-go, but you know how the label is."

"There is no *likely*, Bianca. It's a no," I reiterate. "Don't even try to talk us into that shit. Vegas was my last stop. Never again."

Holding her hands up in surrender, she sheepishly stares at us. "Fine. I'll shut it down. You two have a good night."

"Yeah, I plan to. We're blowing this fucking pop stand," I say to Pansy as I grab her hand and lead us through the party. I don't stop for Bianca or anyone else who calls my name along the way.

The second we leave the party the night improves tenfold. I get Pansy back to my place, alone and naked, and we spend the night devouring each other. I savor every moment, knowing our time together has an expiration.

While our time apart will be brief in the grand scheme of things, it's going to be difficult. I'll miss her like some crazy lovesick fuck, and I'm in no hurry for that.

The vibrating of my phone wakes us at a little past eight in the morning. Pansy's head rests on my chest; her hair fanned out. She lightly kisses my pec and mumbles good morning.

"Morning." I kiss the top of her head before reaching for my phone.

We both sit up, my back against the headboard and her head on my shoulder, fingers splayed on my abdomen, staring at my phone screen. It is an email from Gerald Pilsen.

What does that fucker want now? If he's pushing for the tour, I'm going to walk away now. Fuck the album and the agreement. As my body coils and tenses at the possibilities, her lips brush my chest, causing my balls to tighten and cock to salute her.

I open the email, and there's a video file, nothing else. I tap it, and it opens and starts to play. It takes a few seconds for me to compute what we're watching or, more importantly, *who* we are watching.

"What the fuck?" I yell and toss the phone like it's on fire.

We both sit upright in the bed, alert, with Pansy staring at me like I'm a madman. The familiar pleasurable moans and slapping sounds of sex come from the device lying at the bottom of the bed. Fuck, I was in such a hurry to get rid of it, to prevent Pansy from seeing anymore, that I didn't stop the video.

"What's that, Silas?" Confusion swims in her eyes, but the thick, sinking feeling in the pit of my stomach indicates there's also understanding in her gaze.

I'm mute. I don't know what to say, how to make it all stop. Her gaze flicks from me to the end of the bed and back again. With another gaze to the foot of the bed, her intentions flit through her eyes before she lunges for the phone. I don't stop her.

My gut twists and clenches as a prickle of sweat forms on my brow at the thought that she won't understand.

On her knees, completely naked, she flips the screen to face her, and she's transfixed by the scene unfolding in the palm of her hand. She's watching me have sex. A threesome.

"Jared and Bianca?" She gasps, one hand grabbing her stomach and the other covers her mouth. Like me, she throws the device; it bounces on the mattress before falling to the carpet.

"Once. Ten years ago. It was a mistake. We were drunk, high; you name it. It never should've happened, and I never fucking knew there was a recording of it."

I reach for her hand, but she scrambles back, pulling the sheet to cover her. My outstretched hand hangs there, in the cold, open space between the both of us, rejected.

Staring at her, I wait patiently, intent on catching her gaze. Eventually, her glossy eyes lock with mine. Her skin is pale, and she doesn't look good.

"I don't have feelings for Bianca, not like that. Only as a friend." The gravity of each word hangs between us.

"I know," she whispers, her arms hugging her middle as she sits back on her heels. She cradles herself like a life-raft, the only thing keeping her afloat. Her knuckles are curled tightly, so tight they're white.

"Are you upset?" *What a fucking stupid question to ask.*

I sit on the bed too and gingerly move closer. With my heart lodged in my throat, I'm uncertain how to handle this. I'd go fucking ballistic if I'd just seen a sex recording of Pansy with two other people, no matter if it was yesterday or ten years ago.

"No. I'm..." Loosening her grip around her body, she shrugs. "I'm not sure what I am right now. It was a long time ago, and you haven't kept your past a secret. I knew you were a man-whore."

I flinch, but can't deny it. She's only calling it like it is. Panic glides through me like a shiver -- what if my past fucks up my future with her? Shit, I can't think like that.

"I suppose I just never wanted to see it. I don't like it. And shit, I can't unsee that." Her voice cracks on a nervous laugh.

"Fuck." This time when I reach for her, she doesn't pull away. "I'm sorry."

"It's not your fault. Why would he send you that?" Her fingers are fidgeting within my grasp, and she's nibbling on her lip.

"I have a hunch. I'm sure we'll hear from him."

"So, I guess Bianca really likes cock," Pansy says, again with a jittery laugh, and then she covers her mouth.

My surprise colors the bark of my laugh. "What?"

"Shit, I'm sorry. I didn't mean that! I say silly and inappropriate things like that when I'm nervous."

She is flustered, squirming beside me as her chest reddens, the color slowly climbing to her neck and cheeks.

"It's okay. Why are you nervous?" I tug on her hand, and her eyes flick to mine.

"I don't know if I can ever look at Bianca and Jared the same again."

As she says their names, I realize that I have to call them. I'm pretty sure they don't know about the recording. At least I fucking hope not, or else there'll be hell to pay.

"I thought picturing people naked was supposed to calm nerves?" I say, trying to calm hers.

She giggles and bats at my shoulder. "Not helping."

Sliding my hand around the back of her neck, I bring her closer to me and lightly kiss her forehead.

"I really am sorry. If I could have prevented you from seeing that, I would have," I say. She nods a small smile appears on her lips. "Go get dressed. I've gotta call Bianca and Jared."

I slip on some boxers and grab the phone from the floor when it vibrates with an incoming email. Gerald Pilsen. I growl, and Pansy stops just before closing the bathroom door.

"What is it?"

"It's fucking Pilsen. We now know what he wants," I grind out.

35

VENOM

*P*ansy

My shower is a blur, my mind filled with what-if scenarios and flashbacks to the recording of Silas, Bianca, and Jared. God, I wish I could obliterate the vision of the three of them, naked bodies tangled and fucking, out of my mind.

By the time I'm finished and back in the bedroom, Silas is dressed and on the phone with Eli. I wonder if he's telling Eli about the three-some and Pilsen's blackmail, or maybe the band already knows about their threesome? Did they all sleep with Bianca? Damn, I have to stop this. So what if she did? It's none of my business, and I don't want to think about any of them having sex.

"Okay, see you soon." He ends the call with a heavy sigh.

"Hey, how are you doing?"

He looks as rattled as I feel with his hair a mess from continu-ously running his fingers through it. Pilsen's demand goes against everything that Silas wants. Needs. Trojan must do the world tour or else the tape goes public.

"Fine. They're all on the way. Bianca got an email too. She's upset. Eli and Gray don't know what's going on. We just need to figure out what we're going to do. Fuck, I hate involving everyone, but there's no way around it." His eyes find mine, and I nod in agreement. "I couldn't get ahold of Jared, so I texted him. He most probably has an email too."

Before I even formulate a response -- my mind's still stuck on the idea of the entire band showing up to discuss a sex tape -- there's a knock at the bedroom door. Silas hollers for whoever to come in, and Bianca cautiously enters the room.

Her usually warm olive complexion is pallid, and her eyes are red and puffy. My heart clenches as what I can only imagine she's feeling.

"Hey." Her voice is wobbly, barely a whisper.

"B."

They walk toward each other but stop midway, both looking at me with uncertainty and regret. Seeking permission. I don't want to be in this position.

A part of me doesn't want to see them hug, innocent touching isn't even welcomed right now, even though there's nothing but friendship. Deep in my heart, I know this.

"Guys, it's okay," I finally say, looking away as he takes her into his arms.

"Silas, what are we going to do?" Pain and heartache drip from her every word.

"It'll be okay." His fierce conviction fills my heart, knowing Silas will do everything in his power to make it all right. "Let's wait for the guys to get here. I'm going to jump in the shower. Wait downstairs?"

"I'll wait with her," I say.

Silas comes to me, taking my arm. "You don't have to."

"I'm fine," Bianca adds.

"It's okay." I squeeze his hand and turn to Bianca. "I want to."

Bianca and I are not close. We are civil to each other – for the most part – but now, it's weird to say, but because of the tape, this scandal that could ruin lives, I see her in a different light.

She's just a woman, like me. And woman to woman, I want to be there for her. I don't care if she has threesomes all the time or if that was just one time, a regrettable mistake, it doesn't matter. Nobody deserves to be blackmailed.

"Pansy, I don't know what to say. You must hate me," Bianca starts, grimacing, once we're seated downstairs at the kitchen table.

"No. I don't hate you. This happened years ago. I won't lie, I wish I'd never seen it, but I can't hate you."

"God, that was the worst decision of my life, and I totally regret it."

"Sex with two hot-as-fuck rock stars was the worst decision of your life?" I jest, hoping to stop her self-loathing. "Why? Was it a bad experience? It can't be Silas because he's phenomenal in bed." Her eyes widen, and her mouth opens as I continue, "It's gotta be Jared. What, is he seriously lacking? Pencil dick? Can't get it up? A selfish lover? That would certainly explain his constant scowl and brooding. I might act like him if I was a shitty lover and everyone knew it."

Her laughter starts small and shaky, more an awkward giggle. "I can't believe..." she starts, the giggle building, taking over her speech as it morphs into a full-blown guffaw. She bends over and clutches her stomach.

I join her, snorting and chuckling at my improper comments. By the time Silas comes downstairs, we're two silly girls laughing so hard we're crying.

Each of us tries to talk, but we can't catch a breath, and I'm glad I've helped bury some of this ugliness, if only temporarily. While what I said was funny, it wasn't *that* funny, but she's letting off steam and unloading some of her distress.

Silas is puzzled, but also grateful for the levity. While we get ourselves under control, he makes coffee. Then we sit in silence, waiting for the others.

Eli and Gray arrive shortly after and are filled in. Both are shocked, but as they study Bianca, it's not lewd or disillusioned, but rather with caring and in a protective way.

"You okay?" Eli asks, coming to her side. She nods, but her lips quiver and he pulls her into his arms. "It's going to be okay."

"We'll figure this out. We have to," Gray adds, his tone determined.

As we murmur our agreement, Jared walks into the room, his

dark eyes flicking to each of us. His gaze holds Bianca's deep, dark eyes for a beat longer than anyone else's.

Looking like he just rolled out of bed, his long hair is in disarray, his eyes glassy and his black shirt wrinkled like it's been rolled up in a ball for days.

"Fuck, who died?" Jared asks. "Is everything okay? Why are you crying?" He's staring at Bianca, his voice rushed and rough.

She shakes her head ever so slightly in reassurance. His fingers dive into his mass of hair and curl in a hard grip as he lets out a jagged breath.

"Did you check your email?" Silas asks.

"Email? Who uses email anymore?" Jared responds, pulling out his phone.

In less than a minute, the deep groans and breathy whimpers of the three of them having sex pervade the still kitchen air. Jared doesn't move, and all gazes fall to the floor, or table top. No one dares to look at another.

Silas clenches his hands into fists and his jaw ticks while he tries to catch my eye, but my gaze is on Bianca. She refuses to meet any of our glances, her head hung low, a lone tear sliding down her face.

"Fucking hell! How the hell did Pilsen get this?" Jared roars and stuffs his phone in his pocket.

"Think about it." Venom coats Bianca's words. All her anxiety, shame, and frustration unleashed on him.

"Easy, B," Silas says, patting her hand. "It was the record label's house and their party."

"The place's probably wired with cameras for this very reason, among others," adds Eli.

"They must fucking love having dirt on their talent. What the fuck do they want?" Jared seethes.

Like a trip down memory lane, each of them retells some part of the happenings of the night before at the label's party. Silas, Bianca, Eli, and even Gray add something to the story of how Pilsen wants them to do a world tour. It ends with Silas reiterating his refusal to do it. This time, he isn't as emphatic.

Before they can get to the second email with what this is all about, Jared interjects, "So, we fuck 'em. Let 'em fucking release this. Let 'em do their best. We're fucking rock stars -- we're only living up to our reputation, or down, depending on how you look at it." He chuckles and shrugs.

The room is silent. Jared has missed the point. Pilsen has them right where he wants them.

36

KILLING

*S*ilas

I don't know why I'm stunned. I shouldn't be. Jared hasn't thought this through. He's most probably high; I can't tell anymore.

"If it were just you and me to think about, I'd be with you, but Bianca..."

I hate that I mention her like she's not even there. If he were sober, he wouldn't have overlooked her. Despite the tension and history between them, he cares about her and would never hurt her. Not intentionally.

"Fuck." Jared grimaces and yanks his dirty fingers through his greasy hair. "Bianca, I wouldn't do it. I'm sorry."

"I know," she croaks, wiping her tear-stained cheeks.

And then there's Pansy. She's mine to consider and worry about, but there's no fucking way I'll subject her to the media shit storm that would follow the release of that video.

"You have to go on the tour," Pansy says while grabbing hold of Bianca's hand.

Our gazes lock and her shimmering hazel eyes hold only warmth and compassion. We both know what the tour would mean. I'll be gone for months, possibly even a year.

She'll be in South America, fuck I need to talk to her about that, and then school. We will both be doing our own thing. Apart. But isn't that what I promised myself I'd do? Encourage and nurture her dreams no matter what?

Damn, but why does it feel like I'll be cutting off a limb? A part of myself? "Pansy, are you sure?" Bianca asks, the hopeful lift present in her tone.

"Of course. No question."

While Pansy doesn't say it, we know Bianca will be the whore in this story. The media will rip her to shreds, and it'll be a major blow to her job, if not career-ending. She might never come back from it.

"Okay, it's settled, so now what?" Jared asks.

"We get him to destroy every single copy," Gray grits out.

He's been silent through the whole thing, but now his face is red with fury. His gaze is fixed on Bianca, filled with only compassion.

"Yeah. We've got to get Pilsen to sign something before we agree to anything. Something that makes it impossible to come at us again. I'll get Otto on it."

Once they leave, I spend close to two hours going back and forth with Otto, who does all the negotiating with Pilsen and the record label. I'd like nothing better than to fuck them, but it's not in the cards.

We finally come to a verbal agreement, including Pilsen handing over all that he has. It's not a world tour but close to it with cities on four continents.

It's close to evening when this shitty day goes from shaky to a full-blown earthquake. With the negotiations behind us, Pansy and I head to her apartment to pack her things for my place. The sooner I get her in my bed permanently, the easier I will breathe. Even if it is only for now.

While packing one of the last boxes, she steals furtive glances at me every minute or so. I think I know what's going on. Resting the box on the table, I near her.

"What's up?"

I'm pushing. I promised Pansy that her dreams would come first, and I meant it. She may be second-guessing everything because of what has happened with the tape and the tour.

"I've got to tell you something, and the timing sucks. I should have told you sooner." She's wringing her hands, and I take them in mine.

"Tell me." My voice is soft, coaxing.

"Vinny has invited me on a research trip to Uruguay for six months or so. It's an amazing opportunity, and it changes all my plans, but I ..." She looks away for a split second and then her warm eyes are back on me. "I want to go."

"This is fantastic!" Gathering her in my arms, I lift her feet off the ground and mold her to me. Inhaling all of her. Cherishing her smell. Her feel. Her.

"It is? Did you hear me when I said I'd be gone for six months at a minimum?"

I chuckle, placing her feet back on the floor. "I hear you, and it'll suck, but it sounds like something you have to do. You'd be crazy not to."

Water gathers in her eyes, and she nods as a tear spills down her cheek. I brush it away and pull her into me.

"On one hand, I'm so excited, and on the other, I feel horrible. There's so much going on. You're almost done writing and recording, and then the tour. I feel like I should be here."

I cup her face and tilt her chin up. "You will be with me all the time. And in case you don't know about it, there are ways to communicate. There's this thing where we can video chat, text." She pokes at my side, and we laugh. "And, if I can, I'll come visit."

"You will? Do you think you can?" Her tone is hopeful.

"South America is on the tour. I don't give a fuck what the label says, I will see you." I squeeze the back of her neck.

She gives me a watery smile; her hands cling to my forearms. "The timing sucks, but I do want to go."

"I know, but this is your dream."

"Silas, I have more than one dream. You're my dream too. A dream I never even knew I wanted or dared to have."

"You've got me, babe. And I'll make sure Lucia and Jorge take care of Daisy."

"I kinda already asked them," she says sheepishly.

"You did? You spoke to them before telling me?" I'm trying not to get upset, but I don't understand why she held off telling me, but she's spoken to Vinny, Betty, and even Lucia and Jorge.

A small smile graces her lips as she lightly runs her finger across my jaw. Her fingertips snag once or twice on my stubble, and the tickle of her touch sparks a fire low in my belly.

"I didn't know how to tell you without breaking my heart...and yours." Her strangled voice matches the tears swimming in her eyes. "Silas, I love you."

She is killing me in the best way possible. I can't recall a woman ever saying those words to me and meaning it. Sure, I've heard it countless times from screaming fans or groupies in the throes of climax. All worthless.

But this. Her love for me is everything.

"Pansy, I love you, too."

My lips cover hers, and I kiss her, hard, stealing all her air. Her eyes flutter close as my mouth hungrily assaults her. She greedily pulls me by the waist, bringing her body against mine and my hands wander wildly of their volition. First, gripping her ass, then skating along the soft curves of her sides up to thread my fingers through her silky hair.

I love Pansy more than I love music, and that says it all. She crashed into my life, and while trying to free myself from the wreckage, the disaster that I thought she was; she became the one pure thing in my life. It's going to fucking hurt to say goodbye.

37

GREEDY

*P*ansy

Opening my eyes, I stretch. The cool, soft sheet against my naked body is like a lover's caress, and my thoughts go to Silas and last night. I'm spent and invigorated like only a night with him can do.

We had come back to his place and spent the night alone together. Loving each other with kisses, touches and our bodies entwined. Savoring every moment like it was our last.

A cloud of steam billows from the bathroom door as Silas steps into the room with only a white towel wrapped low around his waist. His chiseled, bare chest is partially damp, and his hair is loose and wet.

He's hot as fuck. I will miss this. My fingertips burn with the memory of his hard, heated flesh beneath them, last night, each scorching moment flashes before my eyes in a kaleidoscope of pleasure.

He stands in his room, in all his glory. Saliva pools in my mouth and I bite my lips to stifle a greedy moan. He doesn't look my way as he walks to the closet and I suck in a breath at his tantalizing back dimples peeking out from the towel. I want to lick them.

What is with me? I'm a horn dog; like I didn't just spend hours getting fucked senseless by this man. I'm insatiable. Silas seems to have that effect on me.

Pulling the sheet over my head, I stuff my face into the pillow and giggle, squeezing my eyes shut as heat rises throughout my body.

"What are you laughing at?" His voice cuts through my laughter, and I peer from under the sheet.

"Um, nothing."

Without warning, the bed dips as he places one knee beside me and lifts his legs over to straddle me. The ends of the towel open for a second and I get an eyeful, enough to tempt me more than I already am.

He yanks the sheet down below my waist, my bare body on display and before I know what's happening, he's tickling me. Oh my God, how does he know I'm insanely ticklish? I buck, kick, and writhe while gasping for air in between my fits of hyena-like laughter.

"Stop!" I pull a large intake of air. "Please stop."

It's not immediate, but with a few more pleas, he relents. His eyes are hazy, glittering with mischief and lust. His palm splays on my stomach, the tips of his fingers graze the underside of my breast, and the heat of his touch and stare makes me squirm. Unable to look at him without conveying my need, my eyes close and I inhale a deep, calming breath.

"Look at me." My eyes snap open at the deep rumble in his voice, and he scoots down, pulling the sheet with him.

With all of me bared to him, his hands roam up my thigh, pulling my legs apart. Laser focused on my exposed sex; he licks his lips like the big bad wolf readying for a meal. He leans down, inhaling my arousal before biting at the juncture of hip and pelvis. My sex clenches at what's to come.

❦

*D*ays. The time we have left together is only days, and while we spend every minute we can with each other, we can't stop it. Or slow it down.

It's bittersweet. I'm excited about the trip, so giddy some nights that I lay awake anxious to hop on that plane. But I dread saying goodbye to the man I love. It's not forever, that's what I keep telling myself. It's the only way I can make peace with leaving Silas. If only I could have both.

I cry like a baby when it is time to say goodbye to Jorge, Lucia, and Betty. Each offers words of love and encouragement. Betty gushes and preens over me, telling me how proud she is, and I haven't even done anything yet.

Then there's Boy. With welling eyes and a runny nose, I bury my face in her soft, warm fur. The dog may not understand, but it's like she can sense I'm sad and she's concerned. Her whimpers mimic mine, as she buries her body into me. Her tail wags, and I cling to her.

Of course, the hardest is saying goodbye to Silas.

Our drive to the airport is silent, much more subdued than when we took Daisy not too long ago. The line to check in moves quickly and I'm ready to go through to the gateway sooner than I'd hoped.

If we were flying directly to Montevideo, it would take over a day with a couple stops. But we aren't going straight through. We have a stop for two days in El Salvador before flying on. Vinny has a friend joining us who lives there. A fellow marine biologist. Then we will fly to our destination. I promise Silas to call him on the way down.

"I better go in," I say. Not wanting to leave, but no longer able to drag this out. I just want to rip off the band-aid.

"Okay." He brushes back my hair and cups my cheek. "Safe travels and enjoy yourself. You're going to be amazing and love every minute of it."

"I better," I smirk.

"I'll let you know when the tour starts. If we can work something out, if you can join us or if I can come to you, we will."

He doesn't sound as sure as he first did when I told him I was going. What if he's backing away from us? From me? What if, while on tour, he forgets about me? Falls into his old ways? The thought never, not once, crossed my mind. Now, the very idea's a throbbing ache radiating from my chest.

"I love you, Pansy." His lips take mine in a deep, long kiss.

Don't forget me. My grip tightens on his sides, and I cling to him, hoping this isn't the last time we will kiss. The last time we will see each other.

38

INEVITABLE

*S*ilas

"Silas, we've got to talk." Otto marches into my music studio in dark jeans and a gray button-down. I didn't think my lawyer did casual. "Bianca." He nods in her direction.

"Hi, Otto," she says.

His clothes may say relaxed and chill, but he's anything but with his jaw clenched and worry lines etching his face. The guy has a shaved head and a solid body. If he didn't wear suits, I'd think he was a bodyguard or wrestler.

"What's up?" Shutting the piano lid, I slide to the end of the bench and turn to face him.

"I'll leave you two alone," Bianca says.

We'd just finished a rough run through of the details for the damn tour, and I ended up telling her about Pansy like some heart-broken school girl, that I fucking miss her like crazy. And it's only been a day. And the worst part of it all? Pansy hasn't called. How the fuck am I going to do this for months?

"No, I think you should stay," Otto says, his tone grave and eyes sharp.

This is serious. Sitting up straight, I glance at Bianca, who is just as concerned as I am. She wrinkles her puzzled brow, but nods and sits.

"There's no easy way to say this." He sits across from me on the couch, his face tight and forehead knitted.

"Just say it." I stiffen my spine and prepare for the blow.

"I was going through your accounts with Jackie." She's my financial advisor. "Pulling together some forecasts for when you leave Trojan, and we came across some discrepancies."

"What kind?"

"Missing money. A *lot* of money, from several accounts. I called the bank, and it took some time, but fuck..."

"Otto." My heart is battering against my ribs, and I'm losing my patience.

"Your parents have a POA on *all* your accounts. And it looks like they've been siphoning monies from them over the past three years, to the tune of fifteen million, give or take. And this is on top of what you've been giving them monthly."

Bianca gasps, her hand covering her mouth, as her healthy olive skin pales.

"Are you sure?" I'm surprised how calm my voice is when my insides are rioting.

"Yeah. I've been on this for a while; I wanted to be one hundred percent sure before I came to you. I even had a forensic accountant look it over."

"How the fuck did they get a power of attorney? I've never, ever signed one."

"That took some time." He pauses and glances at Bianca. "The bank finally went through their records and showed us a copy..."

"It was me," she says in a shaky voice, looking ill. Her hand is trembling, still hovering by her mouth. "Oh, my God, it was me."

My stomach twists as I study the woman I trust with all my financial affairs. She and Otto are the only ones who I blindly allow to call the shots, to make decisions for me. I can't fathom what I'm hearing. Why would she do this?

Otto nods. "What happened?" He directs his question at her.

"Silas, I'd have never done it if I knew... are you sure, Otto?"

"Bianca, how did it happen?" Otto says, now shifting into full-on interrogation mode like the lawyer he is.

"God, Silas, they said you needed to sign it. Your mother told me you knew about it. You were expecting it. I just put it in with the other things I had for you to sign at the time."

"Fuck!" I bellow. Angry at myself, at my parents, not her. I should have seen this coming, they've been around enough over the years to know how I leave all that shit to Bianca. I gave them the perfect opportunity, and I was too naive to think they'd go this far.

It's not Bianca's fault. It may seem that way but she adores my parents, and I've deliberately kept her out of my shit with them. Both she and Otto have no clue about how strained our relationship is, and why.

Bianca lost her family, one by one, over a short and painful period. It was just before we met and while I don't know everything, her family was tight. Her parents were her rock.

My parents quickly filled that void. From the get-go, they treated her like a daughter. Of course, she wouldn't question them or think they were up to anything underhanded. Fuck, she was an easy mark, and I let it happen.

"It's not your fault," I say, consoling her as she cries and apologizes over and over again.

She curls into me and sobs as I rub her back. Rage fills me, but the funny thing is, it's not about the money. I couldn't care less. It's seeing my friend guilt-ridden. My parents used her and had been stealing from me for years. And what for? It's not like I wasn't giving anything to them.

"I'm so sorry. I'm an idiot. I should have said something to you," she says in between hiccups.

"Nope. I'm the idiot. I should read the shit you give me. Both of you." My eyes flick from Otto back to Bianca. "I never do. I trust you've read it and you have my best interest at heart. I trust you, explicitly. My parents took advantage of that trust. Not you."

"Silas, what are you going to do?" Bianca asks at the same time that Otto says, "What do you want me to do? You've got options."

"This ends here." It's time to have the conversation I've been dreading. Deep down, I knew it was inevitable.

"Are you going to get the money back?" Otto asks.

"I don't care about the money. They can have it."

"Silas." Otto uses his stern solicitor tone. "That's nearly ten percent of your net worth. I know they are your parents, but there are consequences for what they did. People have gone to jail for less."

"Otto, I don't care. Besides, it's likely already gone. Now it's my turn to get rid of them."

Bianca arranges a private jet, and we leave for San Jose the next day, first thing in the morning. While at the airport, nervous as hell about my impending confrontation with my parents, a small part of me wonders where Pansy may be. Is she in some South American airport headed for Uruguay?

Bianca and I are silent for the most part as we maneuver through the airport toward the plane. While the Pilsen blackmail crap is behind us, with this colossal shitstorm about to hit, and the part she played in it, Bianca is quiet and subdued.

No matter how many times I say that I don't blame her and that it wasn't her fault, she's lost and remorseful.

"B, we good?"

"Yeah." Her voice is raspy. "I should be asking you that. I feel horrible for all of this."

Her usually stylish hair is back in a messy ponytail, and she isn't wearing any makeup. She's still a gorgeous girl, but she looks nothing like herself. The woman in charge. The powerhouse that everyone knows to take seriously and steer clear of.

"We've been over this. Don't blame yourself. The sad truth is, if it weren't you, they'd have found another way."

She puffs out her cheeks and rolls her eyes. "That doesn't help. Silas, what happened? Why did they do this when you were sending them thousands a month?" She would know, she saw the paperwork.

"I don't know. That's the million-dollar question." We both half-heartedly chuckle. At least, I can still laugh at this fucking mess.

"What do you need me to do?"

"Nothing. Just you being here helps. You didn't have to come."

"No, I did. I want to be here. Are you sure, you don't want me to try and get a hold of Pansy? I could arrange for another flight for her."

"No," I say firmly. "With any luck, she should be on the last leg of her trip or already there."

My conviction is only for show. I feel anything but brave and sure I can do this without Pansy.

Bianca enters the jet first but doesn't go any further into the aircraft. Once on the plane, I glance back at her, puzzled. Why isn't she coming? It's then that I sense her. The air shifts, thickening and intensifying.

I vaguely make out Bianca's "Have a safe flight," as I spin around and come face to face with my heart. Pansy.

39
TOGETHER

*P*ansy

"Pansy." My stomach tumbles and my heart races. "What are you doing here?"

"You needed me. I called you, and Bianca answered your phone. She told me everything, and I got on the next plane back to L.A."

He mutters a *fuck me* under his breath before closing his eyes and furrowing his brow. For a few beats, he forces his breathing steady while his hands curl and uncurl. With a blink, his darkening gaze drinks me in. His jaw ticks as he undergoes an inner battle and I wait. Wait for him to make a move.

"Fuck it."

His hands wrap around my biceps and haul me from the chair and into his warm chest. One hand behind my neck and the other gripping my jaw. My tummy flutters and the hammering of my heart drowns out the white noise of the aircraft.

"I should be pissed you're here and not on some plane to Uruguay, but fuck, you're all I want. If I were a religious man, I'd think my prayers were answered. I need you."

The raw honesty in his tone cracks me wide open. Coming was the right choice, and I'm so glad that I didn't hesitate. His lips crash onto mine in a desperate frenzy, and with each second we kiss, my insides heat and my heart swells.

The stewardess clears her throat, "Excuse me, would you please take your seats. We're preparing for take-off."

Silas chuckles and helps me buckle in before sitting and doing the same.

"Silas, I love you." I should've said it before, sooner. "Please believe me when I say I'm meant to be here, right now. I know this in my heart."

"Okay."

"Okay? That's it? You're not going to argue with me?"

"Is that what you want?" His dimples pop with his sexy grin. "You want to argue?"

Laughing, I shake my head. "No, definitely not." I tug his hand into my lap, interlacing our fingers.

As the plane taxis down the runway, he pulls me in for another kiss. "I love you, too," he murmurs, his warm breath against my face.

Resting his forehead on mine, we stay like that for a while, just breathing in each other.

"I'm so sorry about your parents."

"Me too."

"I'm glad I'm here. I don't want you to do this on your own."

"Me too."

"Is that all you have to say?"

He pulls away and winks. "I need you with me. I can do this alone, but now I don't have to."

"You're not alone."

During the short plane ride, we talk with me in his lap, his head in the crook of my neck.

"Pansy, you need to go back to Uruguay after," he says out of nowhere, a blunt edge to his tone.

"Yes, that's the plan."

"Thank fuck."

I giggle, threading my fingers through his hair. "You expected a fight?"

"I didn't know what to expect. Pansy, you're the love of my life."

I suck in a breath, my hold tightening on him. "I feel the same way."

"I fucking love that you're here, but I won't be the reason you miss out on this trip." He lifts his head, smiling and lightly kisses me. "Also, I've been thinking a lot over the past few days we've been apart, and I've got a theory about all your misadventures as you've put it."

"Really?" I raise my eyebrows, intrigued. "Go on."

"You've been looking at it the wrong way. All the things you did and the years trying out different paths, they aren't failures; you were meant to do those things and learn those lessons." He pauses, his pupils pinning me. "Because it led you to this moment. To me."

"Wow, look at you, Mister Insightful. You've given this a lot of thought," I tease. "But you're right. For all the things I used to regret, or wondered what the point was, they brought me to you, and I wouldn't change a thing."

He draws me closer, his mouth landing on mine in a promising kiss. We're in this together. Finding our way, chasing our dreams, and building a future. Together.

There's only one thing that could ruin this hope we've both discovered. His parents. If they can't see the mistake they've made and recognize their son for the wonderful man that he is, can Silas withstand that kind of rejection? Will I be enough?

40

PRICELESS

S ilas

The drive from San Jose to Gilroy, where my parents live, is relatively quick. I clasp Pansy's hand all the way, and while I'm still anxious, having her by my side quiets my rioting mind.

The closer we get to my childhood home, we pass so many landmarks, so many memories of a time when things may have been harder, but they were also simpler for my family.

Pansy winds down the window. "It smells like garlic."

"Yeah. Gilroy's famous for garlic. Have you never heard of the Gilroy Garlic Festival?"

"Seriously?"

"Yup. Every year, there's a garlic festival, and people from around the world come to taste all things garlic, including ice cream."

"What? Ice cream?" She wrinkles her nose.

"Hey, don't knock it until you've tried it."

"Hmmm, good point." She sniffs the air. "I want to try it. I love garlic, but don't you get sick of the smell?"

"Nah, after a while, you get used to it." I point to a playground filled with kids playing. "That's where I had my first crush. Jenny Tomlin. Some might say my first girlfriend, but I never did kiss her."

"Really?" She leans forward, looking closely at the slides and swings. "How old were you?"

"Nine or ten." The driver slows the car. "And that street over there leads to my high school."

"Wow. I love seeing where you grew up."

"And this is my street." We turn right, and she squeezes my hand as we pull up to the ranch-style home where I grew up.

"You okay?"

"Yes, let's do it."

The driver opens the door, and we walk hand-in-hand to the front door. It feels like walking the plank. Dread, unease, and anger coil and tighten my insides.

I use my key and enter unannounced, heading down the hall and into the kitchen. My parents are oblivious to our arrival, and right away, the truth hits me hard in the face. Here, hundreds of miles away from me, they're living a different life from the one I've been led to believe.

Instead of the staunch savers who live paycheck to paycheck, claiming the money I send is helping with the house, but not much else, they're decked out in designer casual wear. The house is still neglected, but my mother and father look like they're going to a polo match or out on a yacht. The contrast of their high-priced threads and the wear and tear of my childhood home is stark and undeniable.

"Mom. Dad," I say from the doorway.

Guilt colors their faces, and my stomach plummets to my toes as the room feels as if it's closing in on us. No surprise, my father is the first to bounce back from the shock of my unexpected visit.

"Silas! What a surprise." His booming voice is a higher pitch than normal. "And Pansy, is it?" She nods. "Nice to see you, again."

"Hello," Pansy says.

Mom follows his lead and kisses and hugs me. Her bright smile shrinks, fades slightly when her eyes meet Pansy. Her lips tremble, and with all her might, while wringing her hands, she forces her tight smile to grow, but it doesn't reach her eyes.

"Pansy, hello."

"Hi, Mrs. Palmer."

"Come in." My mother pulls at my hand, but I don't budge. With pleasantries out of the way, we stand in awkward silence, the air heavy with unleashed contention.

"I'm not going to waste my time or yours," I say with difficulty. My chest constricting as if in a vise. "I know about the POA. That's now revoked, by the way, and as much as I'd love to hear your excuses, we're way past that. I don't give a fuck."

Their mouths gape at my directness, their eyes growing wide. My mother still worries her hands, averting her gaze to the floor, and my father folds his arms over his chest in response to my determination.

"Silas, let's talk." My father uses his compassionate salesman voice.

"Nothing to talk about. For years I've twisted myself into knots trying to figure out what I did to lose your love. To go from son to a mark."

"A mark?" Mom asks, confused.

"Yeah, a mark, Mom. A target to take advantage of. I could go on."

"I don't understand, honey. What are you trying to say?"

"He's being melodramatic and talking nonsense." My father's tone is hostile.

My sarcastic laugh causes my mother to jump, and I fight to stay strong, to not fall for her clueless act because I find it hard to believe she wasn't complicit in all this. She gave Bianca the POA papers, after all. "Yeah, right. Cut the shit, Mom."

"Silas, stop," Dad commands and I laugh, again, despite the feeling of my guts having been ripped out.

I don't want to be rude to my mother. I love her, despite all this. And some deranged part of me respects my father for defending her, even if I am on the higher ground, but that's no consolation.

"Dad." Sarcasm drips from my mouth. "You don't call the shots anymore. Through all the soul-searching, I finally realize it's not me. It's you. All these years where I've struggled to figure out where we went wrong when it's quite simple. Money. The almighty dollar has been this huge, ugly thing between us. I'm your son, goddammit! Whether I have a million dollars or I'm penniless."

I shake with an overwhelming surge of emotion, all my pent-up rage and hurt rolling off me. I'm letting go of the part I played in this twisted and hurtful relationship.

Dr. Wexford and Pansy helped me realize that even if I unknowingly enabled or encouraged my parents' behavior in some strange attempt to keep them in my life, there's no guilt or shame in that.

I may never understand how our relationship went from unconditional love to this scheming, conniving cesspool of lies and greed, but this demise is on them. I've let this eat at me for far too long. Filling me with anger and tainting every part of my life. It ends today.

Turning my back on them, I grab Pansy's hand, and we exit the room. Mom calls my name while dad orders her to stop, to let me go. He'll likely retreat, to figure out a new strategy for coming at me, but this time, I won't give. I can't. My sanity and survival depend on holding firm.

When we get to the door, Pansy places her hands on my shoulders and stares intently into my eyes.

"I love you," she says in a steady, determined voice. "I'm here for you, and I told myself that I'd stay out of it. I don't know them, only you, but I can't stay quiet."

With a short, firm kiss, she storms back into the kitchen. I follow to a point, unable to enter. If I do, I fear that I may cave. They are my parents, I do love them, even after all this. My heart thunders in my ears as I lean against the wall and will my insides to calm so I can listen.

"He loves you, you know. Even with the way you treat him, he loves you." Pansy's strong and passionate words are a balm to my blistered soul. "Do you have any idea how lucky you are? How much he's already given you?"

From where I stand, my mother wears a bewildered expression, while Dad sneers at Pansy.

"We know that," mom says, stepping closer, her hands interlaced, knuckles white from squeezing them too tight. "It's just that we're not getting any younger, and Silas can help us out."

"And he does," Pansy says, emphatically. "He sends you money, monthly."

We've never really talked about the money I give them, but she did overhear the conversation with my mother. Even without all the details, she's taking my side, defending me.

"True," mom casts her eyes at my father before shifting her gaze to the floor. "But, we've given him so much..."

"That's enough, Alice. We don't answer to her, nor Silas. Who are you exactly?" My father's cutting tone does nothing to Pansy. She doesn't flinch or back down. In fact, she squares her shoulders, standing taller.

"I'm the woman who loves your son. I'll love him for the rest of my life. I know this as sure as the sun will rise tomorrow." Pansy points to my mother. "And as sure as I know that one day, maybe not tomorrow or the next, but someday, you will regret this."

Dad nears Pansy, looking to intimidate, and I push from the wall, ready to step in.

"I know your kind," my father says. "You're in this for the money. That's the only thing you love. Are you the reason he's cutting us off? I've worked long and hard to provide for my family, and now it's his turn to step up. Did you talk him into turning his back on his family?"

He curls his fists and takes another step. Instead of backing down, Pansy inches closer to a man nearly twice her size.

"See that's your problem, right there. Life isn't a game of checks and balances. Silas is your son, not someone to pay you back for the money and time you gave for the privilege of being a father. You expect to be paid back with interest. It's not enough for you to be proud of your son's accomplishments or what a wonderful man he has become. No. you're blinded by dollar signs, you no longer *see* your son. If only you could see what I do. Silas – not his career, or his bank account – your son, his love, is priceless."

Her words knock the air right out of me, and my heart explodes. Pansy then turns on her heel, stalling when our eyes lock. Her stern expression evaporates, and a big, bright smile spreads across her face. Taking my hand, she guides me to the waiting car. We're speechless as the driver exits the subdivision, and once on the highway, I break our silence.

"Pansy, that was ..."

"The truth," she's quick to say with a light kiss on my cheek.

"What you said... it made everything they did bearable. Does that make any sense?"

Nodding, she snuggles into my side, and having her near to my heart is all I need to settle mind, body, and soul. "Yes, it does. And I'm so sorry that what I said didn't make a lick of difference. You may be hurt and sad that you've lost your parents, and you've every right to be, but you're not alone." She pushes into sitting, twisting to face me and cupping my face in her delicate hands. "You haven't lost your family. I'm your family. The guys in the band, Bianca, Jorge, Lucia, we're your family."

"I know."

Covering her mouth, I kiss her, taking my time. Our kiss is long and languid, my lips lingering at the corner of her mouth. I can't bring myself to break away from her fully.

I've no doubt we'll survive the time apart. Her speech to my parents obliterated any uncertainty, albeit small, that I may have had. Nothing will get between us. Now all I have to do is figure out how to get through the next six months without her.

41

DETOUR
ONE MONTH LATER

*P*ansy

Our time apart is filled with long hours, endless lab notes, and countless chores. At first, I'm fascinated and eager to learn, even if some of it is monotonous.

No surprise, the best part is when I get to dive, and despite the barren ocean floor, which is the reason why we're in this part of the world, being in the water makes it all worthwhile.

On top of that, it doesn't help that I miss Silas like a lost limb. No matter how busy or happy I am, there's a part of me that's removed from it all.

Four weeks. That's how long it takes me to face the truth. By the third week, I know in my heart of hearts that I won't last, but I rationalize the urge with the strong need to give this expedition a fair shake.

But toward the end of week four, I finally talk to Vinny despite how much I dread it and fear that he won't understand. He loves research, and in some strange way, he enjoys the long grueling hours in the lab.

No surprise, Vinny is more than understanding and points out that the trip was a success because I now know that research isn't for me. When I hop on the plane, I still feel somewhat guilty for leaving after a month and can't thank him enough for having me on the trip.

During the flight, I make peace with the fact that research isn't my thing, and that doesn't mean I'm a quitter. Research is an unavoidable part of being a marine biologist, and I won't shy away from doing the work.

"Uruguay was not a failure. I narrowed down my interests, eliminating those fields that involve only research."

"Pardon?" the steward asks.

"Nothing." I blush embarrassed to have said it out loud.

The rest of the flight is short and when we land, I quickly determine that São Paulo is intimidating. It's beautiful, but bustling and I feel like every bit the foreigner that I am. Thank goodness for Bianca. She's planned everything. My hardest task is finding the driver at the airport.

The driver navigates the traffic and people like only a native could, and once, at the hotel, I deposit my luggage and change quickly.

Trojan's final tour, Odyssey, has officially kicked off with South America as their first continent on the circuit. This is their third and final night in São Paulo before moving onto Lima. Silas has no clue I'm here.

Standing to the side of the stage, Trojan sings to a sold-out crowd, and I have the best view in the house.

I've been to concerts before, and some have been amazing, but this is different. Surreal. Standing on stage, even off in the wings, the energy is palpable and electrifying. I'm feeding off the continual buzz of the crowd like I've been plugged in. The adoration of the fans is intoxicating. I now understand what Silas means when he says performing live is a high. There's nothing like it.

Of course, the charged vibe is also from the guys. They're on fire, each of them oozing an animal magnetism that rivals the raw and sexy sounds of their music and words. Trojan is on their final encore, and they're dripping wet. They must be exhausted, but they're going strong.

Silas stands front and center. Tall and muscular. Day old stubble, faded jeans molding to his unforgettable ass, and glistening bare chest. His shirt abandoned long ago to the roar and screams of thousands of women. Wet, blond hair plastered to his head. Beautiful.

"São Paulo, you've been fucking awesome! This is the last song of the night!" he yells into the microphone as the crowd screams. "We're playing this one for the first time. It's a special song, releasing tomorrow. Our final release."

Again, the crowd hollers with excitement. "This one is "Clutch," and it's for the love of my life."

My hands shake as I bring them to my lips. Perhaps it's my movement, or maybe he senses me, but Silas glances off stage in my direction. Did he see me? No, he turns back to the crowd.

But like a boomerang, his head whips back in my direction. Eli and Jared have started to play, but Silas just stands there, blue eyes pinning me. Transfixed.

I beam and wave like the crazy fangirl that I am. He still just stares. With a pointing gesture, I urge him to start singing, to get back to his fans.

Jared yells his name, stepping in beside Silas to figure out what has him frozen. Jared's gaze lands on me, and he smiles warmly before bumping Silas's shoulder, breaking the trance.

A slow, sexy grin skates across Silas's face, and he winks at me with a slight chin dip. My knees weaken, and my insides melt. He turns to the crowd, and the throng roars as the music picks up again.

Something magical happens as a lull or hush falls across the stadium the second Silas's sexy voice sings the first few words. The song has a faster tempo than I expect, it's not hard rock or a ballad, but rather something in between. Inspiring and beguiling, the lyrics bring tears to my eyes and my insides heat with a stirring low in my belly.

Again, he's captured our relationship, not only through the words and tune, but there's also an emotion to his tone and vibe of the band. The ideal refrain of holding on, knowing when to let go, but never losing the love.

Happy tears stream down my face at the limitless love washing over me. I'm so far gone that I can hardly see clearly. I wipe my nose with the back of my hand, taking deep breaths and trying to get a hold of myself as the song comes to an end. The guys say their farewell and exit the stage.

Silas runs straight for me, scooping me in his arms. His lips kiss every part of my face, tears and all.

"Hey, you," he murmurs in my ear, his face pressing into my neck.

"Hi." My voice is shaky and hopeful.

My stomach flips as he kisses me over and over again, working me into a mindless mess. All control lost. Combustible need.

His lips move to the side of my jaw, my neck, and the tease of his stubble along my skin intensifies the heating sensation growing low in my body.

"What the hell are you doing here?"

"Is that any way to greet me?"

"Please tell me you're here, not a dream." He nips at my ear.

"I'm here." My voice is breathy with what he's doing to me.

The rest of the band gather around us, Jared stepping in to take me into a quick, sweaty hug. Silas growls as Eli and Gray do the same, but he doesn't stop them. They're my friends too.

"Thank fuck you're here. This guy has been insufferable," Jared says. "Tell me you're staying a while, please." He makes a pleading face and holds his hands in front of him in prayer.

I laugh and nod. "Yes, I'm here for a while. For the rest of the tour, actually." Jared's eyebrows lift as do Eli and Gray's, whereas Silas furrows his, and mashes his lips into a thin line. "If you'll have me."

"Great to see you, Pansy," Eli says, patting my shoulder. And Gray echoes the sentiment before the guys leave us.

"Pansy, I'm fucking ecstatic that you're here, but what are you doing?"

"Can we go somewhere private?" I glance around at the crew and other people milling around. None of them are looking at us or listening, but I want privacy.

Silas nods and takes my hand. "Let me grab my things, and we'll go back to the hotel. Where are you staying?"

"With you. Bianca arranged it all. My things are already in the room."

"Bianca? I should've known." He shakes his head, but I'm not sure if it's in joy or disappointment.

Grabbing his Gibson and bag, he forgoes a shower, eager to get me alone. Security leads the way, and our exit proves to be an ordeal.

The few instances in L.A. with paparazzi or fans were child's play compared to the pandemonium outside. Fortunately, the security guys know what they're dealing with and have a planned exit route.

Surprisingly, steps from the car, we're spotted, and a swarm of fans charge toward us. The four burly guys flanking all sides remain calm but order us to pick up the pace, and somehow, we make it to the car before being swallowed by the mob.

Dozens of women and girls bang on the SUV, chanting "Silas," and some even say my name. I'm shocked they know who I am.

I'm a little jittery on the way to the hotel. I'll never be comfortable with that kind of scene, and Silas keeps me in his lap, refusing to loosen his grip. "Start talking," he says.

"Not everyone gets to realize their dream or even to have the chance to dream." I start big picture, knowing I've got to lay the groundwork for him. He's coming at this from the position of making sure I get back to Uruguay. "I'm fortunate that I not only found my dream career, but I discovered something greater and bigger than I ever dare dream. A family. A man to love that loves me."

He smiles and squeezes me tight.

"The trip was good, but it wasn't for me. Marine biology is still what I want to do, but not research, or as little of it as I can get away with."

He smirks, but nods. "I can only imagine."

"Yeah, Vinny loves that. Making the same daily observations and somehow making sense of all the data or finding the anomaly that could lead to a breakthrough. It's interesting in theory, but for me, it's tedious. And I didn't want to spend six months doing that.

"I didn't jump to this decision. At first, I worried that I was doing the same old thing, taking the easy way out, but instead, I learned something completely unexpected. I know what I don't want to do.

"Vinny was great about me leaving and understanding. I was torn up about failing him, but he said he was proud of me for making that discovery. For being honest with him and myself. I knew I had to come on the tour, be with you. I missed you like crazy."

"I missed you too."

"Life isn't always simple, and you can have a plan, but it's okay to take a detour, or make a pit stop. Life isn't linear. Seizing the opportunity is just as important as having a plan. This tour, doing this with you, is a once-in-a-lifetime opportunity. I've never traveled outside of the U.S. before, and this is your last tour. I want to travel the world with you. I want to be with you."

He kisses me, first my lips with tongue, long and slow, then my neck and by the time we reach the room, he's down to the skin beneath my blouse.

That night, we make up for the month apart. Cherishing and loving each other and reveling in the upcoming months ahead of jet-setting around the globe together.

The Odyssey tour is as memorable as I thought it would be. There are moments where I miss my bed or Boy, or Daisy, or the rest of our family back in California, but I regret nothing.

We plan a hiatus of sorts when Daisy nears her due date, and make it for the birth of my nephew. For the prissy diva that Daisy was most of her life, she is nothing short of amazing during labor. I'm with Daisy for the delivery, and she's instantly a mother in every sense of the word. I've never seen her so warm, caring, and loving. A true mother. And I love her more than ever for it.

Henry Callum Dobson steals my heart the second I lay eyes on him. Eight pounds, six ounces of wailing baby. Daisy names him for our father and tears spring to my eyes, clogging my throat, at how apt a tribute.

My father was always larger than life, and such a caring and loving man. While holding the little man, my heart hurts as I long for something that simply is not possible. I wish my parents were here to meet their grandson. They would have spoiled Henry something stupid.

When we head back on tour, I miss Daisy and Henry. A lot. It's hard to be away from the baby, but I remind myself that he's too young to miss me and Daisy has plenty of help. She isn't alone.

While I will miss some of his milestones like the first time he lifts his head, his first smile, and his first crawl, I'll be there for the even bigger ones.

And being with Silas, seeing the world with him, is where I'm meant to be. We make countless memorable moments, building to the foundation of our love. Moments that I wouldn't trade for the world. Moments that only make me giddy and anxious for our future. Like our time in Paris at the Eiffel tower after Trojan's final show in the city of light.

Silas arranged for just the two of us to come up after hours. Being up there is breathtaking and magical. The city is beautiful, the wind brisk, and the company, the man I love with all my heart, is out of this world.

Standing at what feels like to top of the world, I know no matter what life throws at us, even if we have to be apart again, he'll never let me go. He'll always hold on, and I'll do the same for him.

EPILOGUE
SEVERAL YEARS LATER

*P*ansy

"What do you think? Isn't it beautiful?" I stare at the sparkling sea with the sandbar ahead.

"It sure is." His voice is husky, his gaze lingering suggestively on my backside.

Rolling my eyes, I lightly hit him in the arm. "Silas, I'm serious."

"So am I. Land, air, or sea, you're the best view there is."

Belting out a laugh, I say between giggles, "Oh my, that's total cheeseball."

"It may be, but it's true." Capturing me around the waist, he pulls me into his bare chest.

Our lips collide, his kiss searing. No matter how many times he kisses me, in all the countless and memorable ways, it never gets old. As we break apart, he spins me so that my back is to his front, with his hands splayed over my stomach. "And this is the most beautiful sight there is," he murmurs hotly into my ear before his teeth nip at my earlobe.

I shiver despite the sweltering sun beating down on the deck and the warm sea breeze. "You can't see anything yet," I state the obvious as his hand caresses my belly. There isn't even a bump.

"I don't need to see, just knowing my child is in there is enough for me."

We're expecting. I'd been feeling icky, exhausted, and nauseated for weeks. At first, I'd chalked it up to nerves for my first time being the lead on an upcoming research project, but the more it continued, I knew what it meant.

The two pink lines confirmed it this morning. I'm pregnant, and we're ecstatic, although it drastically changes our plans.

Life is always throwing us for a loop, and it doesn't matter. I'm still in school and haven't quite figured out what area of marine biology I want to focus on, but I'm covering my bases. I'll get there, and the best part is I have an amazing family, the love of the best man, and our family is growing. We're having a baby. Our second.

"Daddy, why you awways kissing Mommy?" Our daughter waddles over to where we stand on deck, with Crystal right behind her.

"Sorry, I tried to keep her busy, but she had to come over," Crystal says, her cheeks flushed at interrupting our intimate moment.

"Hey, Posey, come to Daddy," Silas says, releasing me to pick up our nearly two-year-old daughter.

She giggles, her chubby hands clutching onto her daddy while she tilts her head back. Her strawberry blonde curls shimmer in the sunlight as Silas twirls her around.

"Faster, Daddy, faster," she demands.

Her melodic laugh paints a bright smile on my face and warms my heart. Eli and Daisy join us with Henry in my sister's arms. My nephew's bouncing on her hip, arms outstretched and begging for Silas to do the same to him.

"Ankle Si, me too. Ankle Si!" the five-year-old pleads.

While Henry is super smart, scarily so for his age, he's still working on the pronunciation of some words. I think it's endearing and keeps him somewhat of a baby in my mind.

"Great, look what you've started," Daisy groans, putting down her son, who scurries to Silas as soon as his feet hit the deck.

Eli and I laugh, while Daisy heads for a lounge chair. Eli pulls

Crystal into his side, and she beams, resting her head on her Dad's chest.

"I'm getting too old for this," Silas puffs and sucks in some air while placing Posey back on the deck.

Our little munchkin wobbles and plunks onto her bum, glancing at her daddy with pure love. She thinks the world of her father -- as she should, the man spoils her rotten.

"Henry, turn. Henry, turn," Posey orders her father, and he chuckles.

"Yes, ma'am. Come here, Hank," he calls.

"Hey, his name is Henry!" Daisy calls, and Silas winks at me before picking up his nephew.

Daisy and Silas are tight, but both still love to get at each other.

"Children, cut it out," Gray says, handing Daisy a bottle of water. "Henry's his name, Silas."

"'Yeah, yeah." Silas waves them off before picking up my sweet Henry. "You don't mind Hank, do you?" Silas asks.

"I like Hank," he says, grinning from ear to ear. He's no fool, he wants a twirl and would agree to just about anything Silas says at the moment.

"Honey, you better get in shape if this is wiping you out. You're gonna need it with two," I say.

All eyes drop to my belly.

"What did you just say?" Jared asks as he surfaces from below deck.

"Darn, sorry! Not a great way to tell you all, but we're having another baby!" I say.

Laughter and congratulations erupt from them as they swarm around Silas and me with hugs and kisses. Tears of joy spring to my eyes and Daisy wipes at them with her finger.

"I'm so happy for you," she says. "Little Pose will have a sibling, and Henry'll have another cousin. This is awesome."

"Thanks, Daze. We're happy, too."

"We're more than happy," Silas interjects, slinging his arm around my waist and hauling me against him. "We're just getting started."

"What?" Daisy and I say in unison.

"How many brothers and sisters do you want, Posey girl?" he asks.

Posey's busy trying to rip her diaper off and stops pulling at the tab to lift her head toward us. Blue eyes sparkling, she smiles. "Ten."

I choke, Daisy sputters, and Silas lets out a bark of laughter. "Ten! I say that's a good even number."

"Uh-uh, not happening." I point my finger from Silas to Posey. "Maybe one more, we'll see how this goes. But we're stopping at three. End of discussion."

Posey comes to us, mimicking me with hands on her hips. "Mommy, four a better number."

"She does have a point," Jared adds. "Nice and even."

I stab him with a *shut it* glare, and he chuckles. I have a feeling this is just the beginning of many lengthy discussions. And while I'm outnumbered, I never go down without a fight, and I always play for keeps.

Thank you for reading Clutch! Jared's story is next in Reverb, available at major retailers or grab it here: www.smwestauthor.com.

Thank you for reading and please leave a review on your favorite book site, including tell a friend. Reviews help readers find books!

For exclusive content, a free book and to find out when I have new releases, please sign up for my newsletter at www.smwestauthor.com.

ABOUT THE AUTHOR

S.M. West is a USA TODAY bestselling and award-winning author of sexy, angsty romances about brave hearts, wild love with a few heart-pounding twists along the way.

For new releases, exclusive excerpts, giveaways and more, sign up for her newsletter.

For other books by S.M. West, visit: *www.smwestauthor.com*